GW00759032

CROOKED MURDER

An absolutely gripping cozy murder mystery full of twists

JEAN G. GOODHIND

A Honey Driver Murder Mystery Book 10

Originally published as
Blood and Broomsticks

Revised edition 2022
Joffe Books, London
www.joffebooks.com

First published by Accent Press Ltd
in Great Britain and the USA as *Blood and Broomsticks* in 2014

This paperback edition was first published
in Great Britain in 2022

Cover art by Dee Dee Book Covers

ISBN: 978-1-80405-649-3

PROLOGUE

Gavin Whitmore parked his Royal Mail van directly opposite the pedestrian access to Moss End Cottage Guest House, grabbed the parcel to be delivered from the passenger seat, and sprang into action. A backward kick, the van door slammed shut, and he was off like a greyhound, bouncing across the road on Reebok trainers with two-inch soles.

Usual routine for the 'postie with the mostie': up the path, wedge the parcel between chest and stone pillar of porch, hammer on the door, and wait.

Nobody answered. Not a sound. Enough to make you swear. And he did. Though silently. Just in case there was anyone at home. Three times he'd tried to deliver this bloody parcel, and still no answer.

If it hadn't been imperative to get a signature confirming parcel received, he would have dumped it beneath one of the ridiculously huge urns placed either side of the door. The previous owner of Moss End, Ginny Porter, had been an auction fiend. What had possessed her to purchase these monstrosities was beyond Gavin. They were as tall as he was with nude figures running around the side. He eyed them as he waited and ran a finger over a nubile Greek breast; well, it *looked* like Greek. Historic anyway. And naughty. Might have been fun to know those Greeks.

One more try. Bang, bang, bang.

Chilly old place, he thought stepping back and looking up at the three-storey facade. The house was old; but there was nothing too different about that. A lot of houses in and around Bath were old, this one, however, had a creepy look about it, being set apart from the rest of the village behind walls that wouldn't have looked out of place surrounding one of Her Majesty's prisons. Even the decorative scrolls of the wrought iron gate behind him were covered by a metal sheet made too large to fit comfortably. The proximity of the plating against the hinges caused it to squeal, metal against metal when it was pushed open — the sort of sound that put your teeth on edge.

There it goes now.

'Nobody's there, postman.'

He knew who it would be even before she spoke. Mrs Hicks lived in one of the cottages across the road, a place as old as this one though nowhere near as large.

She was using her whole body to keep the strong spring of the gate from closing, both hands firmly grasping her walking stick. Bright blue eyes sparkled in a face creased with the pain of arthritis. Gavin conceded it must have taken some effort for her to cross the road.

Peregrine, a grey cat with orange eyes, curled his tail and whole body around her ankles. The cat followed her everywhere.

'How are you, Mrs Hicks?'

'My usual self. Old age isn't for wimps, you know.'

Gavin grinned. 'Years in you yet, Mrs Hicks. Years in you yet.'

She chuckled and her eyes twinkled with pleasure.

Gavin stooped down and tickled the cat behind its ears. 'And how are you, Peregrine, me old mate?'

The cat purred with pleasure.

The postman jerked his head sideways in the direction of the big old edifice opposite. 'Nobody in again.'

'You could wait for them at my place. Just in case they appear,' she said, her face shining in the hope that he had some time to spare. 'And if they don't appear — well — you can do what you usually do.'

Gavin smiled. Except for the cat, the old dear lived alone. Most of the residents of Northend were commuters, so she didn't get much company — not in the day anyway. Probably not at night either, seeing as most people would just come home and collapse in a chair with a gin and tonic, or saunter up to the Northend Inn for a bit of banter and beer with the landlord, or some bell-pulling at the church. Funny how townsfolk took to village pursuits that the real locals had no time for.

'How about a nice cup of tea?' urged a beaming Mrs Hicks.

Thirsting for a cuppa, he glanced at his watch. 'I s'pose I could for a while, but only if you've got a biscuit too.'

'Kettle's already boiled.'

Mrs Hicks, the cat, and the postman trailed off in single file across the road.

Once he'd drunk the tea and eaten the biscuits, he asked her if she wouldn't mind signing for the parcel and giving it to the new owners of the old place across the road when she saw them.

'Not at all. Anyway, it's time I introduced myself,' she replied, her eyes lighting up at the prospect of somebody new to talk to.

'You mean you haven't yet introduced yourself to the new owners of the old place? That's not like you, Mrs Hicks, party-going little raver that you are!'

The old lady tittered at his teasing. She always did, loving it when she had to take in a parcel for one of the neighbours. Gavin usually gave delivering a parcel three tries before leaving it with someone — usually Mrs Hicks. So far not one complaint of non-delivery.

He got her to sign the electronic device that recorded signatures on its dull grey screen.

'I'll just fetch my specs.'

'Now you're sure it's no trouble?'

'None at all,' she said, with a shake of her silvery head. 'Anyway, you'll never catch them during the day. I've never seen them in daylight, though I know they're in after dark. I've seen the lights go on. Don't think they get many paying guests though. Strange that. Miss Porter used to do quite well.'

Gavin thanked her profusely and went on his merry way, his head full of tunes from his iPod and his thoughts with his live-in girlfriend, Rita, who he was considering making his wife.

When he looked back at Mrs Hicks's cottage, the orange-eyed cat was sitting on a stone pillar to one side of the gate. It stared at him all the way across the road. Once he was safely seated behind the steering wheel, it appeared to lose interest. Washing one fat paw called for serious attention.

The following week he called in at Mrs Hicks's, meaning to tell her the good news that Rita had accepted his proposal of marriage. The old girl was an incurable romantic and had asked him to keep her informed.

There was no answer. Peering through the windows he saw no glow from the old Parkray she used to heat her house. OK, it wasn't that cold at the moment, but she was getting on a bit and he knew she kept it burning all year round, though low so she didn't get through too much coal. Neither did he espy the gleam of an electric light which he knew she needed if she was reading, which she did quite a lot. She liked reading *The People's Friend* which he picked up for her when it was due from the newsagents down on the main road that dissected Northend from the rest of Batheaston.

More worryingly he couldn't see any sign of Peregrine either. Perhaps she was in hospital or maybe a relative had suddenly remembered her and taken her on holiday. Not likely though. She never saw her relatives, although he knew she did have some. And she wouldn't go away without making arrangements for the cat. If she was away it had to be in a cattery.

He looked around the front garden for any sign of the cat. Nothing doing. On the off chance that the cat was in the back garden, he took the path at the side of the house. A wooden door set in a rickety wooden frame divided the front garden from the rear. He'd never been through it before. He knocked on the mossy green wood just in case Mrs Hicks was round the back doing a bit of weeding or hanging out her washing.

The gate hung loosely on its rusty hinges and scraped the flagstone path as he pushed it open. There was nobody in the garden, just a small shed and a dustbin. A broom, the sort made of willow twigs and used for sweeping up leaves, was propped up behind it.

No sign of Peregrine.

Being an upright chap, he'd done his duty checking that she was all right. But she wasn't there so he couldn't. Someone in the village would enlighten him as to where she was. The worst-case scenario, that she might have passed away, saddened him. Still she'd had a good innings, he thought, then laughed at the saying. Nobody he knew played cricket nowadays. How about saying that she'd shook it up well on the dance floor. Dancing would be far more likely than cricket. But then, surely somebody in the village would have told him if she'd snuffed it. And the cat wasn't around. That fact above all else was the crucial one; where Mrs Hicks went the cat went too.

He paused before getting back into his van to cast a look across the road at Moss End Cottage Hotel. The wall surrounding it was so high that only the upper floor windows could be viewed, the ground floor hidden behind the high wall and the filled in gate.

No lights showed in the upper windows either and although he'd put some letters in the letterbox today, there'd been no sign of anyone being at home. He wondered whether they were taking paying guests yet. It didn't seem like it given the vacant look of the windows, doing nothing but reflecting the cottages with which it was surrounded.

'I've not seen a soul there yet and according to Mrs Hicks she's not seen any sign of life during the daytime,' he said to Rita when he got home. 'The old lady said she only saw a light go on at night.'

'Like vampires,' said Rita. 'That's it. I expect the new owners are vampires and they sleep in coffins down in the cellar during the day, and only come out at night.'

Gavin guffawed and put his arms round her. 'Don't be so bloody ridiculous! Now give us a kiss, but gently now. Don't draw blood.'

CHAPTER ONE

Following an invitation from an old friend, Honey Driver, hotelier and part-time Crime Liaison Officer on behalf of Bath Hotels Association, was doing the 'ladies who lunch' thing at the Pump Rooms. The tablecloths were white, the atmosphere convivial, and a three-piece orchestra was strumming something by Handel.

Overall, it was a good place to lunch. In the eighteenth century the social networking was done over a beaker of warm water and a dip in a thermal pool. Today it was razor-thin cucumber sandwiches, cakes glistening with icing, and fruity scones oozing Cornish clotted cream and strawberry jam. The tea was too weak for Honey's taste but at least it was served in a china pot with a tea strainer and sugar cubes. Giving the tea a good mash in the pot with a teaspoon was a forlorn hope. Adding a few extra lumps of sugar, she decided, might be the best course of action.

She eyed her old friend Alison Brunton over the rim of her cup.

'You haven't changed since we were at school together.' She drowned the half-truth with a mouthful of tepid tea and tried not to grimace.

Laughter better suited to the teenager Alison used to be bubbled forth from lips that had been Botoxed and plastered with pink lipstick. 'No. Haven't lost my youthful looks, have I?' she gushed, preening like a teenager.

'You look good for your age,' said Honey, not quite truthfully, but Alison was an old friend and flattery was part of the must-have survival mechanism for the over forties.

The truth was that Alison looked like a life-size Barbie doll, all pointy boobs, lacquered hair, and clothes erring towards eighties glamour. It was all there, from her purple eyeshadow to her *Baywatch* hairstyle; plus she was wearing platform shoes with four-inch heels. Honey had seen her standing up and was amazed at how well she walked in them.

How did she do that?

It was a wonder her legs don't snap, thought Honey, who much preferred comfy shoes with low heels. You could go faster in low heels, better still in trainers. Who cared if she wore them with a skirt rather than jogging bottoms? Not that she ever went jogging. She had an aversion to it.

Alison, who visited the gym three times a week, did her best to impose on Honey what a great place it was for meeting people; specifically of the male gender.

'That's where I met Maurice. Maurice Hoffman. Big, bold, and beautiful. Oooh, yes! What a man! Abs to die for.'

Honey thought of DCI Doherty's abs. They had the consistency of blockboard, but she sure as hell had no intention of dying for them.

Alison was dabbing a paper napkin at each corner of her Botoxed lips, to which traces of Brigitte Bardot pink clung on regardless of the cream cakes she'd scoffed.

'Maurice has organised everything. My birthday's on the thirty-first of October. I'm holding it at Moss End Cottage Hotel. For some odd reason they refused at first. They said they'd only just taken it over and weren't ready to hold functions or take guests. However, my beloved, hunky-chunky Maurice insisted he'd booked it ages ago with the previous owner. They still refused to honour the booking, but Maurice is a lion when he's roused . . . grrr.'

Alison made lion's claws her hands. Her interpretation of a lion's roar was distinctly on the tame side.

Honey gritted her teeth. The 'Maurice the Lion' thing was bad enough; the hunky-chunky thing made her want to puke.

Alison hadn't noticed. 'Anyway, my darling Maurice, the most muscular man I have ever had the pleasure of . . .' She tittered and pretended to blush. 'Oh my. I am naughty. Now you know what the two of us have been doing.'

Honey resisted the urge to inform Alison that it was no big deal that she and the new man in her life had been playing more than footsie in bed. Instead she said, 'So your friend Maurice the lion threatened them with a lawsuit for compensation and they relented accordingly?'

'Maurice Hoffman, not Maurice de Lyon. And that's exactly what they did. You will come, won't you?'

'Of course I will,' said Honey, before Alison resorted to bending down on her knees and imploring her to come. Mentally she reworked the hotel rota so she could get away. In doing so she absentmindedly sprinkled salt into her tea.

Alison noticed what she'd done and made a pained expression as though it was on the same level as having an arm amputated. 'Honey, poor you! Shall I get you a fresh cup? I say, I say!' she shouted, waving her hand at an overburdened waitress who was presently serving a party of Americans at the next table.

Recognising a ready-made excuse to pass on the tepid tea, Honey gently patted Alison's arm back to earth. 'I'm not that thirsty. Anyway, I'm all agog to hear more about your birthday party. What is it you've got planned?'

Keen to indulge her favourite passion, talking about herself, Alison wiggled her bottom as people do when they're overexcited. Either that or her knickers were too small and too tight. On the other hand she might have merely been making herself more comfortable, but Alison was determined to hold onto her youth as long as humanly possible so it was possibly a yes to a pair of lacy thongs.

Eyes sparkling, her tone verging on the secretive, out it came.

'A themed party especially relevant to the date of my birthday.' She giggled. 'Guess the theme.'

Honey did her best to look as though the theme of Alison's birthday party seeing as it occurred on October 31ˢᵗ, would be a total surprise.

'Vicars and tarts? Naughty schoolgirls, naked men?'

Alison shook her head at both of Honey's guesses, though she did look as though she were considering naked men for a moment.

'None of those.'

'Not even the naked men?'

Alison licked her lips and looked thoughtful. 'Perhaps next year. But this year . . .'

She let out a 'ta-ra-ra' sound that was supposed to resemble a fanfare. From Alison it was kind of squeaky, as though a mouse had got trapped inside a trombone.

'Hallowe'en,' she squealed in the same irritatingly excitable voice she'd had as a teenager.

'Cool. That's really cool,' said Honey. 'Predictable' was more like it, but the woman was almost wetting herself with excitement — like a five-year-old about to tuck into a chocolate trifle.

'And you're a definite yes,' said Alison. Not waiting for Honey's answer, she dived into her handbag — a flashy concoction of leopard skin with an overabundance of brass buckles and zips.

Out came a pink notebook. Pages rustled as she flicked it open with pink-painted fingernails. She produced a pen — pink of course. Worse than that, it was adorned with a miniature pink fairy which wobbled as she scribbled.

'How could I not come? We're old friends,' said Honey, feigning enthusiasm. In reality she would have preferred to break her leg rather than attend, but reasoned that Alison was at a very difficult moment in her life and needed friends.

Her old school friend had only recently moved to the village of Swainswick, just a spit and a promise from the city centre. If she'd stayed in France with her ex-husband, two children, three cats, dog, parrot, and an au pair from Toulouse, Honey could have evoked distance as a credible reason for not attending her birthday party. As it was, Andrew, Alison's husband, had run off with the au pair . . . and the parrot. The au pair was young and pretty so running away with her was understandable. The parrot, however, was a different matter. According to Alison it swore like a trooper, but Andrew was very fond of it and if he had left it she would, in her own words, have had it put down, stuffed, and Fedexed it back to him.

Honey conceded that Andrew had guessed her likely reaction and as he was as fond of the parrot as the au pair, he had no wish to see the poor bird stuffed in retribution for his wandering groin.

'So. What will you come as?' asked Alison, her face bright with childish anticipation.

Honey smiled secretively over the top of a chocolate éclair she'd just taken from the cake stand. 'Not telling. It's a secret.'

She wasn't lying. The costume was a secret to her too. What the hell would she go as? A ghost? A witch? Something purple and indescribable?

The present wouldn't be a problem. Alison was a dyed in the wool chocoholic and Smudger, Honey's head chef, was a closet chocolatier. Handmade chocolates. Sorted!

But the outfit? There was no way she was going to attend dressed in a bedsheet with holes cut for eyes. If she got it askew, she'd end up tripping over the hem. And no way did she want to cover herself in odd colours and wear rubber appendages, or masks, or a hooked nose, or any of those things. She especially did not want to dress up as a spider. She did not like spiders. Anyway, despite the theme she harboured the grim determination to hang on to some kind of normality.

I want to at least be recognisable.

The question of costume stayed with her on the walk back to the Green River Hotel, set not far from Pulteney Street in the heart of the lovely city of Bath.

Spiders, ghouls, goblins, pumpkins, and witches with warts on their noses; none appealed.

Shrugging her chin into her upturned coat collar, she paused to let a plastic carrier bag and a brace of autumn leaves scuttle past.

In the act of pausing, she happened to glance into a shop window display offering 'EXPERT financial advice'. How about expert supernatural advice? When it came to things that go bump in the night, there was only one person to ask. She was tall, gangly, had eyes that were sometimes piercing and sometimes looked as though they'd shot into orbit around Mars.

On arrival back at the Green River Hotel, an early Georgian building of infinite possibilities if only she had the money for development, she sidled behind the reception desk and punched in 07 on the phone. Nobody answered.

Anna was on duty and for once she wasn't pregnant. Currently working out her notice, she was soon moving back to Poland, where she'd invested in a small café presently being run by her mother.

Honey put down the phone. 'Anna, have you seen Mary Jane today?'

Mary Jane was the Green River's resident professor of the paranormal. She knew everything there was to know about ghosts and ghouls. Looking slightly otherworldly herself, she'd flown in from California many years ago (with American Airlines, not on a broomstick) and hadn't gone back. This was because she'd stumbled across an ancestor haunting her room and decided to keep him company. So entrenched was she in her new life with an old ghost that she'd also brought over her car, a 1961 Cadillac Coupe. It was pink, the steering wheel was on the wrong side for driving on the left-hand side of the road, and so too, a lot of the time, was Mary Jane.

'Yes,' said Anna in response to her question. 'She has gone underground.'

Anna slapped a pile of brochures into apple pie order then fanned them in a circle with a sleight of hand that was breathtaking to watch.

Honey stood for a moment admiring the display. She'd never mastered that particular sleight of hand herself.

'How do you do that?' she asked incredulously.

'Fanny dancing,' said Anna. 'I used to do fanny dancing.'

'*Fan* dancing,' Honey corrected — something she frequently did, even though Anna had been resident in Bath for a few years — suppressing a smile. Anna's English was quite good now, but she had an unfortunate tendency to make comments that didn't quite say what she meant. 'Now where did you say Mary Jane was?'

Anna nodded towards the floor. 'Underground. She has gone under the ground. It happened this morning — just an hour ago.'

A sudden cold shiver ran down Honey's spine. 'Wait, you mean . . .' Getting the rest of the words out was like dredging for gold. Had Mary Jane, way past the three score years and ten, finally been united with Sir Cedric, the ancestor with whom she had daily contact?

'Oh my God! What happened?' she exclaimed, fully expecting to hear that Mary Jane and the pink Caddy had gone to that big car park in the sky.

'She went underground because Adrian said it was spooky and that somebody was down there. She is still down there. Adrian has quit.'

Seeing as Adrian was, or had been, a trainee wine waiter, this meant that Mary Jane was down in the cellar. He hadn't been that good a wine waiter but having him quit so swiftly raised the obvious query.

'Why did he quit? Is he scared of spiders or something?'

She could understand it if he had. The cellar was a haven for spiders; cobwebs hung in abundance like torn shrouds.

'No. He said it was soldiers. According to him they wore little leather skirts and armour that went clang, clang, clang when they marched through the cellar.'

'Oh, is that all?'

Breathing a sigh of relief, Honey thanked Anna, dared to touch the leaflet display with an enquiring finger, and scooted as it fell into instant disarray.

The cellar was a gloomy place, mainly because a series of arches supporting the building impeded the distribution of the dismal lighting. White paint flaked off bare brick and spiders lurked in dark corners. Some of them were big — very big!

Wine, beer, and discarded furniture considered too good to dump were stored down here, along with tax records that would never again see the light of day; paper mouldered swiftly away, a victim of damp, mice, and beetles.

Roman soldiers marching through had never been a problem before. In fact she didn't recall anyone mentioning them, not even Mary Jane who could sniff out a ghostly apparition with one nostril blocked. However, Mary Jane had never been in the cellar before.

Honey groped her way down the cold stone steps, ducking cobwebs and keeping her eyes open for furry friends scuttling past when you least expected them to.

This was hardly her favourite place, playing Dungeons and Dragons had never been high on her favourite things list.

Nothing to worry about though. Wimpy Adrian! A nervous type with a thin frame and long hands with very thin fingers. Not strong fingers either. Would they have been able to hold onto a magnum of champagne? Not that they sold many magnums of champagne . . . Creep up behind him and shout 'boo' and he might have dropped them. Now how good would that be for the Green River's reputation?

A cold draught came up the steps, making her skirt into a bell tent. At the same time she slapped at the prickling sensation at the nape of her neck. Or had a spider landed there? If so, where was it now?

She wriggled from the waist in the hope of dislodging the eight-legged creature that just might have fallen down her back.

A light bulb fizzled and blinked out. She paused, one foot poised over the bottom step. Her heart wasn't exactly leapfrogging against her ribs but the frequency of the palpitations she was experiencing were reminiscent of Morse code. She read the dot-dot, dash-dash encryptions easily. They were telling her to get out.

Gird your loins!

The advice came out of nowhere and was less than helpful. It was difficult to be brave with all these cobwebs around and light bulbs blinking out for no reason. Still, there was just enough light to see by.

Taking a deep breath, she called Mary Jane's name. It echoed right back. The following silence was worse than the echoes. There was a terrible emptiness to the silence. As though it was waiting for loud noises to fill it, she thought.

Her heart leapt at a scuffling sound. Her brain was telling her to run back up the steps. Her feet seemed to be buried in concrete.

She held herself very still. Silence. Then more scuffles.

Probably a mouse, she told herself. A mouse she could cope with. But, please, not a rat. She hated rats. How the hell could people keep a rat as a pet?

But that rustling, scuffling sound was too loud for it just to be Robert Burns's 'timorous beastie'. This beastie was far from tiny; in fact it sounded huge.

Narrowing her eyes, trying to focus, her attention was drawn to a particularly dark corner. Another sound came to her; heavy breathing, like somebody struggling to get out from somewhere. Hopefully nobody had buried a vampire down here in the darkness. She tried to recall ever seeing a coffin down here. No. The oblong thing lying to her right on top of a stainless-steel table was not a coffin. It was an old blanket box

15

that used to sit in a small corner on the first-floor landing. If it did harbour a vampire, then his name had to be Shorty. She figured she could handle a very small Count Dracula.

But short vampire or not, her heart had given up on Morse code and was beating like a drum. Her tongue turned to sandpaper when the pitch blackness in a far corner changed shape. Throwing herself back up the stairs to daylight leapt high on the agenda, but she was hedging her bets. It had to be Mary Jane in the corner.

First there was what looked like something hunch backed scrabbling on all fours. Suddenly the paleness of a face pierced the gloom, and the culprit popped out of a hole.

'Honey! Did I scare you? My torch went out.'

Mary Jane came into the light and straightened to her full height. At over six feet tall her stiff curls — orange this month — scraped the flaking paint from the ceiling. Flecks of it showered around her. She looked like a figure from a very large paperweight, one of those you turn upside down to make it snow.

'Mary Jane!' Honey pressed a hand to her chest. 'I was worried about you.'

The Californian professor brushed cobwebs from her hair and shoulders. 'No need to be, dear. It may have escaped your notice, but I'm not the kind to be frightened of the dark. Or spooks. Or ghouls. Or anything ephemeral.'

Honey sighed with relief.

'Did you find anything interesting?'

She said it as though the cellar held no fears for good old Honey Driver.

'Could be a possibility that your hotel was built on an old Roman burial ground. Or an old battleground. We need to do a little research.'

'Lindsey will be pleased.'

Honey had always entertained surprise that her daughter was more interested in history than she was men. Not that Lindsey didn't have her moments. Indeed she did. But if something interesting on the historical front came up, the chance of some guy in tight jeans getting anywhere with Lindsey went down. It was Lindsey who would do the research.

'How very interesting. So you think the buried soldiers are still marching into battle?'

'Poor guys. They probably didn't even get to the battle. Could have been victims of an epidemic. Either that or the natives cut their throats before they had chance to draw their swords.'

'Well, if it's only long-dead Roman soldiers, there really isn't anything to worry about,' said Honey airily. Roman legionaries were far less frightening than spiders and small imagined furry creatures.

'Tea,' said Mary Jane without making comment about what or who else might be lurking in the darkness. 'I need tea. Investigating a haunting is guaranteed to work up a thirst.'

Honey would have preferred something stronger, but it was only mid-afternoon. Besides, she'd come up from the cellar without wearing cobwebs in her hair. A definite bonus!

Nice white tablecloths covered the dining tables in the restaurant. Mary Jane smoothed the sparkling linen with one wrinkled hand after gulping back her first cup of tea which Honey promptly refilled. She was unconcerned that Mary Jane was leaving a trail of white flakes and coal dust whenever she moved.

'There's a tunnel down there,' she said after gulping back her second cup of tea. 'I think I was pretty close to the end of it when my flashlight gave out. Damned shame. I'm sure I was on to something. I could feel the vibes. There are old bones down there, mark my words. It could be that the tunnel links up with the ones below the Roman Baths. Even to those underground places in Milsom Street.'

Honey had it on the tip of her tongue to remark that it was probably only Mary Jane's old bones that had been down there but she managed to hold back.

More flakes of dry paint and dust fluttered in the air as Mary Jane sipped tea and nibbled at home-made lemon drizzle cake.

'Still, I'm so glad you're in one piece,' Honey remarked. 'When Anna said you'd gone, I wondered what she meant. You know how she is muddling up meanings of words.'

Mary Jane chuckled and her eyes twinkled. 'You afraid I wasn't here anymore?'

Honey felt her face turn warm. How could she possibly admit to thinking that Mary Jane had finally joined her ancestor, Sir Cedric, on the other side?

'I would really miss you . . .' Honey began, meaning to go on to say how embarrassed and sorry she was to have assumed that Mary Jane had passed over, but Mary Jane didn't give her chance.

'Don't be silly,' she trilled, her blue eyes looking deeply into Honey's. 'You should know for sure that I am never leaving you and going back to the US. Sir Cedric would be so upset if I did. Nice to think that you would too.'

Honey exhaled a big breath. Phew! What an upset she could have caused. Mary Jane had misunderstood, not guessing she'd thought she was dead. There was no way Honey was going to own up — she was genuinely relieved that Mary Jane was still in the here and now.

'What would we do without you?'

Her remark coincided with loss of tension. It was like having all the bones fall out of her shoulders, leaving the muscles like soft cushions.

Mary Jane said that she was relieved to hear it and what a silly goose Honey was to have thought that she would leave without saying goodbye.

From there she went on to explain about the birthday party and the fact that she had no intention of going dressed in a bedsheet or look terribly purple and ugly as a monster, a spider, or a witch with an overlarge hooked nose.

'I thought you might have an idea of who I could go as. Something spooky but sexy. That's my take on what the outfit should be.'

Mary Jane blinked, put down her cup, and went immediately into a trance — or so it seemed. Closing her eyes, she raised her arms so that her hands were out to each side, palms upwards. She was making a humming noise.

Feeling a tad concerned, Honey snatched at Mary Jane's teacup and took a sniff. She had good reason to do so. Some time back their washer up, Rodney Eastwood, aka Clint, had mislaid a sachet of magic mushrooms that he kept purely for personal recreational use. The restaurant had been busy. The dishwashing had been going at full pelt and Clint had been forced to help out with the beverages. He'd made pot after pot of tea.

After polishing off a pot of Earl Grey, six members of the Swainswick Senior Bowling Club proceeded to dance and behave as they had back in the Summer of Love. On seeing what was going on, the rest of the club demanded to have the same as their colleagues. It wasn't until later that Clint was spotted spooning teabags from pot after pot, searching for his mislaid stash.

Luckily that didn't seem to be the problem on this occasion. Suddenly Mary Jane's eyes popped open.

'Morticia Addams!'

Honey sat back, genuinely impressed. She recalled the American TV show and remembered the gorgeous female lead.

'Dark. Sexy. Recognisable,' she said feeling and sounding seriously impressed. 'That HAS to be me!'

'Right!'

'Long black clingy dress with feathery, shroud-like sleeves. I think I can find something suitable. Pale complexion, dark make-up, and long dark hair. My mother has the stage make-up. The dramatic society are "resting" at present.'

The truth was that a number of members had dropped dead or gone senile, which accounted for the latter so frequently forgetting their lines.

Lindsey joined them, bubbling with the news that the elusive honeymoon couple in one of the suites had finally surfaced, paid their bill, and left a very generous tip.

'They reckoned it was the best hotel they'd every stayed in.'

'How would they know? They never came out of their room.'

Lindsey waved a fifty-pound note in front of her face. 'That's why they enjoyed their stay. They never got out of bed and nobody ever disturbed them. What better honeymoon could they have had?'

After agreeing the point, Honey went on to tell her about the fancy dress Hallowe'en birthday party.

'A lot of parties rolled into one. I'm going as Morticia Addams. I've got a long black dress. It's not too shroud-like, but I can unpick the sleeves and make them more ragged.'

'That should work. If you like, I can get you a long dark wig from Clarissa,' said Lindsey. 'She used to wear it all the time when she was doing art class at college.'

'I didn't know you had a student friend named Clarissa,' Honey remarked with a satisfied sigh. She was feeling incredibly happy now her outfit was on the drawing board — so to speak.

'She was a life model. She posed naked. The long black wig was a modesty thing.'

CHAPTER TWO

Steve Doherty grumbled, between soft caresses and promises of good things to come, that he didn't like fancy dress parties.

'Is it OK if I go as myself?' he wheedled.

'No. You have to be Gomez Addams to my Morticia.'

'Sherlock Holmes?'

'Sherlock Holmes has nothing to do with Hallowe'en.'

Some pretty hot sexual antics weakened his resolve; food might be the way to some men's hearts, but in Doherty's case it was sex. He would accompany her wearing suitable costume and be pleased to do so. As long as she took her clothes off right now.

It was a small price to pay, anyway she was quite keen on getting up front and personal with him. As for the party? Of course he was coming. He was putty in her hands.

Honey should have remembered that the end of October was not her favourite time of year and that the demands of life were not constrained to the Green River Hotel. She had a family to contend with, though that shouldn't have made that much difference. As Smudger the chef was fond of telling her, manure becomes a four-letter word when it falls on top of you.

If her old Citroen hadn't developed a technical fault, and if Ahmed at the oily little repair shop beneath the arches hadn't let her down, then the accident would never have happened.

'There's a gremlin in the electrical department,' proclaimed Ahmed Clifford — son of a Somerset chip shop owner and a widow with three children and a market stall. Ahmed was the only result of their union. He said this while running his greasy right hand through his equally greasy long hair.

Ahmed didn't look like your average mechanic. His glowing skin, glossy shoulder length hair, and long black eyelashes was far more luscious than anything Max Factor could produce. His eyes glowed with dark depths, in a face continually greasy from the cars he worked on.

Honey took the statement on board assuming he was referring to her car's electrical department — the tangle of wiring embedded beneath its metal skin.

'I know she's a little cantankerous, but I do believe it's part of her charm and—'

'—her electrics are lousy. Dangerous even.' Ahmed had a habit of butting in before a sentence was finished. 'It's a Citroen. It's French. Anyone with any sense knows that French electrics are crap. There's a gremlin on the production line.' He had to be kidding. Did he really believe in a green gremlin chuckling wickedly to itself while pulling wires from where they should be and putting them where they shouldn't?

'If he exists, I hope he's well insulated and isn't likely to—'

'—catch fire. The car might. That's the dodgy thing about electrics.'

Ahmed shrugged and lit up another cigarette. The fact that both he and his workshop were coated with flammable substances didn't seem to worry him.

'How soon can you fix it?' She spoke quickly before Ahmed could pre-empt and answer the question before she'd actually asked it.

His sucked in breath made a hissing sound through his pearly white teeth. He shook his head, expression as morose as a down at heel funeral director.

'It's a big job. Not easy at all.'

It was as though somebody had shoved an icicle down Honey's back. A very long icicle. Ever the optimist, she'd expected him to tell her that hey ho, it would be fixed in the shake of a lamb's tail. But she'd heard that hissing before; it was made by anyone in the business of fixing things or rather inferring that something was not fixable. The writing was on the wall; her vehicle needed to stay in the automotive equivalent of intensive care. Hopefully there would be a full recovery. But this was a car and not just a French car. It was her wheels, her mode of transport, imperative to survival.

'I really need it . . .'

'. . . back in a hurry,' he finished. 'Of course you do. Sorry. It'll take a week at least. I'm stacked out with work as it is and tracing an electrical fault takes time.

Honey huffed out a sigh. Bath was a great city for walking, but there were times, such as shopping at the cash and carry, escaping to do serious shopping in London, or driving her mother to somewhere she just had to be, when she badly needed a car. Her gaze scooted over three or four cars parked on the forecourt. Two or three of them sported for sale notices. She wondered whether he hired them too.

'Do you . . .?'

'. . . hire cars? No. Sorry.'

'Ever thought of . . .?'

'. . . running a few cars I can let out to customers whose cars are being repaired? No. Running a hire fleet can be expensive. It's the insurance, you see.'

'I was about to ask if you'd ever thought about going on the stage.'

His teeth flashed white against dark skin and a wreath of cigarette smoke.

'Not stage. Film. I wouldn't mind being a film star. I can do all the dance moves.'

Suddenly he broke into song while gyrating like a Bollywood superstar, rolling his eyes and flapping his hands — all to the sound of a rock and roll number sung in Urdu.

'No,' said Honey once the performance was ended. 'Stage. As a mind reader.'

She repeated all this to Doherty later in the smoky darkness of the Zodiac Club.

'No bloody car and my mother wants me to go with her to meet a friend who's down. I suppose I'll have to hire one—but the cost . . .'

'Is this a life and death kind of visit?'

'You could say that. Her friend's husband's gone off. Left her a goodbye note and said he was going to travel the world to find himself. My mother's offered my services; wants me to find him.'

'PI Driver,' he said with a grin. 'Have you any idea how many people leave to find themselves every year?'

'Lots, I would guess, though not many in their late eighties. And not many with a wife offering five grand to whoever finds out where he is.'

Doherty gulped. Honey wasn't sure whether it was in disbelief or amusement. Probably both.

'And before you ask, Rhoda is also in her eighties. So it is life and death in that both of them have one foot on a bar of soap and the other in the grave.'

'Tell you what,' he said, still looking amused, 'I'm on a course in Reading for the next week. Borrow mine.'

'My,' she said, snuggling up to his shoulder. 'More brownie points for you!'

His grin widened. 'I'll collect them all later.'

Doherty's Toyota MR2 was made for two to share. It didn't boast much room for shopping, but they were off to visit Rhoda Watchpole, one of her mother's oldest friends.

Rhoda lived in a two-bedroomed flat on the second floor of an apartment building catering exclusively for the over-sixties. The broad door guarding the entrance was wide enough to take wheelchairs. It also closed slowly to allow for the entry of slow legs and Zimmer frames. In case of need there was also a warden on duty at all times.

Gloria Cross, splendidly turned out in a damson-coloured suede jacket, caramel sweater, and trousers the colour of Cornish cream, pressed the button for Rhoda's flat. Honey was resplendent in faded jeans, a black sweater, scuffed boots, and a quilted jacket that smelled vaguely of wet dog.

Rhoda's voice sounded through an assortment of squeaks and asked who it was. The buzzing sound that followed happened at the same time as the lock released.

The room they were shown into was stuffy. It was also very beige; light beige walls, dark beige furniture, beige and pink floral carpet.

Honey had seen the woman before when dropping her mother off at some seniors do, but didn't recall her being as fat as she was now. She certainly couldn't recall her having a treble chin. Her hips fitted snugly in the wide armchair.

A box of Marks and Spencer's fresh cream cakes sat on a small occasional table within grabbing range. Half a chocolate éclair sat on top the box, all that remained of four cream cakes if the writing on the side of the box could be believed.

Gloria Cross also noticed the cakes.

'Am I reading right, Rhoda? There were four cakes in that box?'

Rhoda twisted her head and eyed the box over a buxom bosom.

'Were there four?'

Honey's mother grimaced. 'There certainly were. Marks and Spencer wouldn't lie about a thing like that.'

'They're lovely,' said Rhoda just before stuffing the half éclair into her mouth. 'I can't resist. My doctor says I'm comfort eating. I've let myself go, he said, and I really need to take control again. But it isn't easy,' she said, pulling a bunch of tissues from a box stuffed under a rim of fat where a waistline used to be. 'I miss Bert so much. Why didn't he say he wanted to go on one last adventure? I would have gone with him, honest I would.'

A vision of the elephantine woman struggling up Everest or paddling a canoe up the Orinoco popped into Honey's mind. In the first instance she would probably fall and bounce all the way back down again. In the second, her bulk would either capsize the canoe or she'd be stuck in it, never to escape until she'd lost a few pounds.

Rhoda dabbed at her watery eyes and blew her snotty nose. A waste bin near her feet confirmed the fact that crying and eating took up most of her time. It was full of tissues, chocolate wrappers, and cake boxes.

'Never mind, Rhoda. Honey's going to call out an ABC and find that missing husband of yours.'

Taking the opportunity to look out of the window at the neat lawns and bare flowerbeds, Honey rolled her eyes. Her mother was now referring to an APB like she'd heard the cops say on American TV shows. ABC or APB, neither would happen. The fact was she'd never had to locate a missing husband before — and not one in his late eighties who had gone on walkabout.

'So, when did this happen?' asked Honey.

Rhoda sniffed and looked around her. At first Honey presumed she was being secretive about the date for some odd reason, until she saw a second box of cakes. Mr Kipling's apple pies. Honey handed them to her and Rhoda grabbed them with her podgy hands.

'It was at the same time as Margaret Sinclair was taken away in the ambulance. The warden would have the correct date. I think she had breathing difficulties. Anyway, she never came back. In no time at all, her flat was up for sale and all her furniture taken away. Poor old soul. Still,' she said, shaking her head as she ripped open the box of apple pies. 'We're all destined to go the same way, aren't we?'

Gloria Cross was having none of it. 'Sooner rather than later if you keep stuffing back those cakes and pies, Rhoda. For goodness' sake, get a grip! We're here now and Honey is going to find Bert for you.'

The first apple pie paused on its way to Rhoda's mouth. The corners of her mouth turned down. It seemed Rhoda was about to break into tears again.

'I can't help it, Gloria,' she wailed. 'You have to understand. I miss Bert so much. Especially at night lying alone in bed.'

Up until this point, Honey hadn't been too sold on the idea of finding a missing husband, but seeing the woman's copious tears, she couldn't be cruel.

'Look, Mrs Watchpole. I'll do my best to find him. Perhaps that will help you control your comfort eating, at least. Yes?'

Honey's mother was more to the point. 'Look at it this way, Rhoda, if the poor man does come home, you'll still be lying alone in bed — because with all that fat you take up so much room there'll be no room in bed for Bert.'

When it came to making the best of what you had, Honey knew that her mother took no prisoners. There was no excuse for letting yourself go even when you were in your eighties and your husband has gone trekking in the Himalayas or swimming with whales, or whatever.

Initially Honey presumed that Rhoda was about to burst into tears again. But she didn't. She looked up at Gloria with moist round eyes.

'You're right, Gloria. You are SO right!'

To Honey's surprise the apple pie went back into its box and the box into the bin.

Rhoda pulled herself up from her chair and studied her reflection in the mirror hanging on the wall.

'I need to get my hair done before he gets back. Might even have a facial. Definitely a pedicure. My corns are playing me up rotten. Yes,' she said, her eyes shining and fixed on Honey's mother. 'I need to get myself in shape before he comes back. I'll join a gym; I'll go jogging . . .'

They left her there billowing with hope.

On the way out, Honey paid a visit to the warden's flat which was on the ground floor. A man with Mediterranean looks and of the required sixty years of age and over answered the door. His eyes flitted over Honey and then landed on her mother.

His smile was practised pure seduction. 'Can I help you lovely ladies?'

Honey heard warning bells. Her mother had been a big Tony Curtis fan in his younger days, especially in *Spartacus* with Kirk Douglas. It was the short skirt that did it. Oh, and she had a weakness for Italians too.

Honey pushed a protective shoulder between the warden and her mother and explained their reason for being there.

'I've been retained by Mrs Watchpole to find her missing husband. Perhaps you could confirm some of the details, such as when he went missing?'

The deep brown eyes that had been locked with her mother's reluctantly returned to her — almost as though she'd just interrupted a very important conversation.

'Mr Watchpole. Ah, yes. He left a note. He wasn't murdered or kidnapped or anything. He just wanted to get away, I think.'

'I know. I just want you to confirm the date. Mrs Watchpole said it was at the same time as another of your residents was carted away in an ambulance?'

'Margaret Sinclair,' her mother interjected. 'Slim lady with pale blonde hair turning white. Used to be a model in her younger days for Norman Hartnell and Coco Chanel.'

'You didn't say,' said Honey, eyeing her mother in disbelief.

'You didn't ask,' said a smiling Gloria Cross, her faraway look and her enigmatic smile directed at the one-time Italian stallion standing in the doorway.

'Come in, dear ladies,' he said, swinging the door wide. 'I will check the details for you. Can I offer you a drink? Tea, coffee, Chianti?'

'No,' said Honey, quickly.

'*Yes*,' said Gloria gliding past her daughter. 'Wine.'

Honey could hardly believe her ears. Her mother never drank wine at lunchtime. It wasn't that often she drank it at dinnertime either.

Reduced to being a second-rate performer in this particular scene, she followed the elderly couple. At one point it seemed the door would close on her, leaving her outside before she had chance to get in. Luckily her boots had no heel so she was quick on her feet.

'My name is Tony,' he said, her mother's hand in his, his smile still sending a sexual message and his eyes looking deep into hers.

'Anthony. I am so pleased to meet you,' said Honey's mother.

'Antonio. Please. Call me Antonio.' He kissed her hand.

'A beautiful name,' breathed Gloria Cross. 'Italian, of course.'

'My mother was Italian.'

Honey looked at her mother's awestruck expression and she could almost hear her mother's heart racing.

'The date. Could you check it,' Honey persisted as the warden kissed her mother's hand for the second time before enclosing it in both of his.

'Of course,' he said, his smile directed at her while his eyes devoured her mother from head to toe.

Gloria positively preened at the attention she was receiving.

The warden let go her hand long enough to delve into an elaborate bureau of tropical wood with mother-of-pearl decorations. It looked Italian. Just like him.

He retrieved a diary bound in black vinyl, fluttered a few pages, and ran his finger down the dates.

'July 23rd. It was a Tuesday evening at seven o'clock when the ambulance came for Mrs Parsons.'

'At what time was it noticed that Mr Watchpole had gone missing?' asked Honey.

Antonio tossed his black-haired head thoughtfully, eyes rising to the ceiling.

29

'He'd started going to the gym. That's where he went that morning, but he didn't come back.'

'Wasn't he a bit . . . old for the gym?' said Honey.

Both her mother and Antonio fixed her with a pitying look. 'It was a class for the over-sixties,' said Antonio. 'It's geared for people who are not as athletic as they used to be. Stiff knees. Bad hips. Lumpy elbows.'

Honey squirmed a bit but didn't apologise. In her opinion she'd asked a totally reasonable question.

'And the note. Do you know when that was discovered?'

Saving his sugary smile for her mother, from whom his eyes never strayed, he nodded in answer to her question.

'Mrs Watchpole found it tucked inside her weekly magazine which her husband had fetched from the shop on the corner before going to the gym.'

* * *

On the way back to Bath, Gloria expressed a wish to visit John Lewis to buy another friend a birthday present. On the way there they talked about Rhoda and Bert.

'It was all carefully planned,' said Honey. 'Right down to leaving the note and taking a holdall in which he could pack the few things he needed. He must have really been keen to do a bit of soul-searching.'

'It's Rhoda's own fault, of course. She was already putting on weight before he left,' said her mother, her lips pursed in disapproval. 'But now she's worse. I'm of the firm opinion that she hasn't seen her toes for a while, or anything else for that matter.' She paused to gather her thoughts and the thoughts made her smile. 'Hey. That warden. What a dish!'

If she hadn't been driving — and driving Doherty's car at that — Honey would have closed her eyes and counted to ten.

'I'm going to buy Cecily a pair of fish tweezers for her birthday.'

'Not perfume?'

'Of course not. Perfume is so *ordinary*.'

Honey considered how she would feel on receiving a pair of fish tweezers as opposed to a 250ml bottle of Chanel No.5. But she also knew that once her mother had made up her mind about something, there was no point in arguing.

The sales assistant had purple hair and a double chin but was very apologetic. 'We have a very wide range of cooking utensils, but . . .' He shrugged his shoulders and flapped his hands apologetically.

Honey's mother was most put out. 'I know she really needed a pair of fish tweezers. Now what do I get her?'

'Perfume?'

'Don't be ridiculous. I don't want to encourage her wayward lifestyle.'

This was the first time Honey had heard that her mother's oldest friend had a wayward lifestyle.

'Are you saying there's more to the Bath Senior Citizen's Club than old-time dancing and playing bridge?'

Her mother made a so-so kind of face and waved fingers heavy with diamond rings.

'Cecily has been sowing wild oats like there's no tomorrow. She can't help it. In fact she hasn't been right since finding Eric dead in bed.'

Honey couldn't argue with that. The circumstances of Eric dying in bed were enough to unhinge anyone.

On the night in question, Eric had gone to bed early complaining of a sore throat. Two hours later, Cecily had joined him. Before switching off the light she'd asked him how his throat was. He'd made a sort of gargling sound that to her ears was confirmation that his throat had not improved. In the morning she'd asked him if he wanted a cup of tea but got no reply. Thinking a lie-in would do him good, she went downstairs, made a cup of tea for herself and took one up to him an hour later.

He didn't answer when she spoke to him. Neither did he respond when she shook his shoulder. At that point she called the doctor and after the briefest of examination, he had confirmed what she had failed to notice; her husband was dead and had been for some hours.

'Well, anyway' said Honey's mother. 'Poor Cecily. Fancy waking up to a stiff one!'

Judging by the sucked-in lips of the sales assistant, his interpretation of what constituted a stiff one differed from that of her mother and he was barely suppressing his amusement. Honey managed not to laugh, but it wasn't easy so she was glad when her mother picked a plastic apron emblazoned with a female figure of ample proportions and wearing nothing but a garter belt. That, her mother had decided, would do just as well for Cecily's birthday.

A cup of coffee and piece of carrot cake in the in-store café, a trip to the ladies' loo, and they were ready to head home.

The return journey would have been uneventful if her mother hadn't had second thoughts about the apron; not the nude torso, but the fact that it might have a label saying 'Made in China.'

'I need to check. I don't want her to think I was a cheapskate,' she said resolutely.

'Mother, it cost you forty pounds.'

'I know, but the right label says it all. I'd prefer if it said "made in England" or even "made in Europe". Not China. Only cheap stuff is made in China. Everyone knows that!'

The traffic was heavy, cars darting on and off to the main island in the centre of the shopping complex. All roads led to the shopping mall and the profusion of shopping outlets that had burgeoned around it like fungus on a compost heap. Honey concentrated on her driving because, after all, this wasn't her car and Doherty loved his car almost as much as he did her — maybe more. The jury was out on that one.

Then she remembered she could do with a box of screws, so quickly headed towards the B&Q superstore.

Leaving her mother in the car, she dashed in, bought the screws, dashed out again, started up the car, and headed for the exit.

The car park exited onto a busy road where she found herself waiting in a queue to get out.

Grumbles and sharp words about idiot drivers were hard to keep in check. A few cars and cusses later and they'd at last reached the white line. Honey turned right out of the car park at the exact moment that her mother got the apron out holding it up against the windscreen. The voluptuous torso faced forward while she searched for the label.

'Great,' she said after some close scrutiny. Her tone veered towards sarcastic. 'It says made in India.'

'Mother!'

There was a screeching of brakes then a bang that jolted both of them.

Honey groaned.

Her mother was all hurt indignation. 'It wasn't your fault. I should give that man a piece of my mind.'

Honey buried her face in the airbag that had conveniently cushioned the blow.

Doherty's car!

The man in the car that hit them wore an expression of total surprise, but apologised profusely, squinting through the side window at them.

'I was just thinking of how sexy my ex-wife was, when bam! There she was in your car windscreen. A well-built woman with nothing on. Sorry love, but you flashed at me and I was in heaven.'

'Understandable and not entirely your fault,' said Honey while throwing a killer look at her mother.

Insurance details were exchanged.

Gloria Cross shook her head. 'Never mind. There's no point crying over spilt milk. These things happen.'

'Don't they just,' growled Honey wondering what the current sentence was for wilful matricide.

Swallowing her urge to commit murder, she sucked in her breath and punched in Doherty's number. There was no point in putting off the dreaded moment. He answered before she'd mentally rehearsed a really sexy, seductive line that might make his response less angry.

'Hi!' The sexy seductive line stuck in her throat and led to a lengthy pause. A telling pause. Doherty could read a silence as swiftly as he could a lie or a guilty expression.

'What have you done?'

'Well. It's more a kind of learning curve. A bit of information that you'll be really glad to learn about.'

'Aaand?'

The response was drawn out. On top of that she fancied he was counting — three beats to give her the benefit of the doubt.

At last he sighed, resigned that he was going to hear something he wouldn't like. 'Go on.'

The apprehension in his voice was palpable, like when the blue touch paper of a firework smoulders for a bit before exploding.

There was nothing for it but to swallow and dive in.

'I thought I'd just ring and tell you that the air bag on your car works perfectly. So do your crumple zones.'

CHAPTER THREE

Honey made the decision that there was nothing for it but to put Bert Watchpole on the back burner. Wondering if Doherty would ever speak to her again, she set out for Alison Brunton's birthday bash alone, sleekly attired as Morticia Addams in a slinky black dress, a long black wig, and shoes with silver buckles. The shoes also had four-inch heels and were killing her. If only Doherty was here to lean on — literally.

One look at the manic glint in his eyes had been enough to tell her that he wasn't in a party mood and wouldn't be in one for a while to come — at least until the damage to his darling car was repaired.

She could tell by the way his mouth lurched from side to side that he was clenching his jaw to stop a few choice expletives coming out and flying her way. He'd even turned his back on her when she'd offered to buy him lunch, shoulders hunched, fists clenched.

'OK. I'll go alone,' she shouted after him. 'It's not that I can't take care of myself. Or won't have anyone to talk to.'

No response. So that was it. I'll have a great time, she thought to herself. I mean, it isn't as if I can't live without him, is it?

In time everything would be back where it was before the accident. The car would come home and they'd be back together.

Her own car still indisposed, she took a taxi to the venue. Anyway, she recalled that Moss End Cottage Hotel only had a small car park. Six cars and it would be stuffed full.

After giving her wig a tweak and bending down to rub her aching toes, she was ready to roll.

The building dated from the early eighteenth century or at least the middle part did. A wing had been added on each end in Victorian times. The building was big lengthwise but of shallow depth. The centre and original part of the house had three floors topped by a Welsh slate roof — the shape resembling an upturned boat and named after a French architect named Mansard. Two adjoining dormer windows stuck out like an afterthought from a bank of grey-blue slates.

The wings on either end only had two floors and pan-tiled roofs that glowed orange in sunlight, but were dull at this time of night and weren't named after anyone. The whole was surrounded by a high wall split by a single gate as blank and protective as the wall. Someone had stuck a hand-written notice on it saying 'Entrance'. Half a dozen balloons dangled over it.

Smoothing her dress down over her hips and hoping none of the lumpy bits were noticeable, Honey teetered up to the front door. Her shoes were still killing her, but once inside she vowed to grab a chair and sit down. Sitting instead of mingling wasn't usually a good idea at parties, but she had a plan. Folding one leg over the other, she would sit there looking sexy.

The front door of the building was protected from the elements by a stone vestibule. It was just about big enough to house a lone sentry complete with bearskin.

Muted noise filtered from inside. Leaning to her left gave her a good view through a pair of French doors. Judging by the condensation misting the glass, the party was in full swing.

Lifting the big brass knocker, she knocked, glanced again at the French doors and froze. The ultimate faux pas had occurred. Alison — unmistakeably Alison — was looking out and giving her one of those silly little finger waves that people of petrified immaturity are wont to do. She was wearing a black dress, a long black wig — and very pale make-up.

Same outfit! Oh hell! Still, there was no going back. Luck of the draw. Who would have thought it?

She thought about scraping off some of the anaemic make-up Lindsey had plastered on her face. If she did that, maybe she could convince them that she'd come as the wicked queen from Snow White.

There wasn't time. The door was pulled brusquely open by a man who was so tall the top of his head was cut off. Honey did a double take. Was he for real or in costume?

'Let me guess,' she said, cheerfully pointing a finger. 'You've come as Frankenstein's monster as portrayed in Hammer Horror films of the sixties. Am I right?'

Honey felt her neck crick with the strain of looking up at him.

'No. I am the owner.'

She bent her knees slightly so she could see him full stretch. He was tall. Very tall.

'Sorry. My mistake. I'm here for the birthday party.'

'You couldn't possibly be here for anything else,' he said coldly, his voice a dull monotone, his expression as hard as stone.

He stepped to one side and held the door.

'In there,' he said unceremoniously, pointing to a door on the left-hand side.

'Have you come as Herman?' she asked, referring to the Frankenstein-ish dad from *The Munsters*, another American show. 'You even sound like him. Very good, I must say.'

'You're not the first one to joke about that,' he said humourlessly. 'But no. This is how I always sound and always look and I don't think it's funny.'

'No. I can tell you don't.'

What a misery!

'Been long in the hospitality trade, have you?' she continued.

'Six years,' he mumbled from beneath an iron-grey moustache that covered his upper lip and hid his mouth. 'Worked for one of the big groups. Small ones too. All sorts of jobs in the hospitality trade; barman, waiter, beverage manager. I've done it all in my time.'

He made it sound as though it were a prison sentence and didn't even attempt to adopt the bonhomie necessary for someone who was meant to welcome people to their humble establishment. A few minutes with him and most people would want to check out.

'Won't be in it much longer with your attitude,' she muttered. She'd met a lot of people in the trade who didn't have the right attitude but did it anyway, perhaps because it was all they knew.

He didn't hear her because at that moment a top-heavy woman came blustering out of a door to the rear of the reception hall. She was wearing a white apron and her face was flushed.

'Boris! Have you done anything about it? Well, have you?' She froze on seeing Honey. A plastic smile, the sort she must have practised in front of a mirror, stiffened her lips. 'Good evening. Lovely to see you. Come far, did you?'

'Bath. The Green River Hotel actually, I own it so like you . . .'

'Lovely. The party's in there.' Her voice had gone from shrill to sickly cheerful in the space of a nanosecond.

'So I understand,' said Honey, noting that the fists on the ends of Boris' long arms swung like lumps of lead. She wondered if he wanted to knock her head off. Very likely.

'Well go on then. Shoo!' The woman forced a laugh.

Honey made as if to enter the noisy room, though one ear was definitely tuned in to this odd pair. What was it he hadn't done?

The woman, a blonde rinse covering the emerging grey and with huge boobs above narrow hips, opened a door marked private to the rear of the hall.

'Boris!'

There was a great sense of urgency in the way the wife — Doris if she remembered rightly from their Bath Hotels Association membership application — hissed her husband's name.

'I'm coming,' he snarled shrugging his square shoulders so that they looked in danger of smothering his ears.

The door closed behind the pair of them. Which one, she wondered, would hit the other one first?

It turned out to be a squeeze getting into the small room where the birthday bash was being held. On pushing open the door she managed to squash Spiderman against the wall.

'Sorry,' she said.

'No prob,' said Spiderman in a distinctly Australian voice that betrayed the fact that he was three sheets to the wind. 'Bit crowded in here. Turns out my hosts the Crooks thought it was a party for fifteen people, not fifty.'

'I bet that went down well,' shouted Honey above the noise.

'Bet your sweet ass it did. He's been muttering about people not notifying him properly and taking him unawares. Silly bugger. That's why there's not much food.'

'Nor drink?' It certainly wasn't going to be much of a party without drink.

'There wasn't,' said the Aussie, his breath capable of igniting a single match held in close proximity to his breath. 'Me and a couple of the lads went up the pub and bought a few bottles. There'd have been a bloody riot if we hadn't.'

Honey thanked Spiderman for the information.

'Nice and cosy though,' he said, taking full advantage of the crush and pressing his body tight against hers.

'Too cosy.'

Sliding to one side and keeping close to the wall she sidled further into the room.

She surveyed the gathered horde as best she could and had to smile. The locals at the village pub must have had a laugh, seeing Spiderman and some other blokes, possibly

Dracula and the guy with a hatchet through his head, enter the public bar and buy up most of their wine stock.

As it turned out, the wine was palatable, the food miserable, and Boris and Doris Crook never put in an appearance at all.

'Alison is going to complain,' somebody said.

Honey nodded. 'I don't blame her.'

On top of the lack of decent wine and virtually no food there were too many Morticia Addamses for comfort. Plus the wig was itchy, but what could you expect? Lindsey's friend happened to have a cat. What was the betting it was partial to sleeping in the wig?

Wine glass in one hand, she scratched with the other. It had to be the wig. None of the other Morticias were having the same problem.

She managed to stop scratching and smiled when Alison came over to air kiss her on both cheeks.

'Morticia number thirteen, I think.'

'I apologise,' said Honey. 'I should have known.'

'Never mind. I think we all wanted to look beautiful,' trilled Alison.

'We did indeed,' said Honey, aware that Alison was trying to put a brave face on the fact that there was barely enough food to satisfy ten guests, let alone thirty.

'I'm going to sue,' she said lamely, her eyes filling with tears.

'Have you paid the bill?'

'Fifty per cent.'

'Then don't pay the rest.'

'At least the wine's good,' said Maurice Hoffman, who had taken the place of Alison's errant husband and was leaning over her shoulder like half a fur cape. 'Could do with a few more bottles though.'

Maurice was something in the import/export industry and very hairy. When dressed in shirt and tie, his chest, neck, and back hair were apt to spurt out over his collar, so, according to Alison, he kept it at bay with a razor. Tonight was an exception, because it seemed he'd grown it long for the occasion and come as a werewolf.

'No need to hire a costume,' he said to Honey with a toothy grin.

Alison stroked the errant curls as she asked him breathily, 'Darling, we could really do with some more food. Do you think you could press these people for a bit more than a bowl of crisps and a few sliced chorizos?'

Maurice growled and nuzzled her neck before going off to locate the owners of Moss End.

Once Maurice was dispatched on his errand, Alison turned to Honey with an errand for her.

'If you could help me get everyone dancing, Honey, it might take their mind off the lack of food. Do you think they'll collapse from lack of food if they start dancing?'

'I doubt it. Wine is made from grapes and we've got plenty of that.'

It occurred to Honey that it would be difficult to tell who was dancing and who wasn't in the small room they were in, but she promised to do her utmost.

After what seemed like a dance with Spiderman — but could just as easily have been an attempt on his part to get to the booze or up close and personal to her intimate parts — Honey found herself wedged into a corner. Clutching a glass of wine tightly to her chest, she found herself wishing she hadn't come, wishing Doherty was with her, and wishing more than anything that she hadn't gone with her mother to visit Rhoda Watchpole and smashed up his car. Doherty loved that car. How long before he forgave her?

She sighed, eyeing the mix of green faces, hooked noses, and ghoulish masks bobbing like jetsam on a boiling sea. Pieces of purple and red plastic had been fixed over the ceiling lights. The gas-powered wall lights — the originals from the 1890s — flickered and hissed, warming the room and the dancers alike.

The prospects for enjoying herself at this party were not good. If she stayed too long she'd either get drunk or

41

die of starvation. All she'd eaten so far was a few crisps, a slice of salami, and a vol-au-vent filled with something that might be cottage cheese or might just as easily have been baby sick.

Beating her way through gyrating bodies to where the food had been, proved a waste of time. Crumbs, a few cocktail sticks, and a lone sausage roll from which somebody had already taken a bite.

Out of the corner of her eye she spotted three bottles of wine that still looked full. Grapes were food, and weren't five pieces of fruit a day good for one's health?

Holding her stomach in, she managed to slither through more gyrating bodies in the general direction of the wine bottles. At last she got there and was just about to pour when the sound of a familiar voice made her toes curl.

'No police bodyguard tonight?'

She twisted from the waist, looked up, and felt herself swoon.

The tall man, dressed in a black evening suit, a black cloak, and a set of fangs that Dracula would have been proud of, smiled down at her.

John Rees. Prince of Darkness.

Honey self-consciously stretched her neck. If he wanted a bite, the bigger the target the better.

'A little mishap,' she said while thinking how good John Rees looked in black. 'I like your teeth,' she added while giving one of the oversized incisors a stroke with her finger. 'Had the chance to try them out yet?'

'I need a willing victim.' His grin said it all.

Honey felt her knees turning to jelly at the thought of his teeth — and his mouth — upon her neck. 'The victim usually faints first.'

'From fear I take it. Or would it be a desire for sex with a tall man in black?'

'Or the fact that her corset is laced too tight.' Now it was Honey that was grinning.

'I'm good at undoing knots. Corsets are a speciality of mine. As for these teeth, well I think they might get in the way of serious smooching,' he said.

'You'd make a good Count Dracula. The teeth definitely give you some bite.'

The crush in the overcrowded room pressed them closer. Honey could smell his aftershave.

He smiled. 'Cosy.'

'Careful. Those teeth are awesome.'

'All the better to eat you with.'

It was a distinct possibility given the press of the crowd.

The dream was shattered when the formidable incisors dropped out.

'Whoops! I feared I might lose them. They're not my size, but that's it when you buy things without trying them on first. I got them from an online joke shop. I think they were made for a kid of about ten. Bit of a tight fit,' he said and flipped the fangs into a handy plant pot. He grinned again. 'That's better.'

It *was* better. Honey admired his typically American teeth; all of them straight and pearly white.

One long arm snaked through the congestion and lifted a wine bottle from the Edwardian chiffonier that was doing a turn as a wine table. He had to lean across her to do it, almost taking her into his cloak like Christopher Lee in one of the old Hammer Horror films. If this was about to become a fate worse than death, then she was all for it . . .

'So,' he said as he poured a blood-red Shiraz into her glass. 'I take it by his absence that you and the DCI had a falling out.'

'I didn't say that.' She couldn't admit the truth just yet, not until she was sure; not until she'd got used to it . . .

Stroking the rim of her glass with one finger, she studied the blood-red wine rather than face looking at him. He would know what the truth was if she did. Seeing as her face was an open book, he probably already did know. Lying had never come easy to her — not that it was really a lie. At present things were uncertain and until she was one hundred per cent sure, she would not admit that her relationship with Doherty was final. It was in a kind of limbo. That's all.

'I hope that it is over.' He gazed at her. 'You know I've always admired you from afar. Never got in with a chance while the cop was around.'

His comment brought a hot flush to her face. He'd never explicitly said before that he was attracted to her. Both of them had kind of known, but now here it was, out in the open.

John Rees's eyes were ice blue and seemed to have their own cutting edge — like twin laser beams. They were twinkling at her and there was an amused twist to his mouth.

'What?' she asked, unable to stop smiling herself.

'I've got a confession to make.'

She shrugged her shoulders. If this was some kind of guessing game, she was right out of it.

'I did hear a rumour from my local garage that you'd pranged the most important thing in his life. Ahmed collects books,' he added so she'd be in no doubt of the rumour's provenance.

Damn. She'd been found out, but that didn't mean she had to confess. A little bluffing was in order.

'Well, there's a dark horse. I had no idea. I presume the books are on the film industry.'

John shook his head and produced an enigmatic smile over the blood-red wine. 'Nineteenth-century classic erotica — *The Kama Sutra, The Perfumed Garden*, et cetera. That kind of thing. Mostly Asian. He reckons it's an important part of his culture, and so it is.'

'A bookworm . . .'

'And a mechanic. So. There you are. Your secret's out.'

The fact that Doherty had actually declared his car to be the most important thing in his life was galling to say the least. Turning the conversation to Ahmed's book-collecting habits hadn't thrown John Rees off the scent.

'Seems Ahmed is a gossip.'

'He can't help it.'

Honey shook her head. 'I can't believe it of Steve. Did he say that? Really?'

His grin widened. 'Does it mean I'm in with a chance if I say yes?'

John's eyes had always held an obvious attraction. When he looked at her as he was looking now, she felt like a pinned butterfly, an object of attraction in a much-loved collection.

She felt a sudden constriction in her throat and a corresponding fizzing in her erogenous zones. So here it was. At last, out in the open. This was the first time John had actually laid it on the line that he fancied her and suggested that they get close up and personal. Up until now they'd only flirted and skirted around what was going on underneath the morning coffees and book recommendations.

There were no words that would make sense. The proximity of her breasts and his chest overrode the prospect of polite conversation.

The wine was a good leveller. Despite the fact that they were packed tightly together like sardines in a tin, she clinked her glass with his. 'Let's play it by ear. Cheers.'

He clinked hers right back, holding her gaze. 'Cheers.'

It wasn't easy to unclamp from each other, but she needed the bathroom. Getting there meant squeezing around the edge of the room. On the way she got squashed up against the French doors that looked out over the paved patio.

The room was noisy so she didn't hear the metal gate when it opened, but she did see it. The sight of two sheet-covered figures coming up the garden path made her pause. Not much imagination had gone into their outfits; each man — they looked too big and bulky to be women — wore a white sheet, two holes cut in the eye area so they could see where they were going.

The bathroom was along a passage leading to the back of the house. Sprinkling water over her face helped her cool down, but thoughts of John Rees kept her hot. The man was propositioning her in order to be Doherty's replacement. But hey, perhaps she didn't want a replacement. Perhaps there was no need of a replacement; after all, she and Doherty hadn't declared formally that their relationship — their engagement — was over.

Her reflection confirmed that her cheeks were still pink and her eyes were sparkling. The black hair of the wig fell forward around her face. At least it might help hide her blushes; it had certainly hidden a lot more of its owner, Clarissa, than it did of her.

There was nobody in the reception area. The new arrivals had obviously been let in and had joined the party.

John was waiting for her in a handy spot between the drinks and what little food was on offer. One thing would have led to another if they hadn't been in company. The party was in full swing, the singing, laughter, and conversation drowning out any in-depth intimacy.

The absence of food was alleviated with drinking wine but even that was close to running out.

Luckily Alison had brought her own cake and there was plenty enough to go round.

Honey looked at John and whipped a blob of cream off his nose.

'I wouldn't mind another slice.'

Being taller than most people there he peered over heads to check the cake stand.

'All gone.'

Honey's stomach rumbled — at least that was one sound nobody would hear amongst this noise.

She held onto John's shoulder while she shouted in his ear.

'Looks like a visit to either a fish and chip, kebab shop, or McDonald's on the way home.'

With the approach of midnight, the party spilled out into the reception area where a set of stairs ascended up to the first floor and a Sheraton-style desk was set diagonally across the corner dividing the window and the fireplace. Spiderman and a girl in thigh high boots were sitting on it, apparently leaning against each other for support. As with a number of other women there, the girl was sporting long black hair, her face the colour of hoar frost. Unlike the other Morticia Addamses present, her skirt was practically non-existent and the thigh high boots were laced up into something vaguely resembling a garter belt.

No wonder she'd attracted the attention of Spiderman, thought Honey. Those strips of elastic were just waiting for somebody to climb up them.

Once the witching hour had struck and the party was deemed to be over, last presents were handed over, the last congratulations offered to boozy accompaniment before mobile phones pinged into action calling taxis or relatives to take them home.

Honey had already handed over the handmade chocolates Smudger the chef had made. She'd noticed that only the box was left, trodden underfoot. It was bound to happen, a consequence of the lack of decent catering.

'Has anyone seen the Crooks?' Maurice called out. 'I need to pay the bill.'

Alison was hanging onto his arm, positively steaming. 'Crooks by name, crooks by nature. Let them stew!'

'We can't do that, darling.' Maurice patted Alison's arm and just caught her before she fell off her extra-high heels. The birthday girl was well-oiled but still wore a disappointed expression.

Can't blame her, thought Honey. Things had not exactly gone according to plan.

'This is a bit of a crush,' said John as they tried to make their way out into the hall, Honey's hair snagging on the nose of a purple-faced witch. 'Take my hand.'

Maurice shrugged and seemed to change his mind about the Crooks. 'I'm not hanging around. They'll ring me when they want their money.'

'Perhaps they've changed into pumpkins,' offered Honey. 'Or werewolves,' she added, her eyes fixed on the tufts of hair sprouting above Maurice's shirt collar.

'Or gone to bed,' added John.

The last option was the most obvious, but a party had been going on and some were still in a joking mood.

'Perhaps they're real witches and have shot off to go dancing naked round a bonfire,' somebody said.

'Anyone know where that might be? I'm up for that,' said Maurice the Werewolf.

Alison tittered and threw him a playful slap.

Honey gathered up her shoes, dangling them from her fingers; even a witch had no spell for dealing with sore feet.

'I could do with some fresh air,' she said to John. 'The sooner we get outside the better.'

'I'm with you on that one. All these witches and ghouls in one place are making me feel claustrophobic.'

There was a crush of people between them and the front door.

'It's jammed,' cried the man who was trying to open it. There was a rattle of a door being tugged. 'It's definitely stuck.'

Spiderman appeared, flexing his muscles as though he was the real thing. 'Here. Let me have a go. Stand back everyone. Stand back. Give me room.'

There was little room to stand back, but those gathered did the best they could. Honey and John were close enough to see him spitting on his hands then cracking his knuckles.

He fiddled with the lock. Nothing happened. He tugged. The door rattled on its ancient hinges but didn't budge.

There was a thudding sound and more rattling as Spiderman gave it a hefty kick. Unfortunately his strength was pure illusion, gained as it was from half a bottle of Highland malt; the kick sent him sprawling backwards.

He fell into the crowd and crashed to the floor where he lay spread-eagled, his eyes bleary, the scarlet mask askew.

'We're doomed!' somebody cried, then cackled. 'For all eternity!'

The revellers were beyond cracking jokes, concerns being made about babysitters, catching the seven o'clock train to London in the morning, and being fired by their boss if they didn't turn up.

A voice of calm cut through the mayhem.

'It's locked. We need to get the key.'

Looking at John Rees being so calmly confident, Honey felt one of those funny tingles that's a mix of pride when you know somebody brave and the sudden need-to-know them better. This man was so in control!

'That room first, I think,' said Honey pointing to the room she'd seen Doris Crook come out of.

John suggested everyone else stay put while he and Honey went snooping.

'Sit tight, folks. We have the advantage of having Bath's Crime Liaison Officer here with us. We'll get out of here yet. No point in us tramping all over the place.'

'Disturbing the evidence,' murmured Honey, blushing at being introduced in her official capacity.

'No,' he murmured back. 'In their present state they're likely to fall into the nearest bed and not come to until mid-morning. By the way,' his eyes twinkled, 'you're a fetching shade of pink.'

'Down to my toes.'

He grinned. 'Seeing as we're in company, I suppose I have to take your word for that.'

The broad door marked 'Private' through which the Crooks had passed seemed the best place to start. Made by Georgian craftsmen with deference to women who wore big skirts, it opened smoothly despite its age. A tiled passageway lay dead ahead before making a sharp right turn. To the left was a door marked 'Kitchen'.

Feeling as though the air was tightening around her, Honey opened the kitchen door, the tiles cool beneath her bare feet. She'd left the high heels to one side of the front door.

Catering kitchens hold onto the smell of the food prepared there earlier; in the case of the Moss End kitchen, the air smelled as though no food had ever been prepared here.

Honey walked round the stainless-steel preparation table in the middle of the room.

'Nobody here,' said John.

Honey approached the American-style fridge, a huge stainless-steel thing purposely designed for large families — not really suitable for a commercial operation, though, she considered, that all depended on how much business came your way.

John heard her take a deep breath before she opened it.

'Hey. Go easy. You sound as though you're preparing to find a body in there.'

'No. But there might be some food.' She looked. 'Not much. Just a sad looking lettuce, four cartons of yogurt and half a pint of milk.'

'Not tempting you?'

'Are you kidding?' She frowned while eyeing the contents as though they were holding on to some sort of secret. 'It doesn't make sense. This is a guest house. Either they've no guests staying overnight or, if there are guests, the only breakfast they're likely to get is a pot of yoghurt and a lettuce leaf.'

John stood close behind her. Normally his closeness would be welcomed and in the present circumstances, i.e. with Doherty still nursing his wounded car, her mind would have focused on his closeness and nothing much else. As it was she was nursing a sudden feeling of unease. Something was very wrong. Firstly, not enough food for Alison's birthday bash; she simply couldn't believe that they'd got the figures wrong. So why hadn't more food been bought? Even if they had got it wrong, any catering establishment worth its salt would have at least enough stock to last them a week. Moss End didn't have enough to last until the morning.

She pointed this out to John.

'You're the expert,' he conceded.

Satisfied that the Crooks were not stuffed into a handy larder, fridge, or deep freeze, they explored the passageway outside. There were two doors one side, one on the other, and directly in front a large external door which had a glass panel at face height. On looking through they could see a small, gravelled patio and steps leading up to the main body of the garden.

One of the doors on the left was a loo and the other a utility room complete with washing machine, dryer, and iron. There were a host of shelves at one end stacked high with white cotton sheets and pillowcases. Towels were piled on another shelf to their left.

Honey sniffed at the towels and wrinkled her nose.

'Not a very fresh smell. A bit damp, in fact, as though they haven't been used for ages. The bed linen too. I don't think any of these has been touched since the last owner moved out.'

'No key though,' said John, reminding her of their purpose for being here.

The door on the right opened onto a flight of steps.

'A cellar,' said Honey and called out, 'Is there anybody down there?'

'I'll go see,' said John.

He sprinted down the steps and just as nimbly sprinted back up again.

'Nobody. Just wine racks — and they're all empty.'

No food. No wine. Moss End Guest House was hardly a going concern.

Back in Reception, Spiderman was hammering at another door marked private, the one Honey had seen Doris Crook come out of.

'Hey. Come on, people. Let us out of here.'

At the same time somebody shouted from the room where the party had been held that a key to the French doors had been found.

In a hungry tide, the guests flowed from reception back into the dining room.

A man wearing bandages and being a very animated Egyptian mummy, explained the situation.

'There's a small wall between the patio and the front path that we'll have to scramble over and a bit of a drop the other side. We can all manage that, can't we?'

There were shrill protests about the likelihood of laddered tights and damaging clothes from the ladies present but most were easily persuaded with the promise of a fish and chip supper and full use of the credit card the following day to repurchase whatever got snagged.

Honey's attention settled on the door off Reception marked private, the one Spiderman had attempted to open. The door was old, the brass knob worn and loose.

'It's been tried,' said John, following her gaze.

'Leave it to me. Old doors have character. Each one was handmade. These aren't reproductions produced in a factory in the Far East. You have to treat them as individuals.'

She pulled the door towards her before turning the knob. The lock made a scrunching sound, as though it were chewing its metal parts, then opened.

The room couldn't be anything but the Crooks's quarters. A rust-coloured settee sat between two dark mustard armchairs and a large TV screen hung from the wall to her right.

The place was neat and tidy, though strangely bereft of creature comforts; surely if this was to be their home for any length of time, it would have pictures hanging from the walls? Magazines on the dark oak coffee table? The odd plant or two? There was nothing to soften the bare emptiness of it all.

'Anyone here?' she called, though not harbouring any hope of being answered.

A lovely chiffonier sat against the end wall.

'There's something odd about this room. It looks as though it belongs to an old person. The previous owner was elderly. I would have thought the Crooks would have thrown this stuff out.'

'Perhaps they wanted to get a feel for the place first,' offered John.

Honey was about to try the door to the left of the chiffonier when John interrupted her.

'The key fitted OK. They've managed to get out of the French doors. Do you really need to bother looking further?'

'Call it professional curiosity. Know the competition.'

The door next to the elegant piece of furniture opened into the Crooks's bedroom. John was right behind her. It was the first time she could ever recall entering a bedroom with him. Oh well. Perhaps another time, another bed.

Besides the bed there were closets fitted into the wall, a dressing table, a stool, and a single chair. There were also four suitcases at the end of the bed and a fifth lying open on the bed itself.

'Looks as though somebody's got long distance plans.'

She turned to see him lifting one of the cases at the end of the bed. 'Heavy. This weight doesn't say short haul to me.'

'And this one was in the process of being packed,' Honey added, her eyes scrutinising the neatly folded lingerie, rolled tights, scarves, and short-sleeved cotton tops. This was a woman's suitcase and the clothes didn't look typical for an English summer. Where were they going? The Mediterranean? Caribbean?

Honey looked around for any clue as to where they were going; perhaps airline tickets or evidence of a hotel booking.

'Perhaps that's why there was nothing in the fridge. They were off on holiday tomorrow. Though that is odd. As far as I know, they've only just moved in.'

She turned to see John in nonchalant pose with one arm raised above his head and leaning against the door surround.

'Whatever, but I'm uncomfortable invading their personal space.'

'I know what you mean, but you have to agree that it'd odd.'

'Tell you what,' he said, his arm sliding around her waist. 'We can talk about it over supper. I know it's late, but I'm starving. I know you're starving . . .'

This is it, thought Honey. How have I resisted this man for so long? The answer blasted in like a Force 12 hurricane.

Because of your involvement with Doherty.

Ah yes. But Doherty had admitted to Ahmed that he was in love with his car. Not her. His car.

Darling John had thrown his hat into the ring. Why not pick it up?

They joined the tail end of those exiting by the French doors, a press of people dedicated to getting some food from a late-night takeaway. First the wall, although it wasn't just a wall. A row of ornamental pots were ranged in front of them. They looked like the offspring of the two big urns either side of the front door though less shiny and of rougher material.

'I hear Miss Porter attended auction on a regular basis. She obviously liked pots.'

'Big pots. You have to climb and stretch at the same time,' advised John.

Honey hitched up her skirt. 'Here goes.'

'Keep your eyes on your hands. Your knees will follow.'

Dear John. He was so sensible and probably right and she would have done exactly that if she hadn't suddenly remembered her shoes.

'My shoes. I have to go back for my shoes!'

Going over the wall wasn't easy. Getting halfway and suddenly going into reverse was worse. Part of the course was back over those pots which meant her knees sinking into the damp dark dirt.

'I bet there's lots of worms in these pots. Horrible wriggly things. I've never liked them.'

John was right behind her. He laughed. 'They don't bite. At least I don't think they do. They'll probably just leave a little worm curd and dive for cover.'

'Ughhh!'

One knee went into one pot, one in another. The pot wobbled. She let go one pot rim and grabbed another while backing into John's waiting hands — and groin.

One leg bent, knee half-buried in thick black earth, and people behind her shouting for her to get on with it failed to help her overcome her phobia.

'I hate worms!'

Panic set in. The pot, perhaps because its base was broken, wobbled and fell over. Honey ended up flat on her back staring up at John Rees. He bent over her, hands either side of her shoulders, his legs between hers.

'My,' he said. 'This is fun.'

Normally she might have agreed with him, but her head was hanging over the wall.

'I'm OK,' she said, then stopped. Something about the scene between her and the overhanging room was far from right.

Above her to the left of John's shoulders, she could see something sticking out of one of the giant urns. She deduced it wasn't a plant. Too dense. Too dark and too much like a man's leg. Definitely a man. The feet were wearing dark socks and size twelve shoes.

Blissfully unaware of what she was looking at, John Rees was gazing rapturously into her eyes.

'Can I kiss you now?'

She shook her head. 'No. This is neither the time nor the place.'

She pointed to the sight above her head.

'That's a foot and it's attached to a leg.'

John glanced at what she was staring at before helping her to her feet.

'Well that's a spoiler. I suppose he's dead.'

'Very.'

John groaned.

'Sorry, John. I hate having to do this. Perhaps we can do supper another time.'

Honey fetched out her phone. Whether he liked it or not, Steve Doherty was going to have to speak to her tonight.

* * *

Doherty swooped out of an unmarked police car and headed straight for her.

'I might have known.'

'You were invited too. If you'd come it would have saved this journey.'

He shook his head despairingly and looked away. He'd never wanted her on board as Crime Liaison Officer — not at first anyway. He thought the interfering prima donnas of the Bath Hotels Association should keep out of police business. But so far he couldn't complain that Honey had been anything but helpful.

That was until she'd pranged his car.

'I want to speak to all you people,' he shouted. 'Sergeant. Stop everybody from leaving. Now!'

'Some have already left,' Honey informed him.

'Then I want a guest list,' he shouted to the shivering throng who had wanted to be home by now following a take-away supper to fill their grumbling tums. He eyed the crowd dispassionately. 'So who did it? Frankenstein's monster, the Mummy, or the Wicked Witch of the West?'

'A few witches, green monsters, and Morticia Addamses have left; and a few ghosts,' she added suddenly remembering the late arrivals wearing bed sheets.

The usual scene-of-crime team were already at work, sifting, what evidence they could.

Flasher Gibb, the official police photographer so called because he liked the old-fashioned flashlight cameras rather than modern digital ones, climbed up a ladder to take a photograph of the deceased. The ladder was an aluminium fold up type that he used on a regular basis.

He liked to take photographic evidence from a number of angles. The flash went off. First shot taken. He came down the ladder, moved it further around the urn, went back up, and took another.

Finally he moved the ladder around the other side of the urn so he was facing the front door. Poised to take a shot, he suddenly spotted something.

'Oi,' he shouted, his white jump suit crackling with excitement. With one arm around a rung of the ladder, hand holding the camera, he shouted down and pointed at the other urn.

'There's another one in there. Looks like a woman.'

A quick inspection by the Scene-of-Crime Officer confirmed that it was.

The woman's legs were resting against the wall, half obscured by a virulent climbing laburnum.

'Both dead,' said the Chief Medical Examiner. 'Quite a drop of blood swishing around the bottom here.'

Honey eyed each of the urns in turn, noted their position, then took a step back and looked up at the roof. The main roof of the house was directly above them. The two wings were two-storey and had ordinary sloping roofs, one of slate, the other of clay-coloured pan tiles. The middle of the house was three storey, the oldest part and crowned with an impressive Mansard roof.

She pointed. 'They fell from up there. One from one attic window, and one from the other. Each one's aligned with the urn, so they slid down the Mansard roof, over the guttering, and into a pot. Each of them.'

Doherty observed the trajectory. 'Thank you, Mrs Driver.'

Mrs Driver? He'd never called her that before.

'How very formal.'

'How very sick my car looks,' he muttered, his jaw clenched to breaking point. 'Nobody heard them falling from the roof?'

Honey clenched her jaw, unwilling — yet — to comment on his ungratefulness.

'We had just enough drink, barely any food but plenty of loud music.'

'Rave?'

'Rocky Horror Show.'

'Not exactly hip.'

'Neither were the guests.'

Up until this point, Honey had considered begging forgiveness, but his attitude grated. He sounded aggrieved. OK, he still hadn't got over her bashing up his car, but hey, live and let live. At least communicate.

She was about to suggest him letting bygones be bygones, when Doherty's sergeant, little more than a spotty-faced youth, joined them.

Warren Watkins oozed enthusiasm, chewed gum, and fingered his ears, nose, or chin incessantly as if wanting to confirm he hadn't misplaced them.

'So. Looks like the original *Hallowe'en* Horror,' he offered with over-zealous enthusiasm. 'Did you see the film? That one with Jamie Lee Curtis being stalked by that bloke with the white face? Bloody great. Trick or treating with gallons of blood. Fantastic!'

Doherty fixed his youthful sergeant with a scornful look. Watkins swallowed his enthusiasm along with his gum.

Doherty turned to Honey.

'Did you know these people?'

'I only met them today. Their names are Mr and Mrs Crook.'

'First names?'

'Boris and Doris.'

'How much do you know about them?'

'Only that they bought Moss End from Miss Porter a short while ago. From what I can gather, they kept themselves very much to themselves. I think they only attended one Hotels Association event.'

'Any enemies that you knew of?'

'Only themselves. Oh, plus the guests that attended the do. Food was sparse. Drink sparser. Going without party victuals makes people mean enough to murder.'

He arched one eyebrow that she recognised as his tell me more look.

Honey obliged. 'Let's put it this way, they weren't going to make Friendliest and Most Hospitable Hoteliers of the Year. If there had been any real ghouls at this party, the hosts would have been mincemeat by now — literally.'

Doherty nodded slowly, as he did when he was digesting information.

'I need you to answer a few questions.'

'Leading questions?'

'Yes. You and everyone else. I want to know if there was anyone here who harboured a grudge against the murdered pair.'

'I've already told you that. Everyone did. They're hungry.'

He ran his fingers across his chin. As usual there was the faint rasp of two- or three-day-old stubble. Honey loved the sound of it, wanted to rub her fingers across it herself now, but wouldn't offer. He hadn't phoned since the car accident. Or returned her calls. The message was obvious. She had injured the love of his life; the one with two headlights and a curved rear end. OK, she had something similar, but hey, how can a girl compete with a sports car?

She shook their personal relationship from her mind and went with it.

'It was a terrible party. Not enough food or drink. The guests got so desperate they had to repair to the Northend Inn for emergency supplies.'

'That bad?'

'That bad.'

'When was the last time you saw Mr and Mrs Crook?'

'When I arrived. He opened the door and just before I went into the party, she appeared from out of the door leading to their private quarters. She asked him whether he'd got round to doing something. I don't know what is was but she didn't sound too happy. She stopped dead when she saw me.'

'What happened then?'

'After that they disappeared through the door to the kitchen. Goodness knows what they were doing in there. It certainly wasn't preparing food. We were all starving and later when I went to look for them because the front door was locked and we couldn't get out, I checked the fridge and freezer. There was nothing in them. Nothing in the cupboards either except a few tins. No cereals at all. I'm presuming there were no residents in the bedrooms either — I didn't check up there,' she added pre-empting what he was about to ask her.

'Care to take a look now?'

She glanced beyond Doherty's shoulder to where John Rees was giving a statement of events to a svelte policewoman who appeared to be hanging on to every word he was saying. She was also barring the route to where Honey and Doherty stood talking business.

Her eyes met his, and even though she should hate Doherty for not returning her calls, she kept her professional hat on and went inside the house.

The stairs to the first floor were carpeted in an expensive pale green carpet. The upper walls were pale green too, and a thick brass handrail ran up one side of the staircase. The latter was a Victorian addition, as were the pine-panelled walls themselves. The Victorians didn't go in for light colours or redecorating every few years. Décor and furnishings were supposed to last a lifetime.

The stairs came out onto a quarter landing, the first bedroom on their left.

Doherty tried the door. It wasn't locked.

A draught of cold air rushed out.

Honey wrapped her arms around herself.

'Is the central heating off?'

Doherty fingered a radiator. 'Cold. The thermostat's turned off.'

A brass four poster bed dominated the room. The ceiling was vaulted and lined with the same pine panelling as the stairway, although this was in its original colour. Not that the dark varnish mattered that much in what was obviously the Victorian west wing of the house. The ceiling was about fifteen feet above them.

'Somehow I expected a mirror,' mused Doherty with a ghost of a smile.

'A lost cause in this temperature.'

One door to the left of the bed opened into a Victorian style bathroom. The cast iron bath had lion's claw feet, the loo had an overhead flushing system, and the basin was big enough to bath a baby in. There was also a very modern shower cubicle lined with the same Delft tiles as the bathroom itself.

The bed was not made. Just a bare mattress.

'No paying guests,' remarked Honey.

The passage along the landing swooped in a dog leg from west wing to east, passing the older rooms in the original building. None of the beds were made. None of the radiators were turned on.

Another set of stairs led up to the attic bedrooms.

A door went off on either side of the tiny landing. Both doors were open and police-incident taped.

The room to the left was slightly smaller than the one to the right. They peered in. As with the other rooms, the bed was unmade and the room was chilly. A fair-haired girl in a white jump suit glanced over her shoulder.

'The other room's swabbed and sectioned. Not far off finished on this one. As far as we can make out, the woman was dumped out of this window, and the man out of the window in the other room.'

Doherty thanked her. They looked over the tape into the other room. Rumpled bedclothes lay at the foot of a perfectly ordinary double bed. The room was nowhere near as cold as the others.

'Someone's been staying in this room,' remarked Honey. 'The only guest in the building?'

'And it's not likely to be one of the Three Bears.'

A pair of table lamps with pink shades and white onyx bases sat on cabinets to either side of the bed. The main light was a round collapsible white paper shade hanging in front of the dormer window.

'We'll do DNA tests of course, but if the occupant of this room doesn't have a record . . .'

The conclusion was left hanging in the air, but obvious for all that. No criminal record. No DNA record.

'We'll ask around whether anyone saw a third person living or working here.'

Honey nodded, her mind torn between the crime scene and her personal relationship with Doherty, Although Honey ached to ask him why he hadn't phoned, she decided that the question was best left for the moment. Doherty had plenty on his plate without her hassling him.

When they got down to the ground floor, the door to Mr and Mrs Crook's private quarters was open.

Honey nodded in that direction. 'I'm assuming you saw the luggage. Did you find any clues to where they were going?'

His response was professional. 'Yes to the first question, no to the second.'

'Well. They were certainly going somewhere. I presume you're thinking whoever was in that attic room threw the Crooks out of the window.'

'That's about the size of it.'

'Odd though. One from each window, purely so each of them lands in one of those pots.'

The pots loomed large in Honey's mind. Why throw two people out of a third-storey window so they landed in them? It also crossed her mind that the pots themselves might have some significance, though it didn't seem likely. They were just plant pots. Very large urns decorated with a frieze of dancing naiads and satyrs in states of semi-undress. And what's more they looked as though they were made of carbon fibre. Tacky. Not good quality.

'Tell your chairman we'll do our best to put this case to bed,' Doherty shouted over his shoulder.

Honey eyed his retreating back regretting that he'd given no sign of a possible kiss and make up.

John Rees was waiting for her by the pedestrian gate. A large stone had been placed against the damned thing to hold it open. A few people at the party had laughingly remarked about how noisy it was and how sturdy the spring that caused it to clang shut behind them.

She threw John a brief smile. 'Homeward bound then.'

'No kiss and make up?'

She almost winced but instead made herself smile.

'He's engrossed in the case. He'll call me if he needs me.'

Hopefully she didn't sound bitter. She didn't feel bitter. OK, regretful, but not bitter.

CHAPTER FOUR

There was nothing Honey found more irritating about Casper St John Gervais, chairman of Bath Hotels Association, than him brushing imaginary dirt off a chair before sitting down. Deciding it wasn't worth mentioning, she pasted on a happy face even though she was only feeling so-so.

'Coffee?'

'What sort of coffee is it?'

'Just coffee.'

'I do not drink "just coffee". Now these people out at Moss End Cottage Hotel . . . quite unsuitable for the hospitality trade. I can't imagine what possessed them.'

'Casper. We shouldn't speak ill of the dead.'

The long face drooped a little longer and the nostrils in the aquiline nose contracted to no more than pencil fine slits.

'I'm not speaking ill of them. I'm merely stating my first impression on meeting them at one of those infernal association meetings. They were gushing over everyone and wanting to be involved in everything one minute, then hey presto! They never appeared again.'

It crossed Honey's mind that Casper himself might have put them off. His opinion of them would have been obvious. He couldn't help himself. 'Did you see their curtains? And those urns. Who in their right mind would buy such monstrosities as those?'

'Miss Porter bought them. Alistair at the auction rooms told me so. She had a habit of not bidding an actual amount, but just going for last bid. When a bidder does that it means that basically they're willing to buy the item or items at any price.'

'I have been to a few auctions myself. I know what it means,' he said acidly.

'Odd that they ended up potted — so to speak.'

'Indeed. Now what sort of progress are we making on this and are the police getting anywhere with their investigations?'

Honey shrugged. 'I don't know.'

Casper had a way of raising one eyebrow that made her think of a guillotine. Nobody could raise an eyebrow like he could, then drop it from a great height. 'What do you mean, you don't know?'

'I'm kind of . . . excluded from what's going on.'

'You can't be excluded. It's your job to be included.'

Honey squirmed. She didn't want to tell the full story. A *précis* would have to do. 'Well, it's like this. Doherty and I have had a slight falling out . . .'

'Ah! So you and he are no longer on the intimate terms you once enjoyed. Is that what you are saying?'

She nodded mutely. Up until now Casper hadn't exactly been in the need-to-know loop regarding the personal side of her relationship with Detective Chief Inspector Steve Doherty.

'Then you have to make amends — whatever the price.'

'I beg your pardon?'

'Well, we can't have the association being excluded from an incident that could have serious repercussions on the tourist trade, now can we,' he exclaimed, slapping the chair arms with his fine, white hands in an act of finality. 'As I explained to you from the first, the reputation of this fine city is in your hands — yours and mine. My reputation and that of the city are inexorably bound together. So is yours, for that matter. There is no other recourse open but for you to build bridges and reaffirm your relationship.'

The fact was she *wanted* to reaffirm her relationship with Doherty. The stumbling block was a smashed-up car and wounded pride. Forgiveness wasn't going to come that easily.

'What if I don't want to?' Honey said huffily, thinking that Casper was acting a bit like her mother. Her mother strived to get her into relationships — mostly with people who lacked sex appeal but not money.

Casper was unrepentant. Intertwining his long white fingers, he viewed her as a judge might a condemned prisoner. The blade of the guillotine was heading downwards.

'I'm sorry, Honey, but you have to do your best to find the perpetrators of this heinous crime even if it means going behind the police officer's back. My preference is for you to make amends. You must be professional at all times, and so must he. There is far more at stake here than personal relationships. I look to you to close this case. If not . . .'

Down came the raised eyebrow.

Just for a moment, Honey imagined the feel of an icy blade across the nape of her neck. She didn't want to confront the 'if not' scenario. When first handed this post, she'd eyed it as one might a cupful of wine given by the most poisonous of the Borgias. Now the job felt as much a part of her as her chocolate-enhanced thighs. Or her daughter. At a push, even her mother.

* * *

November was rustling to a close, the nights drawing in, and a bracing autumn turning damp and misty. Even the honey-coloured stone buildings of Bath were looking a little grey.

The need to keep a hotel presentable all year round meant that Honey and Lindsey were working hard out in the courtyard that separated the hotel from the coach house they lived in. Dead heading the potted shrubs was one of the few outside jobs of a professional hotelier. Honey was no keen gardener, but as the main skill needed was leaving enough hydrangea to protect next summer's new shoots, she was doing pretty well.

Being out of earshot of staff and guests, their conversation naturally got round to Detective Chief Inspector Steve Doherty.

Honey was skirting around the romantic side of their liaison preferring to concentrate on her ongoing commitment to the post of Crime Liaison Officer.

'I simply cannot relinquish the cut and thrust of crime detection that easily.'

'. . . or your association with a certain police officer.'

'I know I wasn't keen to take it on, but now I'm not sure I can live without it. I just love escaping moaning staff and whinging guests. You get to meet so many different people.'

'Thieves, tramps, the odd murderer . . .'

'And detection means pushing my mental faculties to the limit. You can't push your mental faculties unblocking a bathroom sink or shoving sage and onion stuffing up the rear end of a Sunday turkey.'

'And Doherty?' asked Lindsey, as she bent to tug a limp and ragged geranium from its bed.

'I beg your pardon?'

'I mean,' Lindsey said patiently. 'Do you love him?'

Cornered, Honey chewed on her bottom lip and eyed a half-dead fuchsia. Dead or not dead?

Lindsey noticed her hesitation, placed her muddy glove on her hip and faced her. 'OK. You're undecided. Doherty blew a gasket about his car.'

'It wasn't my fault.' She held her tongue on blaming her mother. Not that it mattered much. Her mother had kept her distance for days. Lindsey knew the score.

'It doesn't matter whose fault it was. You've broken a boy's favourite toy, irritating in itself, but more so because you thought YOU were his favourite toy.'

Honey mumbled something inaudible along the lines of that she wasn't a teddy bear. Or a toy train, and if she was he'd cuddle one and play for hours with the other.

'Muttering to yourself isn't going to fix matters. Make up or move on.'

Honey eyed her daughter sidelong. The look in Lindsey's eyes was catlike and deeply intuitive. There was no fooling her. Lindsey had been born old and responsible. She just had that way about her.

At this particular moment she wasn't so much asking the question as daring her mother to deny what was so obviously on her mind. It made Honey wonder whether the words 'John Rees, Bath Bookseller' were written in indelible ink across her forehead.

Deciding there was no point in lying, she waggled her trowel from side to side and gave in.

'John Rees brought me home. That's all.'

'No big surprise there then. He's always hanging around. Was it really a coincidence that he was at the party?'

'He was invited. I think he knew Maurice Hoffman, Alison's latest muscular mattress.'

'He's always fancied you, and you've always had a soft spot for him.'

'I'm not denying that.' Of course she wasn't, though privately she thought it was more like a hot spot than a soft spot.

'There's no point you denying it. I've seen the way your eyes drop to his . . . preferred areas whenever he calls in.'

Honey threw another frost-bitten plant into the biodegradable rubbish bag. The bag was a Lindsey thing that she had no problem adhering to.

There was no point in denying that John Rees had always rung her bell — not literally. As least, yet. But metaphorically? An unassailable truth. Mentally, he had always been in the running.

There was no point denying anything. 'Well come on then, oh wise and wonderful one. What should I do?'

Lindsey patted the compost from a dead plant root with her trowel. 'As I see it, Mother, the choice is yours and on the whole there isn't much to choose between them. Number one, you can beg Doherty on bended knees to forgive you for smashing up his car — even offer to pay the bill if you wish . . .'

Honey grimaced.

'Number two, you can show him that you're as good a detective as he is by solving the case all by yourself — if that's possible.'

'And number three?'

Lindsey straightened, threw her trowel into the wooden toolbox, and grinned.

'Give John Rees some of your time. Dip your toe into unknown waters. You don't have to dive in. Paddle around at the edge.' She shrugged. 'See what comes up.'

Doherty would come round, Honey thought. She was pretty sure of that, but he'd always been touchy about his car. He loved that car, perhaps as much as he loved her. In the meantime, it was a case of getting on with life. Everything would turn out OK in the end. Wouldn't it?

CHAPTER FIVE

Aubrey Abingdon was doing his best to look nonchalant but wasn't entirely sure he was up to the job. He'd waited until his mother and *that man* were out before making his move.

That man! He couldn't bear to even think of his name. Not naming him made him not quite real, though of course he was. The slug! The slimy toad that had upset his life!

A November mist was a help though often as not all it did was obscure the view of the city.

He checked and checked again. Although there wasn't a soul in sight, he was all nerves, half expecting some nosy neighbour to leap out from the emptiness and accuse him of loitering with obvious intent. Especially Mrs Nobbs, her of the generous bosom and terrible taste in clothes and garden accoutrements.

Again and again his nervous gaze scanned the elegant expanse that was Lansdown Crescent with the same result as before; there wasn't a soul in sight. No pedestrians. No passing cars, no taxis, no service vans, and nobody sitting on sentry duty in any of the few cars parked at the kerb.

Satisfied that the well-heeled residents were either at work, shopping, or catching the rays in sunnier climes, he crept up to the front door of one particular house, plunged the key into the keyhole, and pushed it open.

Once inside he used both hands to close the door, keeping the lock disengaged until he knew for sure it would shut soundlessly. Hardly daring to breathe he listened for the telltale signs of occupation; a voice, music, the creaking of footsteps on the staircase that climbed in sinuous curves to the upper floors.

In years gone by the classic Georgian house situated in an imposing crescent of similar houses had been lived in by one family with an army of servants but had since been divided into fine, elegant flats, two on each floor. Nobody lived here who couldn't afford haute cuisine at a two Michelin star restaurant, season tickets to Covent Garden Opera House, and a yacht in St Barts or a ski chalet in the Austrian Tyrol.

The door to the ground floor flat on the right-hand side of the hallway loomed large and menacing. The couple who owned the flat were rarely in residence; the woman was something in education, the man some kind of business development executive who mostly worked abroad in Arab countries.

Aubrey held his breath as he strained to hear, feeling so nervous that he was almost tempted to bite his nails. Reminding himself that he'd only just had them polished and trimmed stopped him. Burglary, he decided, was all so unnerving.

He waited. Listened. Not a sound. The place was all his.

Even so, he couldn't help tiptoeing over the checkerboard of black and white floor tiles to the Georgian door on the left of the hallway. Like the other it was fashioned from solid mahogany, its surface protected by over two centuries of paint.

Confident now, he took a deep breath, inserted the key into the lock and pushed gently until he heard a soft click, then closed it behind him.

He tutted at the marks he'd left on the brass fingerplate. Meticulous in his drive for perfection, he fetched paper tissues from a drawer in the fragile, fine-legged sliver of a hall table.

Setting down the tan coloured holdall he'd brought with him, the sort used by sports enthusiasts to carry their rackets and freshly laundered shorts and polo shirts, he straightened, sighed, and tapped his beating heart. The bag was a recent purchase for which he'd discarded both the bill and its wrapping into a bin on the way here. It was currently empty.

His mother and that man didn't belong here and even though he hadn't voiced his objections to them living here, he had begun to formulate an insidious plan; one that would sort the pair of them out for good.

Satisfied that no one would hear him, he opened the door to his favourite room which faced due south and was thus flooded with light.

Such a lovely room and one of the main reasons why he so loved the place. Sighing at the prospect of living here alone again, he went straight to one of the three tall windows and eyed the view. The city of Bath was better observed from this crescent than from the more famous Royal Crescent, plus it did not attract the tourists. You had to know where Lansdown Crescent was and luckily the tourists did not. Visitors to the crescent were usually there to call on friends and relatives who were residents; either that or service engineers for boilers, cleaners, or the installers of burglar alarms. Lansdown Crescent was its own private little world, for private and often quite wealthy people.

This flat was no exception. Oils and watercolours of the Georgian period graced walls of duck egg blue, a traditional colour from that time, the paint formulated from an original eighteenth-century recipe.

The furnishings were of the right period too, sourced from every quality auction house throughout the country.

* * *

Setting down the bag, he set about selecting and removing those items of which he'd grown particularly fond but which formed part of his plan. The miniatures were first; a set of four beautifully executed watercolours; rosy cheeked ladies with dimpled chins, their breasts peach sized and shyly peering above lace trimmed collars, their hair set in high flounced curls trembling onto porcelain shoulders.

Three Dresden figures were next into the bag, closely followed by some fine pieces of sterling silver. Two silk covered scatter cushions, the very smallest, were also stuffed into the bag — not because they were valuable, purely to protect the more valuable items. Concerned that two would not be enough to prevent damage, he shoved in a couple more so that the valuables were cocooned in silk covered softness. Finally, he zipped the bag closed, buffeting it both sides with a final pat of his hands.

It struck him then how well things had gone and made him laugh out loud. My, but he was so clever, though not too clever for his own good. Nothing, absolutely nothing, could fail.

Bag clutched in his right hand, he closed the door behind him and made his way to the rear of the house. He listened before unlocking the door that led to the steps going out into the garden. The garden was shared with the other residents and was a peaceful, pleasant area as long as he avoided looking at Mrs Nobbs' collection of garden gnomes. The woman was a philistine. The gnomes were plastic. If they'd been made of traditional plaster he would have smashed them all by now. Every so often he stole one and put it in the dustbin. Mrs Nobbs would complain to everyone that some vandal had climbed over the back fence and stolen one of her 'boys'. Boys! A stupid description for a collection of garish plastic figures.

It was pure impulse that made him grab the nearest monstrosity and shove it into the bag along with the fine artefacts — devilishness in fact. The old crow would leap up and down when she found another of her plastic family had gone missing. He cheered up at the thought of it, finding it strange that it actually made him feel less guilty about what he was about to do.

The garden shed was his and his alone and as such he had the only key. After assuring himself that nobody was nosing out of one of the windows gracing the rear of the house — he knew Mrs Nobbs was at her daughter's this week — he shoved the key in the stout padlock and pulled open the door.

The smell of treated wood poured out of the opening. A pleasant smell, he thought. This was the place where he kept things that had no place in his mother's fine apartment but were part of that other life — the one he kept secret from the people who thought they really knew him.

Bearing in mind that the bag was full of valuable things, he set it down carefully behind a tin chest painted dark purple. A black pentacle graced its lid and astrological signs its sides; his mother had once been into that sort of thing.

He was about to leave when a sudden thought struck him. Grinning with evil intent, he unzipped the bag, brought out the gnome, and took out a battery-operated jigsaw from its box beneath a small workbench.

It occurred to him that it would make a bit of noise, but a lot of the people who lived in Lansdown Crescent were either in residence at other properties they owned, at work, or getting on in years and going deaf.

What a clever boy am I, he thought to himself. When he was a child, his mother had often said how clever he was. In latter years she hadn't been so forthcoming with praise. Well, he'd show her! Look how clever he was now, robbing his own apartment. Well, actually, the apartment belonged to his mother and had only been bequeathed to him in her absence.

'It'll all be yours one day,' she'd told him.

He'd grumbled that by the time she'd snuffed it he would be too old to enjoy it. She'd been unmoved.

But never mind, he thought gleefully. He'd show her how clever he could be. As for that other bitch, Mrs Nobbs . . . my, but these old birds made him sick. Why didn't they just shuffle off the earthly coil or go and live in Cornwall?

His malice propelled his hand movements. The saw roared into life. Nobody would question him doing a bit of DIY in his shed. Nobody would suspect he could be so vindictive.

Holding the gnome tightly around its neck, he glared into its fat, shiny face.

'Prepare to meet thy doom!'

He cackled like he'd seen the wonderfully wicked do in old horror movies. Vincent Price had been his favourite.

The sound of the saw drowned his ongoing laughter. His face lit up with delight as he sawed off the gnome's legs. Next he sawed through its plastic knees. Next through its waist and finally, with a bit of fiddling about so he wouldn't saw off his own fingers, he sawed off its head. Plop! It fell onto the floor.

Aubrey couldn't stop from smiling. In fact it was such a stretched smile that he had to lick his lips to ease the dryness.

All the while he eyed the head lying at his feet. 'Not so bloody cheerful now, are you?'

He gave the head a kick. It rolled over and looked up at him, its cheery face unchanged.

He smile dropped. 'Damn you!'

Even stamping on it failed to dent the gnome's plastic smile. Only when he took a hammer to it and smashed its nose and hammered a chisel into its smile, did it finally look destroyed. Kaput! Beyond repair!

Satisfied at last, he bundled the plastic body parts into a sack, whistling as he padlocked the door and returned the key to his pocket.

A quick shufty around, making sure nobody was looking out of the rear windows of the crescent, he upended the sack amongst an army of gnomes that were still in one piece.

Bits of plastic lay scattered amongst the others. To his mind it looked as though the other gnomes were the culprits, gathered around the debris as they were.

He shoved a fist into his mouth to stop from laughing. Mrs Nobbs would go mad, screeching that murder had been done. The woman paid the inanimate objects the same regard as anyone else might a pet dog or cat; as though they were alive and cared a jot. Stupid cow!

It pleased him to annoy her; what a tasteless woman she was; plastic gnomes indeed!

Never mind. Taking revenge on the world — principally elderly women — had made him thirsty. A nice cup of tea next, perhaps with a couple of digestive biscuits. Yes, biscuits eaten and tea drank before his mother came home with *him*!

His mother's new boyfriend wouldn't be around for much longer. What a joke he was! But tea and biscuits were his just deserts and very nice, but, first things first. He took out his phone and punched in the number of Manvers Street police station.

'I want to report a theft,' he said to the person who answered the phone. She asked for his name and address. He gave both willingly. Next she asked for the time the theft had occurred and details of what was missing.

'There's no need for all that rigmarole; I know who did it, so you can arrest the blighter right away.' He proceeded to give her the name of his mother's latest friend. 'How soon can you be here?'

CHAPTER SIX

The atmosphere was tense.

'OK. You asked me to come in and make a statement. Here I am.'

Doherty appeared nonchalant. He was sitting on his side of the desk tapping a pencil on the desktop, turning it the other way and tapping again.

To anyone who didn't know him, he appeared casual, as though this was just a nine-to-five job and the sooner he was out of here the better.

Honey, however, knew him well. Looking relaxed was all part of the plan. 'People drop their guard if they think you're not paying attention,' he had told her.

He might not remember saying that to her, but she remembered.

As witness to a murder scene, she was feeling somewhat nervous. She hadn't actually been so close to murder victims before. If she'd walked out of the party earlier, she might even have seen it all happen. How scary would that have been?

'Good party, was it?'

She met Doherty's gaze. 'Define good party. It ended up with two corpses on the premises. OK, it was a Hallowe'en party, but the monsters with hatchets in their heads are never real — well, not usually.'

'Perhaps I should have come after all. It might have kept you out of trouble.'

'I'm not in trouble, am I?'

He waved a hand as though batting the question aside.

'If you don't find trouble, it finds you. Take my car for instance . . . which you did take . . .'

'At your suggestion!'

'I should have known better,' he replied gloomily.

'Oh for goodness' sake!'

Folding her arms and crossing one leg over the other, she swivelled on her chair so she wasn't facing him.

'Let's get back to the party. Did you go alone?'

'Yes.'

'There were people there that you knew?'

She threw him a stone hurling glare. 'You know there were.'

'You hadn't arranged to meet anyone there?'

Another glare flew across the desk. 'If you mean did I arrange to meet John Rees there, the answer is . . .' She paused, considering her answer. 'It's none of your business.'

'It is my business! This is a murder enquiry. It's nothing personal.'

She eyed him sidelong. 'Isn't it?'

He shrugged. 'Not really. And it would help if you could focus on what happened. Now, you went alone, you met up with people you knew . . .'

'Of course I did. One person in particular was very attentive.'

'Right. The Yank.'

'He's a bookseller.'

'Of course.'

Look at him, she thought. Sat there looking as though he doesn't care what's going on, and yet . . . She couldn't quite face the rest of the sentence. There was an itch under her heart — and in other places — that just couldn't be scratched. There was only one person who could really scratch that itch, and he was sitting right across from her.

Bloody men. Bloody car. Boys and their toys!

'Give me it from the beginning.'

She groaned. 'I've already told you . . .'

'Tell me again.'

She went through the events of that night, carefully avoiding repeating anything John Rees had said to her and anything he'd done. She also didn't admit to drinking more than two glasses of wine.

When she'd finished, his shoulders heaved in a heartfelt sigh, his biceps threatening to split the sleeves of his shirt.

He shook his head. 'I don't believe it.'

'It's the honest truth. That's exactly what happened.'

'That's not what I meant,' said Doherty. 'Only you could go to a Hallowe'en party that actually manages to provide the gruesome dead.'

'It was obviously meant to be. Mary Jane would say that the fates ordained it.'

Doherty scoffed. 'Unless the fates are some criminal family I am unaware of, they have nothing to do with it. These people didn't end up sliding headfirst down the roof and into those pots by mistake. They were murdered.'

'Well they certainly weren't practising Olympic swimming. So what's next?'

'I'm awaiting the post-mortem reports but it does look as though each was murdered separately — one in one attic room, one in the other, then individually slid down the Mansard to land head first in the pots; one each.'

Honey chose to correct him. 'Urn. It's an *urn*. Or rather two urns. One for each body.'

'Whatever. There was no compost in either pot. Very clean, so some blood pooled at the bottom.'

'I wouldn't expect there to be any earth in there. I shouldn't think they were ever planted with anything.'

He looked intrigued. 'What makes you think that?'

'They're too smooth and clean looking inside to have ever had anything planted in them. Just a few leaves inside and a bit of weathering on the outside. I wouldn't have thought they've been kept outside before Miss Porter bought them. Besides, they're made of plastic.'

'Let's concentrate on the victims. Had you ever met them before that night?'

She shook her head. 'No. I've already told you. I saw them once before at a meeting the Hotels Association was holding at Casper's place. Miss Porter introduced them as the buyers of her property. Couldn't say I liked what I saw very much. They were falling over themselves to impress on everyone that they knew more about the hospitality trade than anyone there. After that, nobody saw very much of them at all.'

'Was Casper there at this hotels' bash?'

'Of course. And he wouldn't like you calling it a bash.'

Clasping his hands behind his head, Doherty looked up at the ceiling, a cryptic expression on his face.

'Now let me see if I'm right; Casper took an instant dislike to them. "*Downmarket types. Not the sort we should encourage to front the hospitality trade in this fair city!*"'

His take on Casper's voice was Al.

Honey stifled a giggle and shook her head. 'He didn't like them but I don't think he murdered them.'

'Just froze them out?'

'Casper behaved as only Casper does.'

On the evening in question, Casper had greeted them first, then, once he'd got their measure, had almost totally ignored them.

There was a marked pause as Doherty leaned forward to study the report sheet sitting in front of him.

'By the way, John Rees corroborates your story. You were together all evening?'

The tone was accusing. So was the look in his eyes when he raised them to look at her from below an untidy fringe of hair in need of a cut.

'So why badger me to know who I was with if he'd already told you?'

'I like to cross all the Ts and dot all the Is. Humour me.'

'OK, so let's recap,' she said, understanding why interviewees lost their rag under cross-examination. Repeat, repeat, repeat! 'To repeat myself yet again, we were together. I didn't know he would be there. We met there, and seeing as I was alone and unattached in fact, it made sense for us to hitch up.'

He tried to hide it, but there was no doubting the wince.

'That was a great outfit by the way. Where did you get the wig?'

'Is this anything to do with the murder?'

'No. I just liked it.'

She ignored this. 'Where did they come from, the Crooks? I take it you looked into their background.'

'Reading. Boris Crook had a business there and enquiries are being made of both his business associates and the neighbourhood where he lived. Hopefully we'll have some background information shortly. Someone's bound to have known them fairly well. Everyone has friends.'

'He might not have had friends. I wouldn't have wanted to be his friend. He had a nasty attitude. And he was tall. Very tall.'

'Height doesn't usually have a bearing on personality, Honey.'

'I think he had an issue with his height.'

'We all have issues about something,' he said, folding his arms. 'So! Had you planned to go anywhere after the party?'

'Home. Where else would I go?' Was it her imagination, or did she detect the tension leaving his shoulders. 'After we'd eaten some supper. We were pretty hungry.'

A nerve flickered beneath his eye. Ah! So he *was* jealous.

'So there's still no sign of any evidence of plans to travel to foreign climes?'

He shook his head. 'None were found.'

'How odd. They were packed and ready to go, almost as though it were a sudden decision. I mean, nobody takes over a business and then does a moonlight flit.'

'We don't know they did a moonlight. Has it occurred to you that they may not have had time to unpack?'

'No way.' She shook her head. 'I might think that if they hadn't presented themselves at the Hotels Association get together. But they did which, despite what we may have thought of their capabilities, means they were planning to make a go of it. For what it's worth, that's my take on it.'

Bringing his hands back from behind his head, he scrutinised her over folded arms.

Honey tried not to notice the biceps and concentrated on recalling everything she could about that evening, small details pinging into her mind like stray ping pong balls.

'Does everyone who attended check out?' she asked.

Doherty nodded. 'We're going through every statement, checking everyone's background, possible motives etc., So far only the flimsiest of leads. Circumstantial evidence abounds.'

'In what respect?'

'Jim Tetman, alias Spiderman, was in the running to buy Moss End. He was going to convert it into flats. Clive Wilson, you may have noticed him bound in bandages . . .'

'The Mummy!'

'That's him . . . he's an estate agent and would have benefitted from the sale of the apartments. Jim Tetman was going to give him sole agency rights.'

'Well there's two possibles,' said Honey who felt somewhat disappointed that she hadn't known this before.

Doherty agreed that there was. 'We also interviewed Felicity Champion who worked for Jim Tetman as his personal assistant. She went with him to the party that night.'

'Young? Long legs? Short skirt?'

'You saw her?' His expression was one of immediate interest.

Honey nodded. 'I think Spiderman was in the process of climbing up her thigh.'

'His wife stayed home. He'd told her he was out of town. They live in Pensford.'

'Whoops! So Spiderman had some explaining to do.'

Pensford was only a few miles away from Bath. OK, it was out of town, but even in the heaviest traffic, it was less than an hour's drive.

'Casper's going to want me to report on this. I would appreciate knowing the details when you have them.'

When he nodded, his eyes were fixed firmly on her face as though waiting for and expecting something from her. Another apology about his car? A confession that she was looking into more than John Rees's shop?

There was pride on both sides, so even though she wanted to ask him about the health of his car she was too miffed by his attitude.

'Can I go?' she asked.

He nodded again.

She got up slowly just in case he changed his mind, or had something else to say; not about the murder but about their relationship. An invitation to dinner, lunch, or a drink would have been considered.

When nothing came, she found something to say herself.

'I think the main question with Boris and Doris was not so much where they were going, but why?'

'Yes,' he said, glancing down at the paperwork again. 'They were definitely going somewhere. Every sign of it. But no tickets. No online reservations. Nothing. We've checked.'

'And in your considered opinion, what do you think happened?'

'A sudden danger? A sudden threat?'

'Wherever it was, they were going away for a long time. Nobody runs their food supplies down like that unless they're off for quite a while. It couldn't have been a holiday.'

'Sounds as though it was planned.'

Honey agreed. 'I'll ask around. Maybe they told some-body where they were going, somebody who works for them or friends.' Not that they were likely to have any friends in this short a time. Or employees, but she'd check anyway.

He grunted something unintelligible and began shuffling papers. She waited for him to look up again and seeing it was late, offer to take her home.

But he didn't.

Double whammy, she thought to herself as she left the building. First I dent his pride and joy and then he finds out I've been in the company of John Rees. No wonder he's not too forthcoming on this case.

It was getting dark when she left Manvers Street police station. Irregular shapes of light blinked from tiers of buildings rising up the slopes surrounding the city. Streaks of white and red streamed from passing traffic; despite the hour, the city of Bath still hummed with life. The smell of old buildings mingled with traffic fumes.

Dodging between the traffic flow, she headed for Henrietta Street. The noise of grumbling engines was behind her. There was room to breathe and to move along pavements broad though rumpled with age.

A tall, lean figure stepped out from the shadows where a battalion of conifers hung over a garden fence.

'Christ! You made me jump.'

John Rees placed one arm around her shoulders and gave her a hug.

'Sorry. Didn't mean to startle you. I spoke to your daughter. She said you'd been called in to give a statement. I gave mine earlier; must have left just before you arrived. I wasn't sure whether your policeman boyfriend would be escorting you home.'

'Oh well. You know how it is. Two bodies and not a shred of evidence — well nothing special. So he's kind of tied up at the moment.'

'Great! For me that is. Hope you're not too disappointed that we have to walk back; no swanky police car with sirens flashing.'

'John, I can't think of anyone I'd rather have walk me home,' she said, slipping her arm through his.

If he'd really wanted to, Doherty would have taken her home. He would have done if he was ready to forgive her. But he hadn't. Deep down she was hurt, but damn it all, she would bloody well get over it! Being escorted home by John Rees was a bloody good start.

* * *

Doherty heaped up his files and got up from his desk. He just about had time to shove the lot into his filing cabinet under lock and key. Security was lately the order of the day direct from on high. The Chief Constable had sent round a missive instructing all personnel to lock paperwork away when the office was empty. This also applied to the woman who organised the subcontracted cleaners. Even a cleaning schedule was deemed a security risk.

He'd had every intention of forgiving Honey for smashing up his car, but the wound ran deep. Anyway, he quite enjoyed making her stew. Now he was the one who was squirming, though he'd tried not to show it.

The thing was, he *had* to forgive her or he might lose her for good. It had come as something of a shock to see her in the company of John Rees on the night of the murder. OK, he believed her that their meeting up had been pure chance, but still. Now, remembering her dressed in black and looking so damned sexy made him want to kiss and make up. Intense kissing, of course, the sort that led to intimacy and a nice warm bed.

If he was quick, he thought, he'd catch up with her and give her that lift home she'd been angling for. It was taking his time with this making up. It would happen, but in his own good time. Perhaps that time was now.

He checked out with the desk sergeant before collecting his jacket from the back of the office door then swung out for home.

The sound of a vacuum cleaner droned from one of the offices he passed on his way out through the tradesmen's entrance — cop talk for 'cops and criminals only'.

The police car he was using for work purposes was already warmed up and running round the side of the building, courtesy of his new sergeant.

'All done, sir.'

Watkins' face looked pink and pinched. The temperature was taking a dive.

'Well timed, Watkins.'

It was indeed. Doherty figured that by the time he drove round the front, Honey would have negotiated the corridors and reception area. He reckoned that by now she would be at the beginning of Henrietta Street, the most obvious route between Manvers Street and The Green River Hotel.

And she was.

But his self-congratulation died a death when he recognised John Rees. They were walking off down the street without seeing him. He slipped the replacement car into gear, debating whether to follow them down Henrietta Street or carry straight on home.

'Damn it!' There was no way he was going to offer both of them a lift. Bloody John Rees. Why did he have to show up now, when things between him and Honey were strained?

Refusing to rein in his pride, he floored the car and headed back to the office. Throwing himself into work would help him through this; that's what he told himself.

CHAPTER SEVEN

Gloria Cross — unexpected, unannounced, and looking like the star lead in *Guys and Dolls* — swept into the reception area of the Green River Hotel as though she were the queen doing an on-the-spot inspection.

She was wearing a silver-grey light wool dress with pink flecks, a chiffon scarf in solid pink that trailed behind her like a cloud at sunset, and shoes with three-inch heels and a rose on each toe. The rose was of the same shade as the scarf. Her bag was quilted. Designer. *Real* designer, none of this pseudo stuff made in the Far East and sold in street markets.

Unlike some women of her age, Gloria still bounced on her heels and she always wore heels. Never flats or those ballerina styles that hinted the wearer was related to Cinderella and was down on her luck — and thus her heels. Gloria would never countenance either situation. 'Ignore the years and they'll ignore you,' she was fond of proclaiming, while wallowing in the flattery that usually followed such a comment.

Honey on the other hand was looking less than glamorous. She hadn't started off that way but due to an overactive little boy from Amsterdam who was staying in the hotel with his parents, the crisp white shirt and navy-blue skirt she'd donned this morning was ruined.

Little Peter, or little pest as she'd mentally christened him, had got bored waiting for his parents to plan their day. To while away the time, he'd taken to whizzing round Reception like Hamilton around Silverstone, though without the wheels. His little legs went like pistons, up and down, racing around.

Unfortunately he was one of those kids who ate on the hoof. His favourite food was chocolate. He never seemed to be without a bar, clutched tightly in his hot little hand. The more he raced around, the hotter his hand became. Inevitably, the chocolate melted.

Honey had been hurrying to answer the phone and Peter had been hurrying to get to the winning post, or whatever. Collision was unavoidable. The melted chocolate around his mouth and in his hands were transferred onto her crisp white blouse which was no longer quite so crisp.

'Chocolates will be banned from this hotel in future,' she muttered as she sponged off what she could in the relative privacy of the small office behind Reception.

Her mother took in the situation in one fell swoop.

'You've had that shirt for years. Ditch it. Buy a new one. Something more glamorous.'

'There's plenty of wear left in this one.'

'It does nothing for you. How can you expect to be a bride again if you don't look glamorous? Haven't you heard of eye candy?'

'I'm in working mode, not seduction mode.'

'OK. Well, you want to look good for your guests, don't you?'

'Not when they're armed with chocolate,' she muttered.

Seeing as her daughter was dwelling on the mishap, Gloria turned the conversation away from work and hotels in which she had no interest whatsoever, to the reason why she was there.

'Now. Everything is arranged. I phoned Antonio — a man I fully admit makes my heart pitter-patter, to let Rhoda know we are coming. She's looking forward to meeting you, so tidy yourself up and we'll be away.'

'Is that so,' grunted Honey, sucking on a chip of chocolate that had adhered to one of her buttons.

'It is indeed. Mary Jane is bringing the car around to the front as we speak so you'll have to hurry. We don't want her to get a parking ticket now do we?'

Honey was unimpressed and unmoved. Grunting was mixed in equal measure with grumbling.

'Why not? I thought she was collecting them for a montage. Should give Damien Hirst a run for his money in the Turner Prize.'

The inference that she was going somewhere she hadn't been informed about, suddenly clicked in.

'Am I going somewhere?'

'Yes. Back to Overton House. Mary Jane has offered to "read" the Watchpoles's room. We're hoping she can pick up a few vibes that might tell us where he is and what he's doing.'

'Mother, he's gone to find himself,' she said firmly. 'That's what it said in his note. People do funny things at a certain age. It's the bucket list mentality.'

Her mother looked at her askance, arched eyebrows flying almost up to her hairline.

'Funny things? Bucket list? What are you talking about?'

Honey attempted to explain about the things you really want to do before kicking the bucket, but she'd misunderstood; it wasn't that her mother was taking umbrage to.

'I do not do "funny things". Neither do my friends do funny things. They're perfectly logical things. It's just that the younger generation hasn't reached our level of wisdom so cannot recognise it as such. Now come on. No more of this nonsense. I haven't got all day.'

Honey was about to counter that with the fact that she didn't have that much time to spare either. Owning and running a hotel was not a lazy afternoon by the pool. After all, she was still working. Her mother had avoided working for most of her life. Her social life, however, was another matter. Her days — and nights — were an unending tide of social commitments.

The door to the office opened and Lindsey's head appeared.

'There's a traffic warden outside about to give Mary Jane a ticket. I told him she was waiting for Gloria Cross,' said Lindsey addressing her grandmother.

'Fat lot of good that did,' said Honey.

'On the contrary; he said he'd be glad to make your acquaintance again. He told me to tell you, love from Les,' said Lindsey, grinning from ear to ear. 'An old flame perhaps?'

'Les?' Gloria gasped. 'Do you mean Les Sutton?'

Lindsey pulled a face. 'Could be. About six feet with silver hair. Navy-blue uniform.'

'Oh my,' breathed Gloria. 'I never could resist a man in uniform.'

A swift tidying job in the mirror, a squirt of perfume, and she set forth like a square rigger going into battle; beautiful but deadly.

Honey kissed her daughter on the cheek. 'Won't be long. Hold the fort, and should Doherty ring . . .'

'I know. You'll ring him back.'

'Are you sure he hasn't . . .?'

Lindsey shook her head. 'He hasn't phoned. I would have told you if he had.'

CHAPTER EIGHT

The drive to Overton House, a building containing purpose-built flats for the over-sixties, passed in a blur of trumpeting taxis, braking buses, and cussing car drivers.

Honey didn't hear a thing. She'd made the last-minute decision to borrow Lindsey's iPod. Music masked the hazards of Mary Jane's driving: the screeching of brakes and cuss words, the screams of terrified pedestrians, the octogenarians suddenly obliged to leap for their lives.

She also closed her eyes; she could hear nothing, she could see nothing. Cutting herself off from Mary Jane's driving helped keep her stomach from turning over, shouting 'I'm out of here', and leaving her body for good. No more chocolate for her!

Nobody had ever pointed out to Mary Jane that her driving was abysmal and hey, hadn't she noticed that the British drive on the left-hand side of the road?

The thing was that Mary Jane was a good-hearted soul, always willing to help anybody out — especially on the psychic front — and no one wanted to hurt her feelings by pointing out her less-than-ideal driving skills.

A professor of the paranormal, seventy-plus years of age, and as tall and thin as a poplar, Mary Jane had arrived at the Green River from California some years ago, suggested that a ghost lived in her room, and promptly stayed there on every visit. Eventually, unable to bear her ancestor being in residence all alone, she decided to move in permanently.

'Blood's thicker than water,' she'd pronounced. 'Sir Cedric is a much-respected ancestor of mine.'

Nobody pointed out to her that he was doubtless all dried out of blood by now and nobody declared that there were no such things as ghosts and that she was deluding herself. The fact was nothing substantial could be proved, though it was rumoured that the hotel, when still a house back in Regency times, had indeed been the home of Sir Cedric Strath-Parkinson. 'He was a knight of the realm,' she fondly said with misted eyes, one hand held over her meagre breast as though mortally wounded. 'He loved ladies. He loved his country . . .'

Lindsey had muttered to her mother that Sir Cedric had been a lusty old roué who'd died of the pox. Nobody put the full facts in front of Mary Jane. She believed in the paranormal, so they let her get on with it. She was a nice person, just a wee bit eccentric, looking like a refugee from a witches' tea party with her liking for pistachio green trousers teamed with a salmon pink tabard.

Once she'd installed herself at the Green River Hotel, Mary Jane arranged for her car to join her. Said vehicle was a 1961 Cadillac Coupe in a delicate shade of pink. The fact that she'd not yet been banned from driving was put down to sheer luck, though Mary Jane insisted it was Sir Cedric and others who had passed into the hereafter guiding her wheels.

Mary Jane hadn't yet crashed or killed anyone. It didn't matter whether it was through luck or judgement. Arriving safely at their destination and not having a nervous break-down during the trip was all that mattered.

Feeling the car come to a standstill, Honey opened her eyes, took out the earphones, and popped them into her big brown bag — the one she carried everywhere which served as a travelling office, beauty factory, and lunch receptacle.

Rhoda Watchpole took some time getting to the door. When she finally did appear she was wearing frog green sweats that fitted snugly over her rotund frame though loosely around her bandy knees. She looked like a toad.

'Sorry. I had to get up from the floor,' she puffed, her cheeks pumping like bellows. 'Exercises.'

One glance at Rhoda's overblown figure proved that exercise didn't cure everything, at least in the short-term.

Gloria was first with the advice. 'Take my word. Lie down in a dark room and consult your inner goddess. Address your mental and physical problems. The answers and the advice will come. I guarantee it.'

'I'll try,' Rhoda said brightly. 'It won't clash with my Church of England beliefs, will it?'

Gloria swung her bag into a chair and proceeded to introduce the resident psychic.

'This is Mary Jane. She's here to help.'

Rhoda looked at her expectantly. 'Are you one of those personal trainers?'

Unfazed by the conversation, Mary Jane was looking around the room from her great height. 'No. No,' she repeated in a faraway voice. I'm a psychic. Gloria tells me your husband left and you want to find him again.'

Springs squealed in protest as Rhoda flopped into a chair. 'I do. We've been together for fifty years. Fancy wanting to find yourself at his age.' She shook her head and reached for a box of tissues. Half a dozen chocolates—Quality Street judging by the wrappers, fell out. 'I just don't understand it. Fancy leaving me all alone at my time of life. I was always good to him — or at least I thought I was. I never had headaches when he wanted sex, not that we'd done it for a few years now; not since my body went glandular.'

It was on Honey's tongue to say that Rhoda was not suffering from a glandular matter. She ate too much. She was fat.

Honey looked for the telltale carriers with the M&S Food logo on the side. There were none, though not seeing them didn't mean they were not on the premises.

She thought about mentioning the bucket list to her as she had to her mother: climbing the Himalayas, swimming with whales, though at a certain age swimming with swans in the Avon made more sense. Cold water, but shallow, so less chance of drowning.

'Excuse me, but do you mind if I use the bathroom?' she asked.

Rhoda gave her directions. Her mother waved her off dismissively.

Honey heaved a big sigh. The room she'd just left was overheated and stuffy and she hadn't wanted to stay there. It wasn't that she didn't sympathise with Rhoda, but she'd seen Mary Jane go into one of her trances before. It hadn't so much scared her as made her feel uncomfortable.

She went as directed along the small hallway and took a left at the end.

Bijou was a good description for the Overton House apartments. Shoeboxes might have been better.

Squeezing around the door that opened into Rhoda's bathroom, she vowed never to put her name down for one of these pokey overpriced apartments — ever!

A pixie would be the ideal resident; somebody slight and small. It might also be best if they didn't own any fluffy towels. There simply wasn't room for anything big and fluffy in that bathroom.

Honey never meant to snoop; after all this wasn't a crime scene as such, but things just passed under her hand and there it was — open sesame!

There were enough pills in the medicine cabinet to tranquilise a hippo. Even before checking the prescription notice, she knew they belonged to Rhoda. Besides pills there were the usual things: shampoo, conditioner, deodorant, tablets for soaking dentures, a little face cream, plus some over the counter medicines. Nothing dramatic.

She closed the door feeling somewhat disappointed. What had she expected to see? A knife dripping with Bert's blood? His decapitated head squashed between the denture soak and a jar of Vaseline?

She reminded herself that Bert had only gone walka-bout, as the Australians would say. On reflection he would wholeheartedly approve of what was happening out in the living room — a little otherworldly wisdom to reach out and feel his vibes.

Thinking of feeling vibes and other things made her think of Doherty. She rang him, clenching her stomach mus-cles at the thought of hearing his voice. Her stomach muscles always cinched in at the sound of his voice. The same thing happened when she was about to tuck into a slice of choco-late cheesecake. Anticipation of something delicious; that was all she could put it down to.

'Nothing much to tell you except that they were dead before ending up in the urns. Their skulls were already caved in. Somebody smashed them both on the bonce with a very blunt instrument before shoving them out.'

'And the blunt instrument?'

'Difficult. It's been suggested that they were both rammed into something solid and hard. Like a wall.'

'The walls up in the attic were paper-thin — old-fash-ioned lath and plaster. Their heads would have gone straight through if anyone had rammed them into those walls.'

'That was pointed out to us, but there is something else in those rooms. Did you notice the boxes up there? There was one in each room.'

Honey recalled seeing the wooden chests. 'They looked like linen chests; roughly made and painted a ghastly shade of green. Are those the ones you mean?'

'That's right, only they weren't linen chests. The wood enclosed the old slate water storage tanks; long replaced of course, but the supply was kept and connected to a hanging basket sprinkler system running around the building. You get the picture? Lift the lid, hold your victim's head under water, then wham! Smash the lid down onto their head.' He paused.

'Oh, yes. I forgot to say. There was water in their lungs. No water in the urns. No potting compost either.'

It was halfway through the afternoon when she was back where she should be — on Reception informing an elderly Russian lady of places to visit that had no stairs — when her phone rang.

'If you could just give me a few seconds, I'll be right with you.'

Her heart was leaping and her stomach preparing to cinch in. She hadn't had time to check the caller, but she presumed it was Doherty.

It turned out to be John Rees and he had a question for her.

'Get back to me as soon as you can.'

She promised she would once she'd checked the hotel was covered.

He'd asked her to dinner tomorrow night. 'A mix of business and pleasure. I've invited someone who knows a thing or two about Spiderman to have a drink in the bar with us beforehand.'

CHAPTER NINE

It wasn't often they got time, but tonight Honey and Lindsey were dining together, a real mother and daughter thing that made Honey feel all warm and mumsy.

'Is the chicken OK?'

Honey nodded. 'Delicious.'

'The carrots?'

'Lovely.'

'Actually they're not really carrots. They're arsenic roots, but bleach them long enough in peroxide and I'm told they're quite harmless. And delicious.'

'Lovely,' Honey repeated.

'And you can't really taste any difference at all between chicken chasseur and caramelised rat, can you?'

'It's nice, lovely . . .'

Finally realising she hadn't been listening properly, Honey set down her fork and dabbed at her lips with her napkin. 'I'm sorry, love, but I just can't seem to concentrate.' She paused. 'It is chicken chasseur, isn't it?'

Lindsey nodded. 'So go on. Tell me what's on your mind.'

Honey took a swig of wine.

'John Rees has asked me to go to dinner with him tomorrow night.'

Lindsey hunched her shoulders and spread her hands. 'So?'

'Should I go?'

'Is there anything else scheduled for tomorrow night?'

'No, it's pretty quiet tomorrow night . . .'

'That's not what I meant. The hotel can take care of itself. You have a fine staff and I'm here. What I am asking, Mother dear, is: is Doherty still on the main menu?'

Now it was Honey who shrugged. 'I don't know. He hasn't phoned.'

'Have you asked him why?'

'No.'

'That is a very sniffy "no."'

'I'm feeling sniffy.'

'Why don't you phone him and ask him out?'

'I can't.'

'Is that pride I detect, or guilt?'

'I have nothing to be guilty about!'

'You smashed up his car.'

'It wasn't my fault. It was your grandmother and that bloody apron. Did you see the boobs on that nude? The man in the other car was severely traumatised, being recently separated and all. Besides, there's something else. He's invited someone along to have a drink with us beforehand. He hasn't said who this person is, except that he knows Spiderman — Jim Tetman — one of the people the police have been questioning. I mean, should I meet this person without the police knowing about it? He's a witness, whoever he is.'

'But that's not it, is it?'

'Pardon?'

'You're thinking that meeting up with John Rees — even if there is a line of enquiry into a murder — may dash your chances of a reconciliation with Doherty.'

Honey opened her mouth to say something. The denial refused to voice itself. She wanted to solve the crime; she wanted to make up with Doherty. The trouble was that she also fancied John Rees.

'Give me your phone.'

'Why?'

'I'm going to phone Doherty.'

'No. You can't have it.'

'OK. I'll use mine.'

'You can't!'

'Go on. You want me to.'

Again Honey's mouth dropped open without a single sound coming out. She was cornered. Why was it that a twenty-something daughter could read her so accurately? Of course she wanted her to ask Doherty why he hadn't called, but what would she do if he offered a plausible excuse and she had to backtrack on her budding association with John Rees? And she knew she should tell him about this person with a knowledge of Spiderman — Jim Tetman.

She considered what his response might be. 'Love me, love my car' was a great truism; 'hurt my car and you hurt me' was right up there with it.

'Hi, Steve. It's me. Lindsey.'

Honey closed her eyes and shook her head. Unbearable as it was, her ears were tuned in.

'Look, I know you're busy, but my mother and you, well, I hate seeing a gap as wide as the Avon Gorge opening up between you. Is your relationship as damaged as your car?'

Another pause.

'Oh! I see.'

Lindsey nodded into the cell phone.

'I see where you're coming from. Getting emotional about your car was a knee-jerk reaction. Best forgotten, soonest mended. It's a very old cliché but a very true one.'

Doherty was saying something again.

'Well I don't think that's true, Steve. John Rees just happened to be going to the same party, that's all. There's nothing serious going on — honestly.'

Honey sat bolt upright and mouthed, 'There might be.'

Lindsey waved at her to butt out.

'By the way, my mother does have a meeting tomorrow night with John Rees and somebody who knows a bit about this Jim Tetman, the man who was dressed as Spiderman. It might be a good idea if you're there too. I understand they're meeting in the Garrick's Head. You're invited.'

Honey's jaw dropped. 'No!' she hissed, shaking her head.

The butt out wave again.

'Yes, I think that's a good idea too. You two are made for each other. You know that, don't you?'

Again a pause on Lindsey's part as Doherty answered. Then she smiled.

'I thought so. But if all that's true, Steve, how come you haven't phoned?'

An answer.

The smile dropped from Lindsey's face. Her jaw stiffened.

Honey immediately that she wouldn't like the answer.

'Oh. Two days ago and you left a message with my grandmother.'

Honey sprang to her feet and grabbed the phone.

'Steve! I didn't get the message.'

There was only silence.

Honey looked at the phone then gave it a shake.

'Steve?'

Lindsey was wearing a guilty expression.

'Um. It's run out of credit.'

'I'll ring him back on mine.'

'Mum! Don't.'

Honey stared uncomprehending. The penny dropped.

'You weren't speaking to Doherty?'

'I was.' Lindsey paused. 'But not for the whole time. I really did run out of credit though. I figured it was the best way to tell you that I caught Gran fielding a call from him. He did ring you, it was just that Gran didn't pass the message on. I picked it up from the call log. I tape some calls. Gran asked to phone one of her friends from Reception. I left her to it. It was only this morning that I checked the call log. I always play a few messages back. There was a call from Doherty to the reception phone.'

'Why didn't he phone me on my cell phone?' Honey screeched.

'In case you were with alternative male company? He could only be certain of having you to himself on the hotel phone. Makes sense.'

'Right,' said Honey. Pushing the chair back and springing to her feet. She grabbed the heavy skillet from the cooker hot plate.

'Where are you going?'

'I'm about to practise matricide and this isn't a skillet. It's a blunt instrument.'

To her credit, Lindsey had a very mature attitude and was able to persuade her mother not to murder her grandmother. The skillet was buried in the dishwasher and, furnished with another glass of Cabernet Sauvignon, Honey obeyed the order to sit down and calm down.

This was hardly the first time that her mother had interfered with her love life. Gloria Cross considered herself more capable of finding her daughter a new man than Honey was. Suitable, as far as she was concerned, meant somebody with a regular job, regular salary, and healthy bank account. Someone who was more of a useful appendage than a red-blooded lover — like a handbag.

Her mother didn't so much hate Detective Chief Inspector Steve Doherty as view him with outright alarm. OK, he had a regular job, regular salary, and his bank account wasn't that bad. It was the rest of him. For a start he was no handbag: not smooth, clean, and content to hang over Honey's arm.

He was leathery; gritty, hard-edged, streetwise, able to take care of himself, and keener to have Honey hang over the edge of the bed than him hang over her arm. Like John Rees he wore tight denims like a second skin, had a strong jaw, a shock of untidy hair, and muscles that bulged through his T-shirt. He also had a way of looking at her that was an invite to bed — 24/7.

Lindsey looked sheepish.

'OK,' said Honey. 'When it comes to picking up vibes, I'm almost as good as Mary Jane. What's the reason for that look on your face?'

'Doherty will be in the bar of the Garrick's tomorrow night. I got the first part through to him before my credit ran out.'

Honey groaned. After thinking it through, she shook her head. 'It won't be easy.'

Lindsey placed a portion of lemon soufflé in front of her. 'Eat that. Lemon soufflé concentrates the mind. The petit fours I'm serving with the coffee will calm you down.'

Honey slipped the first mouthful onto her tongue. The soufflé was light, moist, and tangy. She nodded. 'This is lovely.'

Lindsey was also right about the petit fours; eating each one carefully, melting it on the tongue before swallowing, was amazingly therapeutic.

'The Mayans swore that chocolate was a magic medicine,' said Lindsey.

'They also practised human sacrifice,' Honey responded pointedly.

'Now,' said Lindsey, acting like a carer who was used to dotty people of mature years and so-so love lives, 'tell me about Mary Jane's findings regarding Bert the wrinkly hippy.'

Honey hadn't stayed in the room when Mary Jane was doing her thing, but she'd heard all about it afterwards on the drive back.

'Apparently the letter M was pretty prominent. Mary Jane asked if Rhoda knew anyone with a name beginning with M. She said she knew quite a few.'

'I suppose that was something.'

'Not really. Mary Jane then declared that the letter S was coming through. The initials of something or someone was M and S.'

'Did that narrow it down a bit?'

'You bet it did. M and S. Although recently enrolled on a get fit course for the over-sixties, it seems that Rhoda has been sinning big time. We found a box of M&S cream cakes under the sofa. That's where she hid them when we knocked at the door.'

* * *

The Garrick's Head was only moderately busy. The Green Room, where once actors and members of the LGBT community had rubbed shoulders, had been turned into a restaurant. The main bar was virtually unchanged, a place of pre-dinner drinks where theatre goers could also order drinks for the interval.

A guest had complained of a blockage in the lavatory at the hotel. Armed with a plunger and toilet brush, Honey had gone up there to do battle. The culprit turned out to be a collection of chocolate wrappers made into a ball and shoved down the loo.

Chocolate-loving Peter and his family had been the previous occupants of the room. The culprit was a foregone conclusion; the job of unblocking the loo was an unpopular one.

John Rees was already at the bar when she arrived. So was Doherty. So too was Ahmed Clifford. He was the one with information about Jim Tetman? Honey was surprised.

Taking a deep breath, Honey breezed in.

'Sorry I'm late.'

All three of them looked round.

John bought her a drink. Ahmed was drinking orange juice. So was Doherty.

'I'm on duty,' he said to her unspoken question.

They found themselves a snug corner at a point furthest from the bar door.

The bar was filling up with the theatre crowd; a host of standing figures all talking culture while swigging back their pre-performance drinks.

'I expect you're surprised to see me,' said Ahmed, his white teeth flashing in his glossy face.

'I've never seen you not covered in oil.'

'Professional hazard. How do you like the outfit?'

He looked as though he'd stepped straight from a fashion catalogue; well-cut jacket in a pale shade of yellow; pale green trousers; crisp white shirt. It was simple but amazing. His hair was black and glossy. Better still, he smelled of something that didn't come from the bottom of an engine sump.

John Rees indicated that Doherty lead the questioning. 'I'm only a bystander,' he added.

Doherty sat with his elbows resting on his knees, hands clasped together.

'So. What is it you've got to tell us about Jim Tetman, Mr Clifford?'

Ahmed drained his glass. 'Lovely. Orange juice is good for the vocal cords,' he said, his face beaming. 'So, Jim brought his wife's car in for a service. He never brings his own in, not his Jag. Takes that to the main dealers. But his wife's car's a cheap effort; a Fiat. A "get me about town" type of car. Well, it was like this. He was there with this car wanting me to give it a service when them two that got murdered came breezing past. They'd been shopping. Pushing a supermarket trolley along. Well they saw Jim and Jim saw them. Sparks flew. He called them all the names under the sun. Said they'd bought Moss End from under his nose at a vastly inflated price. And what was it all about? Why do that?

'They rushed past him as though they didn't want to know. Broke into a run still pushing this trolley. Piled up with shopping it was. I thought it was strange. I mean, when people leave Sainsbury's, they don't usually take the shopping trolley with them, do they? Seemed a bit stupid to me.'

Doherty nodded. 'So Jim Tetman was pretty peeved with Mr and Mrs Crook. Did he elaborate?'

Ahmed shook his head. 'Only to say that he was going to get even with them one way or the other.'

Doherty made arrangements for Ahmed to come along to the station to give a statement.

Perhaps Honey would have gone on to have dinner with John Rees. Or she might have stayed put, hedging her bets between him and Doherty. As it was, an emergency had arisen at the Green River Hotel. A restaurant diner was suffering from a severe nosebleed and Smudger the chef was responsible.

CHAPTER TEN

Smudger had always been volatile and although it wound her up and there'd been more than one occasion when she'd considered sacking him, good chefs were hard to come by.

Doherty gave her a lift back to the hotel after she'd promised John Rees that she'd be in touch.

She could tell by his sad smile that he didn't believe her. There was nothing she could do about that. Sorting out the problem at the Green River Hotel was top priority.

On arrival, Honey headed for the restaurant where Clive, the head waiter, was ticking names off his reservation list.

Was the diner likely to sue? Was his blood seeping into the very decent carpet?

'Where's the diner with the bloody nose?'

'Gone, Mrs Driver.'

'In an ambulance?'

'No Mrs Driver. He didn't want to go to hospital.' He nodded in welcome to Doherty. 'Neither did he wish for the police to be involved.'

Honey turned on her heel. 'I'm going to sack that chef.'

'Actually, Mrs Driver, it wasn't the chef's fault.'

Honey stopped.

'What happened?'

'The gentleman complained about every course. I think he was trying to impress his companion who was, shall we say, quite a lot younger than he. September and May — if you get my meaning. The gentleman, having imbibed rather a large quantity of vintage port, then decided he was going to beard the lion in his den. A most unfortunate mistake. I did try and persuade him that it wouldn't be a good idea. But he was drunk and trying to impress the young lady. He marched into the kitchen to confront the chef. Chef responded accordingly. The gentleman admitted it was all his fault when we offered to contact the police and then to give him a lift home. I had taken his business card and it does have his home address on it.' Clive took a plain white card from his diner records and waved it. 'He was quite adamant that he didn't want us to ring anyone and to put an end to the matter.'

'Did he leave a good tip?'

'A very good, Mrs Driver. Enough to wipe out the memory of ever having seen him in here.'

'Sorry,' Honey said to Doherty. 'But regardless of the circumstances, I have to deal with Chef.'

He took hold of her shoulders. For a moment she held her breath, thinking he was going to kiss her.

He didn't.

'Shoulders back, girl. Tell him I'll griddle his meat and two veg if he ever hits anyone again.'

Bereft of a kiss, she eyed his back as he headed for the door where he paused, turned, and asked if she could present herself at Manvers Street round about eleven o'clock. She agreed of course.

The kitchen smelled and sounded busy, pans simmering, meat spitting and pans clattering.

Smudger was whistling as he slid pans of sauce around the flat top, turned steaks on the grill, and checked the contents of his oven.

The casual wave he gave her said that he was unnerved by her stiff stance, her folded arms, her heavy frown.

'Smudger! You're still here only by the skin of your teeth.'

He grinned, his face pink from the heat of hot pans. 'He was an arsehole. He deserved it.'

'He's a *customer*, though probably not a returning one. You didn't have to punch him on the nose.'

Smudger smiled. 'Stay cool. Stay cool. I didn't punch him.'

'So the bloody nose was an illusion?'

'No. I was just filling in the detail. I didn't use my fist. I used a frying pan.'

* * *

Blue sky and fluffy clouds were reflected in the windows overlooking Pulteney Weir and a flurry of fallen leaves were dancing in circles over the pavements.

Honey was walking along wondering why she had ever become a hotelier in the first place. The guests could be aggravating, the staff, notably chefs, aggressive.

How about a career change? Was it a feasible proposition when a woman was on the plus side of forty? But what career could she go into?

Brain surgeon and rocket scientist were out of the question; she wasn't qualified and she didn't fancy studying alongside people half her age. Doing that was ageing in itself.

She aimed the odd kick at the leaves.

The question of John Rees weighed temptingly rather than heavily. A new restaurant had just opened. Both the wine and food were Portuguese, courtesy of the owner having been a recent resident of Mozambique. John had been invited for a preview evening. John in turn had invited her.

'It'll be great. If you're free, that is.'

Was she free? She had nothing on that evening, but did dining out with a man you possibly fancied equate to infidelity?

She pulled a face as she groaned which invited the attention of a few passers-by.

'Never mind, luv. Might never happen.'

The comment failed to raise a smile.

'You look as though you've found a fiver but lost a fifty, hen.'

The second voice was instantly familiar.

'Alistair!'

Honey smiled at the man she had to thank for many of her best auction purchases. He was looking down at her from his superior height. She thought he was smiling, but it was difficult to tell seeing as his flame-coloured beard was as thick as a blackthorn hedge and didn't seem to leave much space for a mouth.

'I heard about the double murder out at Miss Porter's old place,' he said to her.

Honey confirmed that he was right.

'My, but old Miss Porter would have a fit if she knew that. She was there for thirty years, you know. It was her who applied for and got all the planning permission and suchlike to turn it into a guest house in the first place. Went through swimmingly it did. Faster than anyone had ever known. Mind you, it might have been something to do with the liaison she was having with one of the councillors.'

'You're kidding!'

'Not at all. Did you not know that, hen?'

Honey admitted that she had not known that, but then again it was before her time. 'The most recent owners were shoved out of the third-storey windows and landed in two giant urns placed either side of the door.'

'Aye. They would do. Those urns are far too big for the place of course. I recall the day Miss Porter bought them. The old girl committed a double whammy. She was after a smaller pair of urns. Not only did she leave a bid on the wrong ones, she wrote "last bid" in the price column. That meant she had to pay whatever they fetched. They weren't even genuine. Plastic replicas.'

Honey nodded. 'Ugly things. Was that very long before she sold the place?'

'A few months? She had intended to resell them, but I suppose she couldn't be bothered and once the old place was on the market, well, it was up to the new owners to get rid or keep the things.'

'I can understand that. I expect once she'd made up her mind to retire, she didn't care what happened to them.'

'She might have gone on a bit longer I suppose, but when those two that got killed came along and offered her a good price, off she went. I recall her telling me that some other bods were after it for turning into flats. She told me she didn't like that idea, but if they paid enough . . . and then along came the cash offer from the two that are now deceased.'

'Cash! Goodness. Lucky them.'

'And lucky Miss Porter. She almost took their arms off.'

'I take it she met them at the viewing. Any idea what she thought of them?'

He shook his head. 'No. Not the kind of question I would have asked at the time. If it's of any help, I could give her a ring and ask her.'

'That's very kind of you, Alistair. I would much appreciate that.'

Honey patted down the coat collar that she'd pulled up around her neck — not because it was cold, but purely because hiding behind a coat collar was like a barrier behind which her thoughts could flow freely.

'I think she said they were colonials,' said Alistair, his breath writhing like a white mist around his red beard.

'What did she mean by that?'

He shrugged shoulders that were broad enough and strong enough to toss a caber — or anyone who'd upset him, should he be so inclined.

'Well obviously they came from somewhere else before landing here. Not another planet—well—not in the accepted sense. Somewhere abroad in one of the old Commonwealth dominions—Africa perhaps. Kenya, South Africa . . . She didn't tell me much else at the time except that Mrs Hicks, her old friend from across the way, would keep her informed of goings on. They were both members of some women's association.'

'The Women's Institute?'

Alistair scratched the back of his neck as he considered the question. 'Could be.'

* * *

Manvers Street police station, twentieth-century architecture at its worst, had the solid look of a multi-layered slab cake stuck together side on.

At least it was warm inside, though hardly jovial. This place had been built when standing out rather than blending in was what it was all about.

Honey wrinkled her nose. She was very sensitive to smells. She looked around her, her nose twitching.

The source of the smell appeared to be a huge lump of dark tweed. He was heaped in a chair in the waiting area, fingers knitted nervously together.

The duty desk sergeant shook his head when she explained that Doherty had asked her to come in.

'He's not in.'

'Out at the murder scene?'

He hissed through his teeth and shook his head. 'I'm not supposed to tell you that. His whereabouts is police business.'

'But you're not denying it either.'

'Just a minute, Mrs Driver,' he said with an air of authority. 'We're the ones who're supposed to ask the questions, not you.'

She smiled and shook her head in acceptance that he was only joking.

Suddenly the musty, unwashed smell suddenly swept over her, accompanied by a shuffling sound from behind her.

'So are you going to pay me or what?' demanded a loud voice.

Even before she turned round, Honey knew that the huge lump of grey tweed had sprouted legs. His size and the colour of his clothes reminded her of a hippopotamus.

Apologising for gripping her shoulders he pushed her aside so he could better get at the desk sergeant.

Sergeant Lynch, a long-serving member of the constabulary noticeably held his breath.

'Rhino. I said somebody would be with you as soon as there was somebody to spare.'

Honey congratulated herself. Hippo. Rhino. She hadn't been far wrong.

A thick fist thudded down on the desk. 'This is important. I know stuff that could shed light on a serious crime. Ain't nobody here interested?'

'I didn't say that, Rhino, it's just that . . .'

'You want the information for free! Yeah! That's it! You want the information for free,' the street dweller shouted waving one beefy arm. 'Well a man's gotta live, and I ain't giving it for free. And that's final!'

Not only did Rhino own a huge body and wear a huge grey tweed coat, he also wore a scarf that looked capable of stretching the length of Milsom Street. At one time it must have been multicoloured, but the colours were now muted by dirt as though it had been buried in rubble for years.

The end of the scarf twirled around him like some kind of street-based helix.

Honey jerked her head back from the rancid smell as the coat, the big man, and the flying scarf strode for the exit, all the while the man muttering curses and expletives.

The door opened and slammed behind him.

'Phew,' muttered the sergeant as he whisked an aerosol spray around the waiting room.

Before leaving she left a message for Doherty to phone her. Could they liaise on a few points and arrange to meet? Please ring to confirm.

Outside the man mountain Rhino was sitting on the steps looking not so much like a doorstop as a steel door.

He was muttering to himself, describing the local nick with a series of expletives that cast aspersions on the paternity of the boys in blue and their abilities in the undercover sector.

'I knew those crooks. I worked for them for Chrissakes . . .'

Honey was two steps closer to the pavement than Rhino, but mention of crooks made her pause.

Did he really mean crooks? Or did he mean *Crooks*?

She turned round and asked him.

'Did you know Boris and Doris, the people who were murdered?'

The muttering ceased.

'So. Somebody is listening!' He looked her up and down. 'You don't look like fuzz. You got a bit of style. Might even be intelligent.'

'Thank you for your kind comment. So you did know Boris and Doris.'

He eyed her suspiciously. 'What's it to you?'

'I'd be really interested in . . .'

'I bet you would.'

'Not many people seem to know much about them . . .'

'How much?'

She knew what he was asking. How much was she going to pay him for the information. Out and about in Bath, she only had thirty pounds in her purse, one debit card, and a credit card.

'How about thirty pounds?'

She winced as a large globule of snot was drawn into his throat and spit out of his mouth onto the pavement. She had her answer.

'Thirty pounds on account.'

He turned his head to look at her again. 'On account of what?'

Honey wondered what Doherty offered on these occasions and decided he would back her up.

'A considerable bit more, though I have to pass it with my superior officer first,' she responded, two fingers crossed behind her back.

Doherty would back her up. Wouldn't he?

'Make me an offer.'

Rhino was nothing if not determined. Well named.

'Say one hundred pounds — if the information is any good.'

He gave her a piggy eyed look, the sort his namesake animal is rumoured to give before dropping their head and charging.

Luckily she was wearing her running shoes — running as in around the hotel, in and out of the kitchen, and shopping for sausages in Green Street. Whether she could outrun a charging Rhino was another matter.

'OK.' He gave a curt nod and rubbed his nose.

Honey dived into her purse. Three ten-pound notes disappeared into Rhino's chubby hand. From thence they disappeared into an inside pocket in the copious coat.

He sniffed. 'Came to check my haul on a regular basis.'

'Haul?' She frowned, not understanding. 'What sort of haul was that?'

'Don't mess me about, lady. I don't like people who mess me about.'

'I wasn't. I just wanted to know what sort of haul. It must have been quite interesting.'

It crossed her mind that he might be violent and most definitely criminal. In what regard? Rhino lived rough on the streets, but he didn't look like a mugger. Too big and too old to be swift on his feet. A mugger needs to make a swift getaway.

'My haul. I collect stuff and he was interested in the stuff I collected.' He pointed. 'That's my wagon.'

Rhino pointed at the lop-sided supermarket trolley waiting for him at the bottom of the steps. It looked as though it had lost a wheel and was propped up against a municipal rubbish bin.

'Got some real good stuff in there. Real good!'

Honey assessed his haul. Newspapers, cardboard and plastic carrier bags jostled for space. If that was good stuff, valuable stuff, then she was missing something.

She caught him looking at her.

'I note your disbelief, sister. But I'm telling you, I've got good stuff on my wagon. Stuff the likes of the dude from Northend paid me good for. Real good.'

Real good. Right. But who in their right mind paid good money for old newspapers?

'I'll show you.' Rhino struggled up and began waddling down the steps.

Honey followed.

First he rearranged a laminated piece of cardboard that was holding everything in. It had writing on it; 'Members Only.'

Pushing the newspapers to one side, Rhino delved into one of the carrier bags eventually bringing out a few till receipts and screwed up letters — and bills.

'These ain't just any old bits of paper. I range only the best areas. That's what the dude liked about my stuff. "Get me the good stuff from the good addresses," he said to me.'

Despite her distaste for handling the grimy receipts, Honey forced herself to take them from him. They were indeed till receipts and screwed up bills, utility bills. Some of the till receipts were from supermarkets. Some were ATM receipts. Some crumpled, but basically information intact.

'The man from Northend paid you for these?'

Rhino nodded. 'Sure he did. My gear is from tidy addresses, upmarket addresses. No crap. He said he liked collecting them too.'

'And paid you pretty well.'

'You bet.'

'When was the last time you saw him?'

He frowned deeply.

'Blew in paying me for stuff, then blew out again. Short and sweet it was. Bastard! Said he had a better business on the go.'

'The guest house?'

Rhino shrugged. 'I don't know what business it was, but 'e only bought from me for a week or so. Might have been doing a deal with Edna. I said I passed some of my stuff to 'er. We was partners at times.'

Honey took a deep breath. So Boris Crook had paid Rhino for information — information that led in one direction and one alone. Identity theft. But only for a week or so? It didn't make sense.

'So where do I find this Edna?'

'Here and there. Here and there.'

'It must get cold living outdoors all the time. Do you have anywhere to stay indoors?'

For a moment his face was like stone. Suddenly his whole attitude changed.

'Sometimes, but only in the city,' he snapped. 'Only in the city, mark you!'

Rhino got to his feet and shambled off down the steps. The moment his hands were on the trolley, he was off at a lick. Only once did he glance at her over his shoulder. That one action made Honey think he was not telling the truth.

CHAPTER ELEVEN

On getting through to Doherty on the phone, she mentioned her meeting with Rhino and the woman named Edna.

'Look,' he replied. 'I've got too much on my plate at the moment. Ask around. You'll find her.'

'I thought you wanted to speak to me?'

'It can wait.'

She was glad he couldn't see her disappointment and the two-fingered salute she gave him.

He disconnected.

'Bum!' she shouted into the phone. 'Bum, bum, bum!'

* * *

Casper had invited Honey for morning coffee. The coffee was dark and bitter. She thought about asking for a cup of good old Nescafé instant, but realised it was a waste of time. Casper didn't do downmarket.

In order to make it palatable, she spooned in two spoon-fuls of sugar. She was on yet another diet; no sugar, but this was an emergency.

'So how did they die?' he asked.

'Somebody bashed them over the head up in the attic rooms. They were dead before they were shoved out of the windows. It's likely that somebody was staying in that top room and may be prime suspect.'

'For both murders?'

His raised eyebrows and sharply questioning tone had the effect of digging out her own latent suspicions; one person smashing two skulls in two separate rooms — at least that was the way it looked.

She frowned into her coffee. 'Unless the victims were taken by surprise, lured into separate rooms for . . . a reason.'

'It must have been a good reason. My inclination is towards a sexual liaison on the female part — that would put her in one bedroom. The woman and her lover hear the husband coming up the stairs; said lover goes out to meet him before he enters the room. There's a scuffle and a smashing of skull. Wife screams. Lover panics so she gets the same treatment as dead husband.'

Honey studied Casper's superior air, his nose lifted and tilted above the tiny cup of select Turkish coffee.

She thought about asking him if he was into reading crime fiction.

'That's a very . . . interesting scenario, if a little melodramatic.'

'Not at all. Human nature. The common motives for crime are money and sex. As far as these people are concerned, I'm opting for a crime of passion — even though I myself would have failed miserably to feel passionate about either of them.'

'We'll have to wait and see. The detective chief inspector has asked me to call in for an update.'

'He couldn't tell you anything over the phone? I was under the impression that you and he were extremely close, very much "an item", to quote the modern vernacular.'

Casper pronounced vernacular as though there was an 'h' on the end. Vernaculah! It sounded like a song.

'Nothing lasts forever.'

'Ah!'

She gave the coffee another stir in the hope that the sugar would finally win out over the bitterness.

'On this occasion he insists I come into the station. I have an appointment to see him at three this afternoon.'

'An appointment no less!' Casper waved his fine fingers dismissively. 'Whatever. I keep asking myself why I am not so enthused about catching the perpetrators of these murders as I usually am. It must be because based on meeting them when they deigned to attend a hotels event, I found them so obnoxious that it crossed my mind to do away with them myself!'

Honey accepted where he was coming from with regard to the victims, but wasn't feeling quite so dismissive; Doherty had never insisted on telling her the findings face to face before. In the past he'd had no objection to informing her by phone. She took this as a sign that all was not lost between them. There was something good in that, she told herself and even began thinking about what she would wear when they next met.

'It did look as though they were about to leave the guest house, though nobody knows why and there was no indication of where they were going. But luggage was packed.'

Casper leaned forward, one beautifully manicured hand cupped around his chin as though about to impart a great secret.

Lowering his voice, he said, 'I did hear rumours that they brought debts with them and had bought Moss End in the hope of making enough money to clear their encumbrances. One look at them and I cannot imagine them making much of a go of the place. The woman gushed sweetness like an upended tin of treacle. As for him, well, he was so terribly tall, head and shoulders above everyone else—and ungainly with it to the point of having acquired a curvature of the spine. I believe their creditors were snapping at the heels of their downmarket shoes.'

Pointing out that you couldn't hold being round or too tall against a person was a waste of time.

'Do you happen to know who these creditors were?'

He shook his head. 'No details I'm afraid. Pure speculation.'

Honey rolled the bitter coffee around her tongue.

'Still,' she said, smothering a cough with her hand. 'They didn't deserve to be murdered for owing money, and we shouldn't allow a personal point of view to cloud our judgement.'

She had to concede that basically he was right in that a good cash flow was imperative in the hospitality game. Earnings could be sporadic and business dipped in the wintertime.

She winced as she swallowed the last of the coffee before setting it down on the silver tray and refusing a second cup.

'Although debt collectors have a pretty rotten reputation, I've never heard of them upending their prey in potting compost before.'

'Potting compost! Is that true?'

She shook her head. 'No. The pots were quite clean, although one would expect them to contain something.'

'Perhaps they weren't keen gardeners,' said Casper.

'Perhaps not.'

* * *

John Rees had invited her for lunch. She'd declined his dinner offer of attending the pre-opening party at the Portuguese-style restaurant. Not dinner. She couldn't do dinner. Lunch was different. In broad daylight it didn't feel like she was two-timing Doherty. Not as though she was. Not really.

She was undecided whether to wear the navy-blue suit with the slit skirt or the coffee-coloured dress with brown flecked bolero. In the end she decided on the latter with brown boots and mustard coloured scarf.

Before venturing out, she rang Doherty.

'I need to speak to you.'

He grunted a response.

'I've discovered some useful information about our murder victims. I think they were into identity theft.'

An ominous silence met her statement.

'Steve? Did you hear what I said?'

'I've got my car back.'

She pulled a face at the phone and poked out her tongue. Childishly bearing a grudge deserved a childish response.

Recalling Casper's insistence that she hang in there and get this case sorted, she swallowed some of the worst of the sarcastic retorts she wanted to use. Instead, she chewed over the words that she had to say—not wanting to say them, but knowing that she must.

'Look, Steve. I'm sorry. You must know that. If I could turn back the clock I would. But I can't.'

She heard him sigh.

'Well I suppose it's not your fault. Why can't your mother find herself a broomstick to fly around on?'

'Look. Can we get back to business?'

'Go on.'

'Boris and Doris Crook were buying information from that bloke Rhino, the one who gathers all manner of rubbish from people's bins.'

'You mean utility bills? Bank statements? Till receipts?'

'Exactly what I mean, though strangely enough only for a very short time. Rhino reckoned that somebody called Edna had taken over collecting for them.'

'Can we meet up for lunch?'

'Does this mean my sins are forgiven?'

'You may have to remind me of what sins you're actually capable of.'

She imagined his smile.

That was more like it! The old Doherty had returned and was back on form.

Just as she was about to accept, she remembered she'd promised John. Was it greedy wanting to keep both men on board — just in case things didn't work out?

'Sorry. I've got a business appointment. How about dinner?'

'Fancy a sleepover?'

Honey punched the air with her fist. 'I'll bring my PJ's.'

'You may recall I have central heating.'

Lindsey caught her humming to herself.

'You look like the cat that got the cream. Dare I ask whether the delish DCI is back on board?'

'I think he is.'

'So the equally delish bookseller is merely a note in life's diary of events?'

'I wouldn't exactly say that. Let's just say that I quite fancy having a menu choice.'

'Just as long as you don't make yourself sick.'

Despite her daughter's warning, Honey told herself that there was no need to feel guilty about going to lunch with John Rees. They'd been friends for a long while and besides, he asked first.

A change of clothes — a green dress with a wrap-around skirt and cinched-in waist — a dab of perfume behind each ear, a grey checked coat, and a dark mustard pashmina. She was ready for action.

The décor of The Tasting Room was clean cut though still managed to hold on to an al fresco atmosphere. The food was bistro style and the wine well kept.

John was in one of his favourite places that had no dress code. He favoured casual dress and comfortable shoes.

They ordered a fish dish each with a green salad, crusty bread rich with sunflower seeds, and bright yellow butter. The wine was white. Drinking white at lunchtime was a habit Honey much favoured. To her mind it wasn't so heady as red. Red wine was for evenings — and romantic moments.

They talked about the murders and the chaotic party, the range of Hallowe'en themed costumes, and, last but not least, Boris and Doris Crook.

'Did you see how tall that guy was? Taller than me, that's for sure.'

Honey said that she'd noticed the same. 'Straight out of Monsterville. Though I shouldn't say that,' she said after a respectful pause. 'After all, he is dead.'

'I wonder what possessed them to take over a business they had no intention of running?'

Honey thought about it. 'We need to find out where they came from before moving into Northend and what people thought of them in the village.'

'The pub might be a good place to start.'

'How about we head in that direction as soon as we finish this fish?'

'We'll have to hurry. It's a village pub. They don't stay open all day.' Honey glanced at her watch. 'We can take the wine with us. It's Australian. Bound to be a screw top.'

Eating up, paying, and grabbing the half-finished bottle of wine took time. With their eye on the clock, they rushed out.

Honey eyed the afternoon traffic. Nothing seemed to be moving fast.

'My car, I think. It's nearest.'

Dashing off to where she'd parked the hire car, neither one of them noticed Doherty standing on the other side of the road, breaking his lunchtime sandwich into bits and feeding it to the pigeons.

Pigeon wings flapped and feathers flew as the flying vermin pounced on the lunchtime bounty.

'Sort it out yourselves,' he muttered throwing the whole lot to the ground.

* * *

Like many other villages around many cities countrywide, the majority of Northend residents worked during the day. Like lemmings heading for the cliff face, they left the village in droves at around eight in the morning. After some eight to twelve hours, they reappeared once the sun was setting, their homecoming accompanied by the sound of ice clinking in liberal glassfuls of gin in period style drawing rooms.

It was about two o'clock when Honey and John drove into Northend. There wasn't a soul in sight, the village possessing an empty feel, as though the houses were only facades in yet another film or TV period piece.

'Even by day it looks a gloomy old place,' John commented, straining his neck to see over the high wall as they drove past Moss End Guest House.

The police-incident tape was still fluttering outside.

'I wonder who inherits,' mused Honey. 'Not that it's likely to be of much consequence. My money is still on the organised crime scenario; involvement in identify theft.'

'If what that guy Rhino has told you is correct.'

'An open and shut case, though I'm not sure why he did a runner when I asked him about living outside during the cold weather. Someone had been sleeping in that spare room. I wonder . . .'

'A homeless man? Most people wouldn't give him houseroom.'

'Unless there was a reason. It's another question for Doherty to ask when he hauls Rhino in for an interview.'

'If he finds him again.'

'Oh, I don't see any reason why he won't allow himself to be found.'

'That depends whether you gave him any money. Once they have money, they're likely to disappear.'

'Whoops!'

'You didn't?'

'I did.'

Your friend Detective Chief Inspector Doherty won't be pleased.'

She sucked in her lips. 'No. I can see that now.'

The Northend Inn was flush fronted to the road, three storeys high and didn't appear very busy. The décor was pseudo-Tudor and the carpet was red with yellow swirls all over it.

A fruit machine blinked and burped to their left and a set of three steps ascended to their right. The latter gave that end of the bar an upmarket air, reserved for those who had no time for fruit machines or the single dart player who threw disconsolately at the board at the opposite end looked pretty glum. One dart after another flew at the board and still he couldn't check out.

The landlord was slender, of average height and had discriminating eyes behind wire framed spectacles. 'What sort of microbe are you?' his glance seemed to say.

Honey played the same game, saw he was drying a glass with a linen tea towel — the same glass over and over again.

Business is slow.

'Yes?' he said briskly finally deciding the glass was dry and setting his hands down on the bar. 'What will it be?'

John ordered half a beer. Honey settled for an orange juice.

Must be alert!

Besides themselves there were only two other people in the bar; the barman and a young man playing the fruit machine.

'I thought you might have been busier on account of all the recent excitement you've had in the village.'

The man behind the bar fixed her with a less than warm look. Like the glass he'd resumed drying, his spectacle lenses shone clean and bright.

'You journalists?'

He fixed them with a suspicious glare, his lips a tight, firm line.

Honey shook her head. John nodded.

'Yeah. I work for a specialist American magazine. We . . . I . . . was wondering what your impressions might be of the people who were murdered. There's been a lot of rumours about what they might have been involved in. Would I be right in thinking they didn't mix much?'

The man sneered. 'Don't tell me. You're another one of the nuts who thinks they were vampires. Right?'

John was floundered.

'Ahh . . . well . . . not exactly . . .'

Honey leapt in to help him out.

'Funnily enough we were at that Hallowe'en party. As you can imagine, finding dead bodies right outside the front door was a little disconcerting.'

The thin man eyed her incredulously. 'It was you that found the bodies?'

'Yes. I did. I mean if I hadn't looked up I might not have noticed them. Those urns were huge.'

'Look. I'm Sid Small, lord of this pub and mine of village information. But, and note this well, me hearties, I wasn't the one who said they were vampires. It was him. Gavin the postman.'

He pointed to the young man who was feeding the fruit machine as though it would eat him if he stopped.

'He's the one who started that vampire business. As I told him, this is Northend, not bloody Transylvania! No wonder he gets the postcodes all wrong.'

A sudden deluge of coins erupted from the fruit machine. The postman, looking as though he'd won the Euromillions Lottery, not a handful of coins, scooped them up into his hands, and went to the bar.

'I don't want small change, Sid. Mind changing them for pound and two- pound coins? Put this lot in me pocket and me trousers are likely to fall down.'

Sid Small did as requested. 'I told these people 'ere that it was you who started that vampire business, Gavin. They're journalists and they reckon they were at the party that night. Now there's a thing!'

Honey smiled at the fresh-faced postman. 'I'd like to talk to you about the people who owned the guest house. It was me who discovered the bodies.'

The postman shook his head disconsolately. 'I'm not sure I can tell much more than you already know, but you're welcome to have a chat.'

'Can I buy you a drink?'

Gavin nodded and asked for half a lager. Honey still had enough orange to see her through and John was only sipping at his lager.

They took their drinks into a far corner at the top of the stairs and next to a glowing log fire.

Sid Small hovered, looking peeved at being left out of the conversation.

Gavin had pink cheeks, corn-coloured hair, and baby blue eyes. Although he had to be in his late twenties, his face was round as a baby's and he had amazingly clear skin. She'd seen his like before, the sort who never would look his age; a perennial Peter Pan.

'Did you often deliver mail to the guest house,' Honey asked him.

'Yep. 'Course I did.'

He took a big draught of his drink, seeming to relish the rush of it going down his throat, as though that would help him find the answers to whatever questions they were about to ask him.

'What were they like?'

He shrugged. 'Beats me. Never saw them. I put the letters into the box, and that was it. It was only when I had a parcel to deliver that I knocked at the door.'

'So you saw them then?'

He shook his head. 'No. I didn't.'

Honey frowned. 'Did any of those parcels need a signature?'

'Yep. But they never answered the door. So I left it with Mrs Hicks from across the road.'

John was surprised. 'Are you allowed to do that?' he asked.

Gavin looked at him as though unsure whether he was accusing him of lacking responsibility or whether as an American he didn't know much about Royal Mail postmen.

'Look, mate. There's nobody here in Northend during the day. Everybody works so they can pay their mortgages and for their kids' private education. There's only a few old stagers here during daylight hours; retired people that have lived here all their lives. Like Mrs Hicks. Been here forever, she 'ave. When I couldn't get a reply, she'd step forward, sign for receipt of said parcel, and make sure it was delivered. She never failed me. Never.'

He looked down disconsolately into his drink and shook his head. 'I just hope she delivered it this time OK.'

'What did Mrs Hicks think of the murder victims?' Honey asked.

Shaking his head he wiped the foamy beer from his lips.

'She said she never saw hide nor hair of them during the day. The only things that convinced her somebody was there was that the lights went on at night.'

'Was that the first parcel you'd ever delivered there? The first one that Mrs Hicks had delivered for you?' Honey asked him.

'I'd delivered parcels there before when old Miss Porter owned the place, but this was the first one for the new people.'

'So where does she live; this Mrs Hicks?' Honey asked.

'Just across the road. Number four. Only she's not there. I haven't seen her since she delivered that last parcel. Bit odd, that. I've never known her not be there. She's always there. Always has been.'

Honey could see that he was genuinely concerned. 'Perhaps she's gone on holiday or to stay with relatives.'

Gavin shook his head. 'That's what I thought, though she weren't known for gallivanting around. I don't think she had any relatives, and if she did, they didn't bother much with her. I've asked around. Though they say she pops off now and again, she usually says for a short holiday, something like that. But this time nobody knows where she's gone. Perry's gone too. Where she goes, he goes.'

'Is Perry her husband?' asked Honey.

'No. Perry, Peregrine, is her cat.' He paused, his big eyes opening even wider. 'You don't think they dragged her inside and buried her in the cellar?'

It was John who shook his head. 'I went down into the cellar on the night we attended that party. There was nothing down there.'

Gavin wolfed down his drink and shook his head again. 'That's a relief, though it's still a worry where she might have gone — if she's gone anywhere. What worries me is that there she was delivering a parcel on behalf of the Royal Mail, and after that, no sign of her. My girlfriend reckons they must be vampires seeing as nobody saw them except at night. If so, I feel guilty for getting the old dear to do my job for me. Real guilty.'

CHAPTER TWELVE

Sitting in her car sipping from a wine bottle across from Moss End Hotel, wasn't exactly Honey's idea of fun, but her brain was buzzing. Old Mrs Hicks hadn't been seen since the day before Boris and Doris Crooks were killed. This gave rise to two particular questions; where was Mrs Hicks now, and what had been in the parcel?

John had suggested doing a door-to-door enquiry — just like the police. Honey pointed out to him that seeing as nobody was at home at this time of day, there didn't seem to be much point. Anyway, it was the police's lot to stick to normal procedure; it was theirs to be more radical in their approach.

John rang the Royal Mail sorting office to ask if there was any way of finding out what was in the parcel. A curt voice on the other end told him he had no chance whatsoever. 'Unless it was insured.'

'And you'd tell us then?' John asked.

'Only if it got lost and the sender needed to make a claim. Are you the sender?'

'No, but . . .'

'Sorry. No can do.'

The connection was sharply cut, almost as though the person in customer service on the other end had a pair of scissors to hand in case of such eventuality.

Sid Small, the landlord had pointed them in the direction of a few elderly people in the village. 'Old Tom Pratt might have some idea. They were close years back so local gossip tells.'

He'd winked at them to emphasise the point that the old folk of the village hadn't always been keen gardeners and whist players, but slim, sexy, and hot for action.

Old Tom looked after the gardens of people who had no time to look after gardens themselves. It was his daily habit that once he was paid he took himself along to the Northend Inn for a quick pint before closing time. Town centre pubs might stay open all hours, but the village local stayed open purely to fit in with the habits of the residents.

They'd had it on good authority that he would totter through the village shortly en route for his habitual pint before taking an afternoon nap. Sid Small had assured them they would catch him just right if they parked where they were now.

Honey regarded the reflections of clouds from first-floor windows of the building across the way. The two attic windows looked like blank square eyes. The ground floor windows were totally hidden behind the high wall and the solid metal gate.

'I can hear you thinking,' John said to her.

'I was thinking about the signs of occupancy in one of those attic bedrooms. I wonder if Mrs Hicks had been kept there before . . .'

'We don't know that she's been abducted or killed.'

'We don't know that for sure.'

'Do the police know of her existence?'

Honey shook her head. 'No. I don't think so. After all, she was supposed to deliver the parcel the day before they were murdered so any questions relating to that parcel are irrelevant to the case in hand, I think.'

'Though you're not sure.'

Honey offered the bottle of wine to John. He declined and she screwed the top back onto the bottle and slid it beneath her seat.

It was nice being with him, but suddenly she wanted some distance. She needed to think, and not just about the case in hand. Still, John had been good enough to come along. It must have ruined his after-lunch plans. Perhaps that was why she wanted this over. The after-lunch plans were no longer attractive.

'What next?' he asked.

If it was a personal question, she wasn't answering it. Stick to the crime.

'We still have Rhino to consider, when Doherty catches up with him.' She twiddled her thumbs as she eyed the house opposite. 'Wouldn't it be just great if we could look over that place again now there's nobody at home.'

'Are you suggesting something illegal?'

Her eyes and a mischievous smile slid in his direction.

'We could wait until we speak to old Tom.'

John nodded to an elderly figure walking along the length of the wall. 'Which, according to the description we were given, seems pretty imminent.'

Old Tom was using a walking stick to propel himself along. One of his legs was stiff, swinging out to one side with every step.

They got out of the car.

'Mr Pratt?'

The old man looked taken by surprise.

'Do I know you?' he asked while peering at them through thick spectacle lenses.

'We're looking for a Mrs Hicks. We've knocked at her door but can't make anyone here. You don't know where she might be do you?'

Old Tom, Mr Pratt, blinked as though he were processing what they'd asked him.

'She don't go nowhere.'

'Well she isn't there now.'

'That's her business. If she don't want to be there, then she don't need to be. Now push off and leave 'er alone.'

'We're just concerned . . .'

He lifted his stick, brandishing it as he might a garden hoe at a particularly pernicious weed.

'Push off!'

Sat in the safety of her car again, Honey got to thinking. As far as she could make out, there was only one option left as regards finding the whereabouts of Mrs Hicks. She had to hand it to Doherty on a plate. Tonight at dinner.

She felt John's eyes on her. 'You're thinking again.'

'I tend to do that now and again, and the funny thing is that once I start, I just can't seem to stop.'

She laughed lightly, unwilling to let John know she was meeting Doherty this evening.

Honey started the engine and turned the wheel for home. Tonight would be the first time she'd seen Doherty socially since she'd bashed up his car. Tonight would be dressed to kill night; pull out all the stops. Red carpet dress over minimal underwear. She only hoped it would be enough to make amends.

Avoid conversation about the car; stick to the job in hand. She would not admit to having had lunch with John of course. As far as Doherty was concerned, she had used her own initiative and asked questions out at Northend all by herself.

CHAPTER THIRTEEN

Honey told Doherty all about Mrs Hicks' disappearance.

'Do you know the identity of the person dossing in the attic bedroom?'

'We've taken fingerprint samples and DNA, but one thing I can tell you is that it wasn't Mrs Hicks. It wasn't a woman. Big fingers. My guess is that it was Rhino dossing there after doing one of his "deliveries". The fingerprints will confirm that.'

'Ah!'

'Do you know what was in this parcel she delivered?'

Honey shook her head. 'No idea and the sorting office wouldn't tell me.'

'You rang them?'

'Of course I did. It seemed the logical thing to do.'

She carefully avoided looking at him while telling the lie. Phoning Royal Mail had been John's idea.

'So! You've had a busy day what with asking questions at the pub in Northend. It's a wonder you've had time to eat. You must be ravenous. I've ordered the full four courses. Their prawn starter is huge. Then I've ordered a rack of lamb each and all the trimmings followed by a trio of desserts. I know you have a sweet tooth. And then it's chocolates and coffee with cream and a liqueur. With wine of course. White to start with, then red . . . how does that suit?'

There was something disconcerting about his smile.

'That's quite a feast.'

Too much! She'd had a good lunch. She'd intended having something light — smoked salmon, omelette, perhaps fish. And just the one course.

He patted her hand. She was instantly suspicious. Doherty didn't pat her hand. Ever. Other parts of her body, yes. But not her hand.

'I presumed you wouldn't get much to eat seeing as you had a business appointment.'

He was up to something. He was definitely up to something.

'So what did you have for lunch?'

There was something about his tone that was too smooth, too cajoling — as though he were planning something or had planned something.

'Oh,' she said, shrugging her shoulders. 'Just a quick sandwich. I was so keen to get out to Northend and ask a few questions. Apparently the postman was in the habit of having Mrs Hicks sign for parcels and leave them with her to deliver. By the way, have you managed to have a word with that man Rhino yet? I mean, he'd bound to show up shortly isn't he?'

She said it as brightly as she could preferring to steer him away from the subject of lunch. In case she looked guilty. In case she let something slip.

'Shortly? Well that depends.'

'On what?' she asked without dropping her smile.

'On how much you gave him for the information. You did pay him for the information didn't you?'

'Ummm.'

'How much?'

Honey cleared her throat, fully prepared to make a clean breast of it.

'Thirty pounds.'

'Shit!'

'Did I do that bad?'

Doherty leaned back in his chair. He'd only picked at his meal, but the wine was going down well.

'Rhino can live for a month on thirty quid. We need to find him. This deal he had with the Crooks has to have some bearing on the case. You should have told me sooner.'

'Your uniformed people should have listened to him. They dismissed him just because . . .'

'Because?'

'He smells.'

Doherty pushed his plate away and looked disconsolately around the room, an elegant space with white table linen, soft music, and seemingly unchanged since the Prince Regent was a lad.

'OK. I admit errors were made. But you should have told me sooner. Obviously you were preoccupied with other things — and other people.'

'Your car,' Honey began hesitantly assuming this was what he was referring to. 'Is it fully recovered?'

She bit her lip as she regarded him from under a lock of glossy dark hair.

'It's fully repaired, thanks to Ahmed. But not thanks to you.'

He narrowed his eyes and fixed them on her. She felt like an insect being pinned to a board.

Honey sighed.

'I've said I'm sorry, I explained . . .'

Doherty held up a hand, palm outermost. 'Spare me the details. It's water under the bridge and before you offer me your body and everything else to get back in my good books . . .'

'Now just a minute. You are not the be all and end all of a girl's dreams . . .'

'You can't resist me. Go on. Admit it.'

'You've got a nerve . . .'

'What are you doing tomorrow?'

The question was unexpected and knocked her breathless. 'I've nothing planned except that my mother was wittering on about her friend who's mislaid her husband . . .'

'Seriously?'

'He's gone walkabout. To find himself. And in his eighties at that. He left a note.'

'You've got to take your hat off to the guy.' Doherty nodded in that understanding way men do when they figure they've discovered a kindred spirit.

'His wife doesn't quite see things that way. She's seriously into comfort eating at present, though she is fastidious in her taste; Marks and Spencer cream cakes only.'

'They're the best. She hasn't reported him as a missing person?'

Honey shook her head. 'No. What with the cakes and believing he'll come back when the weather turns cold, apparently she still has his bedsocks, she hasn't felt the need.'

'Good. I've got enough on my plate at the moment. Would you believe we've got a chainsaw maniac on the prowl?'

'Oh my God! I hadn't heard or read anything about it. Who's he sawing up?'

Doherty poured himself another glass of wine. 'Gnomes. Plastic garden gnomes, and all at the same address.'

Honey digested the information. She decided she could feel quite sympathetic about old-style clay or plaster gnomes being sawn into pieces, but plastic gnomes? Somehow they deserved it.

Honey pushed her hair back from her face and took a deep breath. She felt relieved. Casper would have preferred becoming an all-in wrestler rather than face a real serial killer doing the rounds.

'Unfortunate for the gnomes,' she said. 'But hardly important. So to get back to the job in hand; what have you got scheduled for tomorrow?'

'Miss Porter has agreed to be interviewed, but insisted I brought you with me. She knows you, apparently.'

Honey fingered the stem of her glass and nodded. 'From Bonhams Auction rooms. We sometimes used to be rivals, though not for those dreadful pots she bought. Whatever possessed her I don't know. She used to be so discerning with her purchases, though determined too. Once she'd set her mind on something, she went all out to get it. Hence why she entered "last bid" on those two urns: it must have been a senior moment. Definitely a case of approaching ODAF.'

He looked at her for enlightenment.

'Old, dotty, and forgetful.'

'A genuine mistake?'

'Possibly. I don't know what she paid for them, but one thing's for sure, they're carbon fibre. I'm thinking they were made for a film set, a shop window display, a photo shoot — something of that ilk. Alistair would be able to enlighten us on where they came from.'

'The bloke from Bonhams?'

'That's right.'

They both fell to silence, each harbouring thoughts that had as much to do with each other as with the case in hand.

Honey felt in something of a quandary. She asked herself, should I break the ice and admit to going out with John Rees?

The ice was broken for her.

'So. Bought any good books lately?'

She squirmed. The question had popped up from nowhere and that look of his was pinning her to the back of her chair.

She attempted to laugh it away. 'Now when have I got time to read a book? The odd download I suppose when I'm lying in bed . . . *alone* . . . with nothing else to do.'

The inference was obvious; there was nobody in her bed at night — just her and an e-book.

It was no good. Those eyes were dissecting her thoughts. Either that or he was having a go at telepathy and she was receiving the message loud and clear.

'OK,' she said finally. 'I own up. I had lunch with John Rees.'

'I wasn't asking,' he said, falling back into his chair as though it had been a purely casual question.

Rubbish. Of course he was asking. The tension had left his face the moment she'd admitted the truth.

'Yes, you were. And yes, we did dash off to Northend and ask a few people some questions.'

He leaned forward, his look intense, his fingers interlocked in front of him.

'What questions?'

'About Boris and Doris Crook. It seems that they were quite reclusive. Even the postman had trouble. He tried to deliver a parcel the day before they were murdered, but nobody answered so he did what he always did in such circumstances and left it with a neighbour. She signed for it and promised to deliver it the moment she saw they were at home. According to Gavin the postman, she'd intimated that there was only any sign that somebody was living there at night.'

'But she delivered the parcel.'

'As far as we know.'

He leaned across the table, cupping her face in both hands.

'Clever girl. I knew you wouldn't let me down. Let's go out there tomorrow and ask this obliging neighbour.'

'We can't.'

'No such word as can't.' He maintained his smile, but then he hadn't heard the rest of it.

Honey forced her smile to stay put and for her eyes to appear wide open and innocent — something she hadn't been since for a long time.

'In these circumstances there are. Nobody's seen the neighbour since. I asked at the pub and was directed to an odd job gardener of her whereabouts.'

Doherty's expression was less exuberant. 'And you found out the neighbour is away on a world cruise.'

She shook her head. 'Not as far as we know. She's a very elderly lady, a Mrs Hicks. The fact is . . .'

'The fact is you're going to tell me something I don't want to hear . . .'

'The fact is . . .' Honey took a deep breath. 'The fact is she hasn't been seen since the day the parcel was left with her.'

Doherty's face was now ashen, disappointment etched all over it.

'That's why I asked about the identity of whoever was sleeping in that top room,' Honey added.

'And I said it was definitely a man.'

Honey nodded. Something tickled her all the way down her body when he looked at her that way. Past misdemeanours were forgiven. She was sure of it. She was melting.

'We need to get together on this.'

'Yes!' He'd said exactly what she'd wanted him to say.

Heaving a big sigh that made his chest expand and detail his six pack to feel-good proportions, he grabbed both her hands and held them in his.

'And now to bed.'

'Yes! Yes,' she responded keeping the volume to a level only he could hear.

'So we'd better both shuffle off early. I'll pick you up in the morning.'

CHAPTER FOURTEEN

Gloria Cross was being her usual, forceful, no-nonsense self. Knights of old wore suits of armour when they were being charging into battle. Honey's mother preferred Ralph Lauren.

'I thought you were coming with me? We have questions to ask. Rhoda is depending on us and Antonio has offered to help in any way he can. The man is bending over backwards for us.' On the one hand her tone was demanding, on the other it held just the right tinge of disappointment to make her feel guilty.

Honey had phoned her mother first thing, even before serving up breakfast, Doris being away on one of her frequent short break holidays. When needs must, the owner mucks in which included serving platefuls of full English breakfast.

'Mother, I think Antonio is bending over for you, not for me.'

'The bending is mutual. Cute bum, huh?'

Honey decided to move the conversation along. Talking of bums before breakfast was too much to deal with.

'Look, I've got a few errands to do this morning. How about tomorrow morning?'

'How about today?'

'Mother, it may have escaped your notice, but I have a business to run.'

'You're the owner. Delegate! Isn't that what you employ people for?'

'Look, I have to . . .'

'I quite understand,' she said stiffly. 'This morning your policeman lover has priority over your own mother. He gets the morning so I'll have to settle for later today. I'll be round at six.'

'I can't . . .'

'I have a plan. I've written a list of where we can look and enquire further. For a start there's that Maggie person. She was being trundled off in the ambulance at roughly the same time as Rhoda's husband fled the nest. She may have seen something.'

'I thought the poor woman was having a heart attack? And I thought she'd died?'

'Apparently not. Antonio confided in me that he'd received notice of her giving up her apartment. She'd decided to return home. She has a flat in Lansdown Crescent. Goodness knows why she took a flat at Overton House. Unless her son forced her out of course. Children can be so ungrateful. Anyway, if I can trace the ambulance driver, he might have seen something. Maggie will know who it is.'

Honey wasn't sure about any of this except that reference to this person's son being ungrateful was a double-edged barb, the inference being that Honey too was an ungrateful child.

* * *

'So what do I say to John Rees if he phones?' asked Lindsey. 'Are you about to burn your bridges, or should I maintain a drawbridge-position?'

Lindsey was well into history. Honey was just in a state of indecision; the prince . . . or the prince?

She sucked in her lips and thought about it. 'Tell him I'm a bit over my head in this case. Something's come up.'

Lindsey fixed her with an accusing look. 'Yes. Doherty is back on the scene. Did Gran ask how his car was?'

Honey looked at her blankly.

'Point taken,' said Lindsey. 'Incidentally, our new receptionist is starting tomorrow morning. I'll take it you'll be here for that?'

'I most certainly will. Clint is badgering me for full details.'

Lindsey grinned. 'Hopeful that Anna's replacement will be as obliging as she was, no doubt.'

'He'll have to be introduced, of course. All the staff will.'

'Just promise I'm around when you do it.'

They had a plan in mind, a surprise for Clint that they'd cooked up together. They eyed each other in mutual understanding. This would be fun.

'Are you fit?' Doherty was standing in the doorway, his elbow resting against the frame, his fingers playing with the three-day old stubble that was as familiar to his body as the black T-shirt and leather jacket he wore. His denim jeans were faded and fitted his legs like a second skin.

It was a vision that crept into Honey's dreams when he wasn't there—sometimes without the jeans but always with the stubbly chin. But there was nothing like the real thing. When he moved he gave off the aroma of real man, fresh soap, and that subtle come hither smell; pure testosterone.

She followed him out to the car with a spring in her step. As usual he had parked it on double yellow lines, the police sticker on the dash almost daring the parking attendant to give him a ticket.

He hadn't mentioned her looking nice, but Honey reckoned she did. Today she'd favoured a plum-coloured Jaeger top matched with a pair of olive Betty Barclay jeans. A chiffon scarf of plum, mustard, and red provided the link between everything. OK, Doherty hadn't complimented her on her outfit, and the fact that her hair was glossy and her face a picture of the cosmetic industry's best products. But the way he'd looked, blinked, and adopted an expression of casual indifference told her that he had noticed. He was toying with her and he could toy with her any time he liked.

Alistair didn't so much stand behind the payment counter at Bonhams as loom. He was tall, broad in chest and face, and he was wearing a kilt — clan McGregor tartan, if Honey remembered rightly.

'Is there some Scottish celebration on today that I don't know about?' she asked him. It wasn't meant that seriously. Alistair didn't need a reason to wear a kilt but always had a ready-made excuse if asked whether there was some specific reason.

'No, hen. It's the central heating. The thermostat's gone and we can't turn it off, and what with it being milder than a Highland winter this blower under my counter here just isn't needed. Warm enough to roast chestnuts, it is. Wearing the kilt keeps everything cool.'

She tried not to visualise or connect roasted chestnuts with Alistair's more personal accoutrements. Luckily Doherty seemed willing to accept Alistair's explanation without hesitation; a man thing of course.

'You may recall I phoned you about the Greek-style urns in which two very dead bodies got planted, in a manner of speaking. Can you give us any background on where they came from?' asked Doherty.

'Aye,' said Alistair flicking open the pages of his ledger. Although records at Bonhams had long been placed on the computer system, Alistair would not ditch his old ledger. 'I keep it on computer and written down,' he explained. 'Close at hand so to speak.'

He slid a handful of spade-ended fingers down over a column of copperplate handwriting.

'Ah, yes. They're only plastic of course. It seems that Miss Porter needn't have put a last bid on these. They were never likely to make top dollar. And they came from a nightclub up in London. One of those places featuring erotic dancers.'

'You mean exotic,' Honey corrected him.

'No. I mean *erotic*. Women wearing no clothes and dancing in a suggestive manner. They probably popped out of the urns for some bloke's birthday bash, that type of thing.'

Honey and Doherty indicated that they got the picture with a series of silent nods.

'They were certainly large enough for somebody to pop out of,' Doherty commented. 'You don't suppose Miss Porter was the sort to use them for the same purpose?'

'She'd need to give herself an all over iron to get rid of the wrinkles first,' remarked Alistair as he stroked his nest of a beard.

'It's pretty obvious she bid for the wrong urns,' said Honey. 'It's the most logical explanation.'

'More than likely,' said Alistair. 'She only paid three hundred pounds for this pair.'

'*Only* three hundred quid!' Doherty's face exploded in disbelief.

'It's not out of the way,' said Alistair. 'As I explained, they were plastic and a lot heavier than they looked. Though I suppose they had to have stable bottoms seeing as what they were used for. Wouldn't want them tipping over and the girls spilling out. Not that they were what Miss Porter wanted at all. She was really after a nice little pair no more than eighteen inches high. Reproduction of course; probably brought back from Greece by some tourist in the seventies. But her eyesight was going so she wrote down the wrong number.'

Doherty shoved his hands in his pockets and looked down at the floor, swaying his shoulders from side to side before turning towards the door.

Honey lingered. There was a question she just had to ask of this man she thought she knew well.

'How did you know girls popped out of those pots?'

'My cousin Hamish told me. He used to work at the place. He was staying with me around the time of the auction and wandered in. Recognised them immediately. Surprised that they'd ended up being for sale. He remembered seeing them in the club, standing there in pride of place. Then suddenly they were gone. The girls were still there though — eye catching, lovely . . .'

'Nude,' added Honey.

'Well, Mr and Mrs Crooks weren't nude or dancing in them,' said Doherty from his place at the door. 'Just dead.'

Honey commented that they would probably be passed on to a new owner once the police investigation was over with and the infamy of Moss End Guest House had died down.

'I need a list of everyone who was at that party. Your friend Alison has promised to oblige. The murderer or murderers had to be among the guests. Do you recall anything odd about any of them?'

'Well, let's see,' said Honey slipping her hand through his arm as they walked from Bonhams to his car. 'Quite a few women, including yours truly, were wearing long black wigs, pale make-up, and a slinky black dress. Others sported green noses, pointy hats, and warts on their noses. Oh, and quite a few were armed with broomsticks. Some of the men were swathed in bandages, quite a few sported fangs that Dracula would have been dead proud of. I vaguely recall a Frankenstein monster complete with a bolt through his neck, one Spiderman, two people who I thought were right cop-outs wearing nothing but bedsheets . . .'

'Ghosts,' said Doherty. 'So nobody saw their faces.'

Honey said nothing. Referring to the ghosts had popped out without prior thought. She tried to think whether she'd seen the 'ghosts' later on in the evening.

'That's an odd thing. I only saw them when they arrived at the door.'

'And the hosts let them in . . .'

'I'd forgotten about them. After that . . .' She shook her head. 'I never saw them again. Not at the party. I never saw either the late arriving guests or Mr and Mrs Crook again.'

Doherty stopped. Honey looked up at him. He was wearing his deeply thoughtful expression.

'There had to be two perpetrators to restrain them, smash in their skulls, and tip them out of the window. More damage was done it slid down the roof, the back of his head catching on one of the metal tangs holding a loose slate in place.'

Honey shivered. 'Nasty.'

'Yet nobody saw or heard a thing.'

'Unless our friend Mrs Hicks she saw them arrive. They must have come in a car and lovely as she may, or might have been,' said Honey swiftly correcting herself, 'she's a nosy but well-meaning neighbour. She was sure to have noticed the car colour at least, perhaps even the registration number.'

'It's a possibility.'

'And she was the sort to go poking her nose in, making herself a little too obvious perhaps? It is likely that she may have been eliminated. Unless she really has gone on a cruise or something.'

'We're making enquiries as to relatives and whether any-one saw her going off anywhere or whether she told anyone she was going away. In view of ongoing enquiries, it strikes me that we have enough of a reason to take a look around her house.'

He reached into his pocket and took out a key.

'Steve Doherty, you are such a dark horse!'

'The postman had it. She gave it him in case he couldn't rouse her anytime. He popped in there for tea most days. Thought about popping in there when he knocked the other day, but was in a hurry. He was meeting his girlfriend in town and once the murders happened, he didn't think it would be wise.'

'So he was suspicious even then?'

'Concerned was the word he used.'

'Trip to Northend?'

'Seems like.'

She was careful folding herself into Doherty's car. Fearing even to leave a greasy finger mark, she rubbed the car door with the cuff of her coat sleeve.

Mrs Hicks's cottage was chilly but didn't smell at all musty as a place does if somebody is away for days.

A large vase full of Michaelmas daisies sat on a tripod table in front of the window. The chairs and settee were old and had bun feet at each corner, the cushions were fat and green. A pair of firedogs; black ironwork griffons with snarling mouths and clenched claws sat either side of an old-fashioned Parkray coal burner.

The decoration was subdued but warm, an old person's place but with a touch of eccentricity.

A series of corn dollies looked as though they were dancing along the high slate mantelpiece.

Doherty touched the glass panel on the front of the Parkray.

'Stone cold. Hasn't been lit for days.'

The smell of beeswax evidenced well-polished furniture. A mahogany sideboard graced one wall, the curtains were green velvet, and every shelf and surface seemed to be taken up by feline figurines, though there was a frog and a couple of rabbits as well.

Honey admired the daisies.

'They're still pretty fresh. There's a big bunch of them growing in the garden. Strange that she bothered to pick some if she was going away.'

Doherty was straightening a picture of a beautiful woman, a cat draped like a mink stole around her shoulders.

'Gorgeous creature,' he murmured.

'The cat or the woman?'

'Both. Now retrieve your claws and get looking.'

'For what?'

'I don't know. Anything useful.'

A large mirror hung on the back wall reflecting the front garden and the upper floors of the house opposite.

'The Lady of Shalott,' murmured Honey.

'I know. A poem. I vaguely remember it from my schooldays. It was about a woman who was cursed and could only view the world via a mirror. She went along with it until she saw Sir Lancelot riding down to Camelot. That's the bit I remember the best. I think I was eleven years old and fancied myself as Sir Lancelot. You know . . . horse, sword, suit of shining armour.'

'Written by Alfred Lord Tennyson.'

Doherty turned to her and grinned. 'That's the bit I didn't remember.'

Each room of the house was neat, tidy, and there was no sign of a struggle. Rows of clothes hung in the wardrobe in the front bedroom; a patchwork quilt lay smooth and brightly coloured on the brass bed and the clothes in the chest of drawers lay undisturbed.

The dressing table was of the same vintage as the sideboard downstairs. Honey caught sight of herself in the triple display via the one central and two folding side mirrors.

A pair of candlesticks sat on the main part of the dressing table where most people kept their hairbrush, face cream, and fancy box of cleansing tissues. No cleansing tissues. Just a paperweight.

Honey picked it up and shook it. 'No snowstorm,' she said. 'I'm disappointed. All paperweights like this have snowstorms.'

'Put it down and continue looking.'

She had one last look at the scene inside the glass globe before putting it down noticing that it held only one solitary figure; a small, crooked goblin with a leering grin and misshapen eyes.

She pointed it out to Doherty.

'He's ugly.'

'And not relevant.'

Honey placed it back where she found it only to see that she was now looking at the back of the globe rather than the front — and a bare bum.

She laughed. 'Why, you cheeky little beggar!'

The ugly goblin was mooning at her!

After setting the grotesque back in its place, she headed for the bathroom while Doherty took a look around the rear bedroom.

'There's something missing from here,' Honey called out. 'No toothbrush. And no toothpaste.'

'Perhaps she wore dentures.'

'No Steradent either.'

Doherty frowned.

He hadn't needed to bring Honey with him, but it seemed the only way to make up. Not that he'd been going to rush at making up, but seeing her with John Rees had forced his hand. There was no way he would admit to himself that he was jealous — but he was.

'So she was travelling light,' he called back. 'I think that under the circumstances we can stop worrying that she may have been abducted. Nobody abducts an old lady then takes her toothpaste and brush. If they were being that considerate, they would provide her with that kind of thing — which isn't likely. Abductors and kidnappers aren't known for being considerate. They tend to concentrate on the money, and that's the other thing; what would be the point of abducting her?'

He shut the door of the bathroom cabinet, leaving his handprint on the shiny mirror.

Honey had to agree with him that the parcel must have been delivered and no harm had come to the old lady.

'She must have gone away without telling anyone.'

'I think that's about right,' stated Doherty while testing the bedsprings with one hand. 'Very comfortable, these old beds. Makes you want to dive in and give it a test run.'

'And more cats.' Honey nodded at the two felines portrayed stretched out. In the middle of them was a small vase. Doherty looked at each ornament in turn, pausing at the vase.

'No flowers. Just water.'

'There was one in the downstairs window ledge too. And one in the main bedroom.'

She frowned. There was something significant about that, something she should know.

'Just a minute.'

She went back into the main bedroom.

'Just a bowl of water?' asked Doherty.

She nodded, teetering on the edge of thoughts inspired by past conversations with Mary Jane. Feng Shui set a lot of store by having a bowl of water in a room. Even her central heating engineer had suggested doing so from a health perspective.

'Come on. There's nothing else in here to interest us.'

'Except for him,' said Honey, pointing at the glass globe containing the ugly goblin.

Doherty picked it up. 'A crystal ball. Perhaps Mrs Hicks does a bit of fortune telling on the side . . .'

'A *crystal ball*?'

Doherty tossed what she'd thought was a paperweight from one hand to the other. 'Looks like one — except for the bare-arsed cheeky little chap inside . . .'

'Shhh. I heard something.'

Doherty looked out of the front window then drew abruptly back. 'Uh-oh! We have a problem. Mrs Hicks has come home.'

They stood at the top of the stairs looking down. Mrs Hicks was standing there with the door half open, her key still in the lock, a small overnight bag on the floor next to her feet along with a wickerwork cat carrier.

'What are you doing in my house?' Her voice was high-pitched, her face pink and angry.

Doherty, feeling distinctly awkward, told her he was a police officer.

'Proof of identity! I must see proof of identity.'

Her voice had turned more strident.

Doherty showed her his warrant card and explained they'd been worried about her whereabouts.

'Mr and Mrs Crook over at the guest house were murdered,' Doherty explained. 'We were also told that you never went anywhere. The postman was worried.'

'Silly fool,' she snapped.

Her tone was surprising seeing as it seemed they were friends.

Honey butted in. 'We were wondering if you'd seen anything; perhaps a car on the night of the party arriving after everyone else.'

'They were murdered, you say? Please. Let me get this door closed and my coat off, and you can tell me all about it.'

They told her everything over a cup of tea and buttered crumpets. The cat lay the centre of the room, eyeing them with its bright orange eyes.

'Did you get to deliver the parcel the postman left with you, Mrs Hicks?' Doherty asked.

'Most certainly.'

'At what time was that?'

'About seven thirty. It was dark and they always come out at around seven thirty.'

'Really?'

'Yes. That's how I knew it was seven thirty. The church clock used to chime the half hour but it doesn't do that any-more — either that or my hearing has got worse. I have to depend on the bats.'

Honey refrained from the urge to exchange a sly glance with Doherty. Bats as a clock.

'How did they seem?'

'Seem?'

'Mr and Mrs Crook. Were they composed? Nervous?'

'Scared?' Honey added.

'Nothing specific,' replied Mrs Hicks, offering them more crumpets.

'Was it Mr Crook who answered, or Mrs Crook?' Honey asked while Doherty munched.

'It was Mrs Crook. She thanked me for my trouble in a very polite manner. I told her the weather was about to turn unseasonably warm. She told me that the weather forecast hadn't said as much. But there you are. I was right. They were wrong.'

'And how did she seem?'

Mrs Hicks looked up at the ceiling as she gathered her thoughts.

'Vague. Yes. I think that's the best way to describe how she was. Vague. As though her mind was on something else.'

'Do you recall anyone arriving late for the Hallowe'en party?'

'Oh no. I wasn't here you see. It's that time of year. I had a convention to attend. It was Hallowe'en after all.'

'Where was this convention,' Doherty began.

Honey placed a hand on his arm.

'Mrs Hicks is a witch, Detective Chief Inspector. Isn't that right, Mrs Hicks?'

The pink-cheeked face glowed with secretive pride. 'How did you guess?'

'Certain things. The water-filled dishes on the window ledges, the cats, the corn dollies . . . oh, and the crystal ball complete with guardian spirit.'

Mrs Hicks screeched with laughter. 'Oh, him! Isn't he just the naughtiest little goblin you've ever seen?'

'Wicked,' Honey responded, laughing.

On their way out Doherty asked Mrs Hicks if she wanted him to return her spare key to Gavin Whitmore, the postman.

'No. I think I'd better take care of it, at least for the time being. Poor Gavin. He has an overactive imagination. Fancy thinking I'd been abducted. The silly boy. He even got it into his head that the people at the guest house were vampires! Fancy that! I don't think those people were totally up front, but they certainly weren't vampires!'

'Why do you think they weren't up front, Mrs Hicks,' Doherty asked.

'They had dealings with strange people. I saw a big man over there. He didn't belong.'

'Can you describe him?'

Mrs Hicks closed her eyes. 'Big, broad, and black. It was dark. And he had a smell. Most people do. But his was different. And the other men. They came in a car. They didn't go inside the house, though. They sat in their car at the top of School Lane, watching the house. Just sitting there.

Watching. And before you ask me about the make of the car or the registration number, I don't know. I know and care little about cars. I don't like them.'

'And the men? What were they like?'

'Dangerous,' she said. 'Very dangerous. I didn't see their looks. I only detected their auras.'

Once they were outside, Honey explained the evidence that pointed to Mrs Hicks being a witch.

'Water-filled dishes placed on the window ledges so evil spirits would trip over the rim, fall in, and drown. Cats of course, the witch's close companion. Corn dollies on the mantelpiece, a crystal ball — you got it right. I kept thinking it was a paperweight. I should have known better. Mary Jane taught me better than that.'

'Not your mother?' Doherty asked grimly.

'I'll ignore that remark.'

'She seems quite a nice old girl. Bit of a surprise really. I thought witches wore pointed hats, rode broomsticks, and had warts and big noses.'

Honey pulled her coat sleeve down so that her fingers wouldn't leave marks on the car door handle.

'No. Some of them *are* bewitching . . . gorgeous. And a taxi is far more convenient.'

'Right.' Doherty grinned. 'And plastic surgery on warts is better than ever.'

CHAPTER FIFTEEN

Clint was wearing blue checked trousers, a clean white tunic, and a crisp white apron. In short, he looked everything a good washer up should, right down to his plastic clogs.

Honey was checking the meat order with Smudger. Lindsey was perusing the kitchen staff rota for the following week.

All three of them were in collusion, though Clint wouldn't know that.

Suddenly there was the clatter of a dropped pencil.

'Blow it. I seem to be all fingers and thumbs today,' Honey muttered, bending down to capture the rolling pencil. 'That poor receptionist out there. I did promise a cup of coffee. Poor thing . . .'

'Leave it with me!'

Clint leapt into action, spreading a lace doily over a stainless-steel tray, adding a coffee pot, sugar basin, cream jug, and finally a cup and saucer.

Lindsey surveyed his work with an aura of surprise.

'Are there no mugs washed?'

Honey kept her head down so Clint wouldn't see her smile.

Clint adopted the pose of a maitre d', certainly not a run of the mill washer up.

'The Green River Hotel extends a warm welcome to our new receptionist,' he declared. 'Start as you mean to go on; that's what I always say.'

Folding a fresh tea towel over his arm, he grabbed the tray and headed for Reception.

Honey, Lindsey, and Smudger dropped what they were doing, heading on tip toe for the door that opened onto the hallway that in turn opened into Reception.

The receptionist was not in sight, still ploughing through the employee particulars that needed filling in.

Clint's palm hit the brass bell fixed to the counter.

'Coffee is served, fair lady . . .'

His voice fell away as Eugene, a svelte figure in tight trousers and a neat waistcoat, appeared from the back office.

'How very kind,' he said, his slim hands reaching for the tray. 'You must be Clint, but I will call you Rodney. You may call me Gene. Pleased to meet you, Rodney,' he said, apparently unaware that Clint's hand was as limp as a melted packet of peas. 'I know we will be the best of friends. As friendly as you were with Anna, my predecessor, perhaps?'

Clint coloured up. 'Right, mate. Right.'

He hightailed it back to the kitchen.

'Ha bloody ha,' muttered Clint, scowling as he pushed past them en route to his saucepans and the spluttering, steaming dishwasher.

Clint had had more than a friendly relationship with Anna, their last receptionist. To say it had been fruitful was an understatement. As it turned out, Anna was more of a free spirit than any of them had realised. Planning to invest her earnings in a roadside café with letting rooms, she'd taken the children and moved back to her hometown in Poland where, rumour had it, a brand-new road was going to be built — courtesy of European development funding.

'Call me Gene' was settling in nicely. He was quick on his feet, highly efficient, and as sleek and neat as a Siamese cat.

'He's gay,' Clint muttered to her, up to his arms in soap suds.

Honey was in no doubt that Gene's sexual orientation had nothing to do with Clint's dislike. What he really meant was that Gene was not female.

Lindsey was standing next to Gene in Reception, going through the booking in system when an angry-looking woman with what looked to be the beginnings of a toothbrush moustache banged through the swing doors into Reception.

She was wrapped warmly against the winter weather, held a walking stick in one hand, and a large shopping bag in the other. Her hat was big and beige and had a very large brim. The hat coupled with the predominant colour of her outfit made her look like a large mushroom.

'Young man!'

Her voice was as loud as a sergeant major calling a battalion to attention.

Neither Lindsey nor the new receptionist had time to open their mouths.

'I wish to speak to this Driver person. I have a little job that needs sorting out. Now come along. I don't have all day. Go and tell her that I'm here. Right now!'

'Of course, madam. Who shall I say requires her presence?' Gene asked, his vowels rippling with a soft French accent.

Lindsey was impressed.

'My name is Mrs Gertrude Nobbs. Perhaps you would be so kind as to tell her that I have been referred to her with reference to a crime that has been orchestrated upon my person.'

Lindsey thought about asking her whether she didn't think the police would be more helpful than a hotel owner, but somehow she knew that wouldn't get anywhere.

'If you'd like to take a seat, Mrs Nobbs, Eugene here will give you a cup of coffee while I fetch my mother. I think it's my mother you're looking for,' Lindsey said.

Mrs Nobbs bottom lip shuddered as though she were blowing a half raspberry. Fixing her watery blue eyes on Lindsey, she nodded and said that she would forego the coffee but would take a seat while she was waiting.

'I don't think I know her,' said Honey after thinking about it, peering through an inch gap in the office door. 'Did she say who referred her?'

'No. All she said was that it was to do with a crime.'

Honey frowned and put down the cup of coffee she'd been drinking and popped the last smidgeon of chocolate digestive into her mouth.

'Bring her in.'

In the privacy of Honey's office, Mrs Nobbs settled herself down into the best armchair without being invited and told Honey to do the same.

'I don't speak to people who are standing up. I like to face people eye to eye,' she stated. Accordingly she fixed Honey with eyes that were only just holding onto a hint of colour.

'I live in Lansdown Crescent. Have done for some years.'

'Very nice,' said Honey adopting her warmest smile and looking suitably impressed because people who lived in Lansdown Crescent expected non-residents of Lansdown Crescent to be impressed.

However, her intuition, in the form of a nervous fluttering in her stomach, told her she was about to be asked to do something she might not wish to do. Still, she was cornered. It seemed there was nothing to be done except to pull up a chair.

'Before you tell me I should go to the police, I have already done so and was given short shrift. Do you know what that means, young woman? Short shrift?'

Honey opened her mouth to respond that she did, but Mrs Nobbs was too quick for her.

'They more or less told me that they didn't have time to provide a round- the-clock vigil over my property. It wasn't high enough priority. Poppycock! I cannot express it strongly enough. Poppycock!'

Poppycock was hardly that strong, but given that Mrs Nobbs was of a certain background and a certain era, Honey supposed it was as strong as it got.

'This policeman you saw . . .'

'Rough-looking sort, though no doubt attractive to a certain kind of woman. The sort with loose morals whose blood runs hot at the sight of such a rough diamond.'

The description of Doherty was spot on. Honey refrained from blushing at the thought of being the possessor of loose morals. She also wondered at what Mr Nobbs might have been like and entertained the sudden thought that the pair of them had never undressed in front of each other — well, not with the light on. Hence, Mrs Nobbs' morals had never hung loose at the sight of a man like Doherty.

'And the crime that has been perpetrated against you?'

'My boys! They have been attacked and most badly disfigured. Just one or two of them at first, now half a dozen or more occurrences.'

It was like a little bell was suddenly ringing in Honey's head. Either this woman was nuts, grossly exaggerating or Honey herself had grabbed the wrong end of the stick.

Crossing her hands neatly in her lap in an effort to both feel and appear calm, she asked, 'Can you explain the nature of these attacks, the extent of injuries and when and where they occurred?'

'I can do better than that!' exclaimed Mrs Nobbs, her bag landing with a thump on the floor. 'I've brought the latest casualty with me, or at least, what's left of him. I can't bend down to get him out. You'll have to do it.'

This, decided Honey, is one of those quirky days that will have you and your dinner guests laughing over the cheeseboard. Either that or one of those horrific scenes like the boiling bunny from *Fatal Attraction* will have you running screaming from the building.

She eyed the back with cold anticipation.

Please don't let there be bloody doggy or kitty parts in there.

First there was a head, then a torso, followed by lower limbs: all made of plastic. Mrs Nobbs was reporting a crime against her gnomes.

The urge to burst out laughing, mostly with relief, was hard to suppress.

'There! Look at the poor thing! His body parts were scattered in bits amongst my other boys — those that are left that is. This isn't the first time my boys have been torn limb from limb. These evil people want to put a spell on me. First they chop up my boys and then they'll chop me up.'

'Right . . .'

Being at a loss for words wasn't usually a problem for Honey. She prided herself on being a woman who could converse with anyone from any walk of life; sewer cleaner to secretary of state, not that the latter had ever stayed at the Green River Hotel. Nor the former for that matter. The odds for her taking this case on were pretty long.

'I want something done about it and I'm willing to pay.'

The odds on Honey taking it on had shortened.

Fixing her lips between her teeth she nodded. This was the second private case offering to pay her money for her services. Her fame was spreading, her ego expanding.

'When did this last incident occur?' she asked Mrs Nobbs.

'Hallowe'en!' Mrs Nobbs voice dropped to a hushed whisper and her eyes bulged with a look of secretive horror. 'I think Norman was a sacrifice to the old gods, cut into pieces in an effort to arouse Beelzebub and his legions.'

Honey's resultant nodding was now on automatic. Norman, she assumed, was the name of the gnome; a phonetic alliteration that suited him.

'So six of your . . . boys . . . have been brutalised?'

'*Murdered.* I don't consider murder too strong a word for this terrible deed. All in the last fortnight. The run up to Hallowe'en, you see.'

'Trick or treaters don't usually come knocking until Hallowe'en itself . . .'

'Not children! Children wouldn't — *couldn't* — do this much damage.'

Honey surveyed the rough edges of the plastic.

'You could be right. I think I should get this examined by an expert who can advise as to what would have cut like this. Do you mind leaving your . . . Norman with me?'

Small piggy eyes glinted at her from over plump cheeks. Mrs Nobbs was weighing her up. At last she nodded.

'I think I can trust you. Now, what about organising a stakeout? I'm willing to pay you fifty pounds per night plus expenses. It seems about the going rate for people like Philip Marlowe once you allow for inflation over the years. When can you start?'

It wasn't easy trying to explain to Mrs Nobbs that sitting out in the cold on a November night wasn't likely to achieve much. Besides which, she pointed out, Marlowe might have been more inclined to ask for fifty pounds as an hourly rate not a day rate.

Honey persuaded her that it made sense to first obtain an expert to look at the damage done to Norman the gnome.

'You may call on me the moment there are developments. Here's my card.'

Mrs Nobbs had blown in like a March wind and went out pretty much the same way.

Honey slumped in her chair, white card flung onto the desk.

'What did she want?' Lindsey asked, sticking her head around the door and grinning.

'Mrs Nobbs has a fetish.'

'Really?' Intrigued, Lindsey sat in the chair on the other side of the desk. 'My word, older people never fail to surprise me. What is she into?'

'Gnomes.'

'*Gnomes?*'

'Plastic gnomes. She wants me to find the person who's been sawing them into bits.'

'Plastic gnomes are horrible.'

'So are politicians, but that's no reason to saw them into bits.' Honey paused. 'Is it?'

CHAPTER SIXTEEN

Doris was back on duty when Honey's phone rang just before breakfast was served.

'I just thought you'd like to know. We've found Edna.'

Honey had known Doherty long enough to read the sound of his voice without needing to see his face.

'You've found her but she's playing dead?'

'Worse than that. She is dead. I'm in Keynsham. Edna was found in a skip outside a house that was being renovated.'

'What? In Keynsham? What was she doing there?'

Keynsham was one of those towns to the west of Bath that had grown up from a village sixty or so years ago. Now it was an urban sprawl, a mix of housing and a busy high street where traffic was king.

'Well she wasn't having an away day with friends.'

He gave her the address.

First stop was to phone Ahmed to check about the health of her car.

His sigh said more than words ever could; noisy and full of dramatic intent.

'Alas, poor car. French, *n'est-ce pas*?'

'Point taken.'

She closed her eyes and took deep breaths. When her car was incapacitated, only one person could oblige at short notice. Mary Jane was, as usual, ready and willing, had eaten a bigger breakfast than anyone else, and declared herself raring to go.

'Get you there in no time,' she declared, 'and I won't spare the horses.'

Honey gulped. Mary Jane's response was exactly as feared.

While Mary Jane went to fetch her pink peril of a car, Honey went into the bar where she reached for the gin bottle, poured, and swallowed a swift snifter.

Back in Reception, her daughter Lindsey eyed her with amusement from beneath a heavy fringe that this week was brandy brown — more or less her natural colour.

Looking and feeling as wooden as a Dutch doll, Honey stopped in front of the reception desk.

'Do you think I should write a last will and testament before venturing out?' she asked her daughter.

Lindsey patted her mother on the shoulder. 'You'll be fine, Mother. You don't need to make a will. I'm perfectly capable of sorting things in your absence without you needing to direct me.'

It wasn't funny. Being a passenger in Mary Jane's car was never funny.

Honey was aware that her legs had turned to jelly and a host of flying fish were windsurfing in her stomach. She kept telling herself that Keynsham was only a few miles away.

Unfortunately, this was one occasion when she couldn't get away with listening to her iPod; she had to give Mary Jane directions. The west side of the city was an unknown quantity to an out-of-town person.

'This the right way?' Mary Jane shouted as they whizzed along the Lower Bristol Road.

Honey opened one eye. 'Yep. This is the way.'

Alternating eyes was tiring but somehow being able to see only flashes of dangerous driving halved the fear.

By the time they were parked outside the address Doherty had given her, Honey was convinced that her eyes had been shaken loose from their fixings and were rolling round in her head like glass marbles. Lindsey had told her that breathing exercises could help overcome anything. Honey tried it but decided that Mary Jane's driving was a notable exception.

'Do you want me to come in?' Mary Jane asked.

'No,' Honey responded fervently. 'I'll be a while. I can get a lift back with Steve or one of the other officers.'

'I can wait for you if you like,' she replied eagerly.

'No need,' Honey said hurriedly.

Mary Jane leaned out of the driver's side window. Lowering her voice, she said. 'Well, you be careful who you drive with. Those cops just love driving fast. They're trained to do it. That's how come you see all those car chases on TV and blockbuster films.'

Feeling distinctly unsteady on her legs, Honey trotted towards the right house, a big stone semi-detached with a huge garden, big bay windows, and a gable at one end.

A large skip was pulled up onto a concrete covered drive outside.

By modern standards the house was huge, big enough to accommodate three estate style semi-detacheds. By the look of its squared off bays, it had been built round about the beginning of the twentieth century.

Incident tape fluttered across the gap where a hedge had been rooted up to make way for the builder to park his skip and his van. A little further along the road she spotted Doherty's car hugging the kerb. A few crisp leaves, the last of this autumn, came fluttering from a walnut tree to land like splayed hands on the car's gleaming paintwork.

On the other side of the tape, Doherty was talking to a few of his team. He saw her, waved her in, looked deep into her eyes, and said, 'You look a little pale.'

'Mary Jane drove me over.'

'That would do it.'

'Not as pale as our friend Edna, no doubt.'

164

'Edna was the outdoor type. Slept outdoors summer and winter.'

'She was found in there?'

Honey jerked her chin at the builders' skip.

'It was only half full,' Doherty explained. 'One of the builders' labourers was about to shove some more rubbish in there when he saw our lady of the highways and byways. Do you want to see her?'

Honey hesitated. Quite frankly it was something she preferred to avoid but on this particular occasion she was right there and couldn't really avoid it. The crew had just transferred the victim from skip to stretcher. Just this once her stomach would cope with it. Afterwards it would be nil by mouth until supper time.

Doherty pulled the zip down. A knitted woolly hat that could easily have doubled as a tea cosy appeared first. A small, wizened face came into view beneath it. The face was heart-shaped and high-coloured, as though it had been wind-blasted and sunburnt for years. Both face and clothes were unwashed, the strong smell masking the stench of death.

Honey swallowed the bile that rose in her throat. 'And nobody noticed her?'

'The ME reckons she's been here for a couple of days. The builders were working on another job during that time. She wasn't discovered until this morning.'

The body was resealed in the body bag.

Honey stepped back, unable to take her eyes away from the small bundle that used to be a woman.

'Small, isn't she?' she said, noting that the woman's feet stopped a few feet short of the bottom of the stretcher.

She joined Doherty to peer over the iron side of the skip, the cold of the metal biting into her hands.

Doherty was wearing his serious, thoughtful expression, the ironclad one that once adopted didn't disappear until he'd thought things through.

'There wasn't much in here, so nobody would have seen her from the road. She was right down the bottom. Amongst the rubbish.'

Honey eyed the outline of a person drawn onto blood-soaked pieces of plasterboard. Each piece was being photographed and logged before removal from the scene for further analysis.

Although she'd never met Edna, Honey felt a great sadness come over her and couldn't help the big sigh that escaped with her steamy breath. Who had killed her? Why had they killed her?

Doherty read her mind. 'We don't know who killed her, but there are a few possibilities as to why, number one being this business of identity theft. If that is the case, then I think the only person that may be able to answer our questions is Rhino.'

'And he's disappeared.'

Doherty's hands were clasped tightly together and his eyes were narrowed.

'Something's scared him, and once he finds out about Edna he's going to bury himself so far underground, nobody's likely to find him. The man's scared of somebody. We need to find out who.'

He understood she needed a lift back to Bath and eyed her warily before offering.

'Just don't touch anything,' he said as she fastened the seatbelt. 'And don't distract me from my driving. Distraction is what causes most accidents.'

She promised not to touch anything. Promised not to distract him.

A seasonal mist was starting to descend on Saltford, like Keynsham once a village and now a busy road crowded with houses on both sides.

Not very interesting scenery. There had to be something she could do, something she could talk about that was both professional and amusing. Mrs Nobbs and Norman the gnome sprang instantly to mind.

'Do you recall telling me about the decapitated gnomes?' Honey asked Doherty.

'I do.'

'You didn't follow it up.'

'The woman's mad. Do you know what she wanted me to do?' Doherty said incredulously.

'Arrange a stakeout to see who was carving up her boys?'

For the briefest of moments it seemed as though he was going to look at her. The urge was strong, but he kept his nerve, eyes fixed on the road, hands gripping the steering wheel as though it might fall off if he didn't. My, but he loved his car.

'She came to see me,' she said in answer to his unasked question. 'She wanted to pay me fifty pounds to sit outside in her garden all night. I declined of course.'

'I should hope so.'

'I told her my rate was fifty pounds an hour.'

'That's exorbitant!' he exclaimed. 'You're not a real detective!'

'You told me I was pretty good.'

He just about managed to slide his eyes from the road for a few seconds.

'We were in bed at the time and I'm not sure it was your sleuthing prowess I was referring to.'

'I promised her I'd get expert advice as to what weapon was used to carve up Norman and the boys.'

'Norman?'

The car went into a slight wobble, kissing the white line in the middle of the road before straightening out.

'That's the name of the latest victim. Mrs Nobbs believes he was the ultimate sacrifice to the dark forces of Hallowe'en. Some of her other gnomes were vandalised in the weeks before, but she reckons Norman was their greatest prize.'

Doherty was shaking his head and murmuring that he didn't believe what he was hearing; that riding the two horses of being a hotelier and crime liaison officer had finally sent her round the pipe.

'You and I both know that I can't possibly sit out in her garden all night in the hope of catching whoever did it. I've got other things to do.'

'Like find this ageing hippy who's gone to meditate in India or something?'

'Bert Watchpole is not an ageing hippy,' she said firmly, 'and Rhoda is worried about him. He's left his medication behind.'

'Then he can't have gone far; either that or he's got access to a fresh supply.'

Honey sat back and thought about it. 'You're right. Why didn't I think of that? He's either managed to get his hands on a fresh supply or he's dead, or ill, or something.'

'Is his wife charming?'

Honey pursed her lips. 'Let's just say that she's into comfort eating.'

'You mean she's fat.'

'Well, I comfort eat sometimes.'

He grinned and glanced at her without losing control of the wheel.

'You work it off, and I don't just mean at the hotel.'

She cleared her throat. 'About the weapon of choice for sawing up plastic gnomes . . .'

'A chainsaw. I think I told you that when I first mentioned it.'

She pointed out that he'd referred to it as the 'Tasteless Chainsaw Massacre'.

He snorted. 'Plastic gnomes! A bloody good description. I mean, how tasteless is that?'

'So it was a chainsaw?'

'Absolutely.'

She sighed. 'I can't do a stakeout. It's not practical, but she does need to be reassured.'

Honey fell to thoughtful silence. Did she need to ask him to oblige, or would he offer? The old Doherty, her Doherty, would offer.

'You want me to have a word with her. Right?'

The old Doherty was still in situ!

'Right.'

'OK. Lansdown Crescent it is. As it happens I can kill two birds with one stone. I've another case to follow up, that's if you don't mind waiting for me once I've set Mrs Nobbs's nerves to rest.'

CHAPTER SEVENTEEN

Despite the mist that was slowly turning leaves soggy and pavements slick, Lansdown Crescent looked as opulent and breathtaking as ever. The honey-coloured stone never failed to glow even in November.

Bearing in mind that his car doors were wide and the entry low, Doherty parked his car at the end of the crescent where the pavement was almost level with the road.

They found the right house where bay trees in tubs stood either side of a white front door with a brass knocker and letter box. The sash windows were tall and wide, and reflected views of the city.

Someone had neglected to close the front door properly so they didn't need to buzz into the security system. The door opened into a wide hallway. A handsome balustrade curved with the stairway up to the next floor. At the far end of the hall a glazed door looked out over a patio and a patch of green grass. Without needing to see it in more detail, Honey realised that the garden would be like a slice of countryside in the heart of the city, a tasteful oasis where birds nested in the spring and flowers bloomed in perfumed splendour, spoilt only by a collection of plastic gnomes. She'd probably have taken a chainsaw to them herself.

An elderly woman with snow white hair and wearing a grey woollen dress answered the door of the ground floor apartment, right hand side. Her expression tightened.

'Oh! It's you.'

'I'm not here to see you, Mrs Sinclair. I'm here to see Mrs Nobbs. Is she at home?'

'Yes?' she replied while her hands played nervously with the cameo brooch she wore at her throat. 'I was invited in to have coffee with her. But I'm going now. Who shall I say is calling?'

Doherty explained why they were there.

'The vandalism. Oh dear. Yes. I see. Then I'll leave you to it.'

They divided as she darted through them leaving the door of the apartment wide open.

'Maggie? Who was it at the door?'

Mrs Nobbs appeared, stocky and purposeful, and without the aid of a walking stick.

'Where did Maggie go?' she asked sharply.

'The lady went that way,' said Honey, pointing to the door on the other side of the hallway.

Mrs Nobbs grunted something about not finishing a perfectly good cup of coffee. 'Flighty type,' she explained, although neither of them had asked anything about the woman.

'You're not using your walking stick. Is your leg feeling better?' Honey asked, assuming a pleasant opening gambit would elicit pleasantness from Mrs Nobbs.

'There's nothing wrong with my legs. I always take a walking stick out with me. It's a useful weapon should I need one.'

'I'll pretend I didn't hear that, Mrs Nobbs,' said Doherty. 'Mrs Driver suggested I come along to put your mind at rest about the vandalising of your gnomes.'

'Oh, has she now! Well, Detective Constable or whatever you are, you're both too late. I've got rid of the lot of them. I've heeded the warning. After weighing up the evidence, I decided that they had to go. They attracted evil. My garden will be none the worse without them. I've decided to collect stone mushrooms instead. And frogs. Clay frogs.'

Honey and Doherty exchanged surprised looks and a light laugh once the door was shut in their faces.

'Mad as a box of . . .'

'Frogs!'

'So what's the story with the other woman?' Honey asked him as they made the descent back to town.

'A bit of a domestic. The woman's son from her first marriage reported some things missing. He blamed the man she's had move in with her for taking them.'

'And had he?'

'There's no evidence. Prior to his mother moving back into the apartment, her son lived there alone. Lived there like a lord from what I can gather. Then his mother came back and brought her beau with her. A quick search of the premises and we found the missing items stored in a box out in the shed. Mr Abingdon, the son, insisted he had nothing to do with it, but I have my doubts. I think he wanted the old chap thrown out. He could probably cope with his mother moving back in, but not her lover.'

Honey's phone warbled something that sounded like bubbles being blown into water. It turned out to be Casper.

'I've been thinking. If you and this policeman person are not an item again, perhaps it's time for you to step aside and let somebody else take over. Compatibility is of prime importance in a working relationship.'

'Everything's fine, Casper. In fact there has been a development in the Crooks case.'

'That's good?'

'Well actually it's another murder, but . . .'

'*Another* murder in this cultured and eminently refined city?' he spluttered.

'Not exactly. It was in Keynsham.'

'I'm glad to hear it.'

There was nothing to be gained in pointing out to Casper that the people of Keynsham wouldn't be glad to hear it. The chairman of Bath Hotels Association's focus was on the city he lived in and loved.

'That was Casper,' she said once she'd closed the connection. 'He was very glad to hear that the murder occurred in Keynsham not Bath.'

'Well that's Casper for you; all heart,' quipped Doherty with wry sarcasm.

Honey gazed at her fingers without really seeing them. She was thinking of her relationship with Doherty; they were warming to each other again. She liked it, but her pride wouldn't let her rush it. Not yet at least.

What it boiled down to was that Doherty came with extras; not just his body, but their occasional working as well as playing together. It counted for something. In fact, on thinking seriously, it counted for quite a lot.

'So,' exclaimed Honey deciding to play it totally professional. 'The method of dispatching Edna was identical to that used to dispatch Boris and Doris Crook, without her being thrown from a great height.'

'Then thrown into a skip rather than two urns.'

'It all goes back to Moss End Guest House and the two men I saw that night.'

'Men? Are you sure they were men?'

'Men. Big, ungainly men with no imagination. Women would have given more thought to their costume. I went into a lot of trouble to choose mine. I'm betting they were the same men Mrs Hicks saw hanging around.'

'The thing about these two men is that it wasn't really a costume, was it? It was a disguise. The question that I'm bound to ask is why they bothered to come disguised at all.'

'And who informed them that it was a costumed Hallowe'en party?' Honey added.

The seasonal mist was turning into a fine drizzle, splattering the windscreen. They both stared straight ahead at the traffic as it wove from one lane to another.

At the precise moment Doherty switched the wipers on, they both exclaimed in unison.

'Somebody at the party told them it was!'

'An inside job.'

'But who?'

The reason why the Crooks had been killed was still something of a conundrum, though there were definitely a few pointers.

She dragged her eyes from the road and studied Doherty's profile. He was concentrating hard on his driving. She recalled he'd specifically asked her not to distract him, but so far nothing they'd talked about had distracted him. Obviously police business didn't distract like personal stuff. So stick to that, she told herself.

'Did you find out whether the victims were being chased by creditors?'

'There does seem to be a question mark over their financial arrangement. Mr Crook had been in business with a Mr Belper. Mr Belper claims that his partner went off with half a million in company money, but swears that due legal process was in operation. In fact he stated that Mr Crook had made a firm promise that the money would be paid back very shortly.'

'And was it?'

'No. It was not, though he didn't seem that worried about it. The company money bought Moss End so legally the place will be resold and the money returned to the company of which Mr Belper and Mr Crook were directors.'

'Do you believe him?'

'Everything seems in order so I've no reason not to.'

'So if he didn't send in the heavies, then who did?'

A flash of light distracted Doherty's attention. Frowning he glanced into his rear-view mirror.

'Who the bloody hell's flashing their headlights?'

Honey looked over her shoulder. Her face paled.

'It's Mary Jane.'

'Christ!'

'I think she's just saying hi.'

'I don't want her to say hi. I want her to keep as far from the tail of this car as possible,' said Doherty with grim-faced finality.

Honey gritted her teeth in sympathy with Doherty whose jaw looked close to cracking under the strain. She closed her eyes.

Doherty noticed her action.

'Don't take your eyes off her!' he cried.

He sounded frantic. Understandable. Mary Jane had that effect on everybody once she was behind the wheel of her car.

'Sorry. I always close my eyes when I'm driving with Mary Jane.'

'You're not driving with Mary Jane. You're driving with *me*. I'll keep my eyes looking forward. You keep your eyes on her.'

'I don't think I can keep my eyes swivelled for that long.'

'That's an order, Honey!'

The traffic lights ahead of them changed to red where the Lower Bristol Road divided from the Upper Bristol Road. Doherty took the left-hand lane and shot down into the Upper Bristol Road.

Mary Jane looked as though she were pulling up in the right-hand lane.

'We've lost her!' shouted Doherty with a whoop of relief.

More used to Mary Jane's driving than he was, Honey expectantly regarded the pink Caddy over her shoulder. True to form, the Green River's resident professor of the paranormal swerved in front of the traffic in both lanes and followed them into the Upper Bristol Road.

Honey broke the bad news.

'She can't do that,' Doherty yelled.

'She has . . . she's right behind us.'

Honey saw him look at the road ahead, then his speed-ometer, then back to the road ahead.

Honey saw the beads of sweat on his forehead and read his mind. 'You can't outrun her.'

His knuckles were white, his eyes staring.

'Steve! Cut it out. It's only Mary Jane, not the hounds of hell!'

His face remained stiff, his eyes glazed over.

She was getting frantic. 'You're a cop. A cop who could get nicked for speeding.'

Some sense of her words seemed to get through to him.

'If I stop she'll ram me. I've only just had it repaired, for Chrissake!'

'No! No! She wouldn't.'

Riding with Mary Jane was like white water rafting on half a surfboard; exciting and exceedingly hazardous. Imagining Doherty's worst fear was unattractive because she couldn't be at all sure of the consequences. Better to eye the parked cars and the neat driveways of solid-looking houses they were passing in a haze of speed.

She tried to reassure him. 'She's never had an accident. Never hit anything. Not a car. Not a person. Not even a bicycle.'

'Is she still behind us?' he asked.

Honey pushed back at her sweaty hairline and nodded. 'Yes. And she's waving. She obviously has something she wants to tell us. How about you pull over and hear what she's got to say?'

She saw his tongue lick at his dry lips before he nodded in agreement. Thankfully his knuckles became less pronounced. She took this as a sure sign that he'd agreed to her suggestion.

Mentally, Honey went through the instructions given her on the first driving lesson she'd ever had.

Mirror, signal, manoeuvre. It kind of happened that way, but not very accurately.

They came to a stop. Doherty looked as stiff as a board and refused to get out of the car.

'You see what she wants. I'll stand guard. Just in case.'

'She's not going to ram you.'

'I thought you said she'd never had an accident. Never hit anybody.'

'It's true.' She looked at his knuckles. There was no way she was going to prise those fingers from that steering wheel. 'OK. You stand guard. And even if you feel the urge to bark, please don't bite anyone.'

Mary Jane was hanging out of the driver's window, which seeing as the Caddy was an American car, happened to be on the left-hand side. When she was animated as she presently was, her face seemed to fill out, her wrinkles diminishing to fine lines.

'The moment I saw you in that car, I knew it was a sign,' she said enthusiastically.

Honey's stomach clenched. She wasn't one for having premonitions herself. The last thing she wanted to hear was anything that might hint at another prang to Doherty's car.

'A sign of what?' she asked.

'That the premonition I had last night had firmed up. I thought I'd forgotten it, but the moment I saw you it came back to me in a flash.'

Honey's thoughts darted around from one possibility to another.

Mary Jane's eyes had narrowed. She was holding her hands together as though she were in church and about to ask the big guy on high a very personal question.

'I saw him somehow connected to small people? I don't know how he was connected to them, but I know for sure that he is.'

Honey shook her head as her forehead creased. 'Can you clarify that, Mary Jane? Who or what exactly are we talking about?'

'The missing husband. He's somehow connected to very small people.'

Honey frowned. 'You mean children?'

Mary Jane closed her eyes and pursed her lips against her fingers as she considered this.

'No.'

'Dwarves?'

This time the thought process was less lengthy.

'No. But similar.'

So! Bert Watchpole was involved with the little people. Honey concentrated on that aspect then burst out with her conclusion.

'Ireland! Perhaps it means he's gone to Ireland. They call the fairies and leprechauns little people in Ireland?'

'Say!' said Mary Jane, her wrinkles reappearing as her face relaxed. 'That could be it. Yes, you're right. The little people live in Ireland.'

'Some do.'

A cold clammy feeling suddenly grabbed Honey by the throat. She grabbed the Cadillac's wing mirror.

'Mary Jane. Grab the wheel. Your car's moving forward. You haven't got the brake on!'

A grating sound accompanied the wrenching of the handbrake.

'All OK now,' Mary Jane said brightly.

Honey felt her knees give way. On running a swift inspection she saw that there were only inches between the Cadillac and Doherty's pride and joy.

Audacious was a good word to call what Honey did next. She actually placed herself between the two cars. Actually, dangerous was a better word. If Mary Jane did roll forward Doherty's car would be safe but Honey's knees would need replacing.

Honey slid back into the passenger seat of Doherty's car, breathing a sigh of relief that her knees were still intact. Mary Jane had driven off without a scrape on her powder pink paint.

Doherty was sitting with his hands laced over the wheel. He straightened on seeing the tail lights of the Caddy blink on and off some way down the road.

'So what was that all about?'

Honey repeated what she'd already told him about Bert Watchpole, plus Mary Jane's latest statement.

He blinked at her as he attempted to digest the reference to small men, like leprechauns, and the conclusion that Bert had gone to Ireland.

'And before you say it, I don't really think that she's lost her marbles.'

Doherty stared at her in disbelief. 'You don't?'

'I just think she just wants to be helpful and is applying herself to the problem.'

He went back to staring out of the windscreen. It wasn't like him to dwell on things and it worried her. A little flippancy was in order.

'At least she didn't hit your car. Did you see how willing I was to sacrifice myself for the most important thing in your life? I actually placed myself between the bonnet of her car and the boot of yours. I hope you appreciate it.'

He snorted. 'Nobody asked you to be a martyr. It's only a car for Chrissake!'

'*Only a car*? Hey, this is the love of your life you're talking about.'

'Who told you that?'

'Ahmed at the garage said . . .'

'Honey. Ahmed reckoned that Bristol Rovers were going to win the European Cup.'

Honey looked at him in surprise. 'That's rubbish.'

'Let that be a lesson to you. Never trust a man who wears a shower cap when he's repairing a car and a jock strap over his overalls.'

Before she could ask, Doherty answered.

'In case something spoils his hair or falls onto his wedding tackle.'

CHAPTER EIGHTEEN

'John Rees called. I told him you'd call him back. Are you going to?'

Lindsey was putting the finishing touches to a flower display. Gene was helping her. Being a sensitive soul, their new receptionist cottoned on to the fact that this was a girl-to-girl *tête-à-tête*.

He flapped his hands. 'I see a girl thing. Well you carry on. I'll just go to powder my nose.'

Honey flopped into a chair and toyed with an elastic band. Making cat's cradles with her fingers didn't fool Lindsey.

'I know all the signs. You and Doherty are rekindling the old flame. Our delicious American bookseller is still a contender, though compared to your policeman, he's just an appetiser. Doherty is still the main course.'

'You sound pretty certain of that.'

'You're my mother. I know you well.'

'How's Dominic?'

Dominic was Lindsey's latest boyfriend. 'Friend' was the operative word; Lindsey had a lot of friends who just happened to be guys. She didn't enter into many relationships. Not that she was actually saving herself for Mr Right, it was just that she liked having boys or men who were first and foremost friends.

Lindsey waggled a long-stemmed lily at her mother. 'You're trying to change the subject. You know very well that I haven't seen Dominic for two weeks. He's gone skiing with Sophie. You may recall that Sophie and I went to school together.'

Honey pouted. 'Fine. I have to let John down.'

'He's a grown man. He can take it.'

'But I did give him cause to be hopeful. At the party and all that.'

'Alison's party.'

'That's right.'

'You had a call from her too.'

'What about?'

'Annoyed that her guests are being interrogated by the police again. She wondered if you could do anything about it.'

The lily flopped onto the reception counter from the flower vase, neck broken.

'Oh, sure. I'll waltz into Doherty's office and insist he keeps his hands off my friend's friends. I'm sure he'll oblige.'

However neither the chance to phone John Rees or Alison occurred. In a flurry of angry agitation, Maurice Hoffmann, Alison's beau, crashed into Reception with Alison trailing behind. Both of them looked as though they meant serious business, despite the fact that Alison was wearing pale cream pants, padded jacked, and palomino-coloured accessories. Barbie probably had the same outfit herself this winter, though somewhat smaller.

'Well, some friend you are . . .' Alison began.

Maurice pointed an accusing finger only inches from Honey's face. His own face red with anger.

'Do you know how long they had me down at the police station? Do you?'

Honey shrugged. 'I've no idea . . .'

'Four hours. I have been interrogated for four hours and been asked some pretty stupid questions. When did I book the party, how did I pay for it? And then why hadn't I paid for it? Because the people I should be paying are both dead. You'd have thought the police would have noticed that by now wouldn't you?'

'I don't see what that's got to do with me . . .'

'You were at the party. You've given them every scrap of information about who was there and added to it.'

'You made up lies,' bleated Alison, her heavily made-up eyes welling over with angry tears. 'We gave them a list of everyone who attended and what costumes they were wearing. But you added two. You said there were two people there who were dressed as ghosts. You're a liar!'

'But there were . . .' Honey began.

'I saw no ghosts,' said Maurice. His fine mane of tawny hair showed flecks of grey when he shook his head. 'Two extra guests that didn't exist. The police want this case closed and they'll place the blame anywhere they can in order to get it wrapped up pronto.'

Honey didn't like Maurice's brusque tone, nor the way he took up position between her and Alison. If she had direct access to Alison, face to face, she was sure her friend would understand.

She tried anyway.

'Look, I'm truly sorry about this, but there were two guests who turned up late but never joined us — not properly. They appeared at the door but were never seen again.'

Alison's face turned white. 'Are you saying they were the murderers?'

Honey pushed her hair back behind one ear, a sure sign that she was getting serious.

'We don't know but they're the only people unaccounted for so it's very likely. That's why the police are re-questioning everybody. So far it seems as though I was the only one to see them.'

'This is awful,' cried Alison, burying her face in her beautifully soft hands, nails perfectly shaped, varnished, and embellished with twinkly little stones.

Since becoming Crime Liaison Officer for the Hotels Association, Honey had never divulged any information imparted to her but on this occasion she decided to make an exception; after all, Alison was one of her oldest friends.

'Look. How about we sit and talk about this over a cup of coffee?'

'A brandy!' Maurice exclaimed. 'I'll have a brandy.'

Maurice looked to be taking no prisoners. Still, the brandy might help him relax.

After ordering the drinks, she took them into the conservatory. A watery sun infiltrated the glass, fooling the indoor plants into thinking spring was on the way. Poor plants, thought Honey. They had to get through Christmas first.

Over coffee and brandy she told them a little of what they'd found out so far.

'It seems Mr and Mrs Crook were likely guilty of fraud,' she began. 'They bought the guest house with a chunk of capital they embezzled from a company of which Mr Crook was a director.'

'That's as may be, but what's that got to do with us? The guests at the party were friends and acquaintances — like yourself. It was my darling Alison's birthday and I wanted her to have fun,' said Maurice.

Honey wondered which slot she occupied, friend or acquaintance.

Her eyes followed the massive hand stroking Alison's arm with the back of his hand. A physical man. A strong man who shunned working in an office.

'My darling poppet,' he cooed.

There were terms of endearment and terms of endearment; being called 'poppet' was right up there with 'sweetie pie' and in cutesy-tootsy puking territory.

On reflection it suited Alison's Barbie doll dimensions in body and mind. She was that type. She liked being pampered. In another life she might have been a Persian cat or a handbag dog.

'It also appears they may have been involved in identity theft.'

She awaited their reaction.

Alison tensed, hands clasped tightly over her teeny-weeny leather bag which was no more really than a purse on a rope.

'You mean they stole credit cards? Oh, Maurice!' she said, turning to the man at her side and laying her perfectly painted fingernails on his sleeve. 'They didn't take your card details, did they? After all, my gorgeous guy, you did pay a deposit for my lovely, lush party.'

Honey began to wonder why Alison had ever been her best friend. Once a blonde bimbo, always a blonde bimbo, she thought. Still, there was no sense in prolonging the agony; there was only so much vomit-producing dialogue a girl could take. She had to explain as much as she could.

'I won't go into detail, but it didn't quite work like that. And the two extra guests may have had something to do with it, hence the questions.'

Alison looked relieved. 'So it's not really anything to do with us? None of my guests had anything to do with killing them?'

Maurice patted her hand. 'It seems your fears were groundless, my darling delicious doll.'

He was a big man, Honey thought, no doubt a man's man, used to working in rough conditions. His clothes were well-cut and smart; a russet-coloured jacket, dark beige trousers, a cashmere sweater.

Everything about him was smooth and dependable — except for his terminology. Whatever possessed him to call a woman coochie coo, darling doll, and other sick-inducing terms?

Still. Alison's choice, not hers.

* * *

Rhino poked his nose out of the door and sniffed the air like a dog.

'Nice night,' he muttered before backing into the plastic boot that was now his home.

The boot had once graced the play area of a pub down by the river. The pub had become a bistro, so no room for kids or a playhouse made in the shape of an old boot.

Rhino's new home was sited in the corner of a field where folk of the gypsy kind stored anything they didn't have a use or punter for at the present time. The field was full of junk; old car chassis, defunct boilers, caravans without windows and dodgem cars from funfairs and slot machines in need of paint and refurbishment.

The plastic boot — just big enough for Rhino to squeeze into and sleep warmly, was thrust behind a metal contraption of burst bulbs that had once graced a fairground carousel. For the moment it was forgotten and unloved except by Rhino. He'd wanted a place to hide away from the city streets where everyone knew him. Even the travelling folk didn't bother with frosty fields when they had a warm caravan and a flat screen TV to watch. Spring was the time for fields.

Rhino settled down to eat the tin of beans he'd just opened. He'd eat them cold tonight, though that wasn't always the case. There was a caravan just a few yards away that was occupied in warmer months and it had a single gas ring and a long tube leading to a red canister. There was just enough in it to warm up things he didn't want to eat cold. He'd brought plenty of tins with him and there were a few in the caravan. He'd survive for a time up here out of sight with a nice view of the city and a few pounds for emergencies. He'd made enough money and didn't regret handing over his business to Edna, that business being in the form of his Tesco supermarket trolley and all its contents. He was finished with that, at least for now.

Unrolling his bedroll, he tucked it about his lower limbs and pulled his coat around him. The tin opener grated its way around the can of beans to the halfway mark. Halfway was enough. Taking hold of the spoon he'd taken from an inside pocket of his copious coat, he shoved it into the beans and drew out a mouthful.

He pulled a face. The beans weren't just beans; they had sausages in with them; small skinless ones that tasted like wet slugs when they were cold. But, from experience, he knew they'd taste fine warmed up. There was nothing for it but to use the gas ring that he knew was in the caravan opposite.

Shoving the spoon into the tin, he pushed at the yellow plastic door of the boot and looked out. Nothing moved and the only sound was of two owls hooting to each other across the fields and the sound of the odd car down the hill where the houses started and the fields finished.

If the boot had been a bottle and Rhino a cork, there would have been a popping sound as he pushed himself out of the tiny door on all fours.

Once out in the fresh air, he stayed on all fours, his hands and knees in contact with the frosty grass. He hadn't survived this long on the streets by being careless.

Satisfied that nobody was around, he got to his feet, reached back into the boot, and felt for the tin of sausages and beans.

The door to the caravan might once have had a proper lock but didn't anymore. The padlock that was supposed to keep it secure opened easily. It merely looked like a padlock; it didn't actually lock anything.

The moon was the only light he needed to cook by and the gas ring was immediately to his right and just inside the door. The bloke who owned the caravan — a swarthy scruff named Frank — had conveniently left a box of matches behind.

Rhino turned on the gas and lit a match. He didn't bother with a pan but placed the tin directly onto the gas ring, giving the contents a minimal stir with his spoon.

'First rate! First bloody rate,' he muttered and licked his lips.

He peered up at the moon suddenly, thinking it had got brighter suddenly. It hadn't done any such thing; in fact a shard of cloud covered it like a ripped shawl, thin with age.

The sudden light was due to car headlights. Somebody had turned into the dirt track that led from the lane to the field.

Rhino uttered a string of serious expletives, leapt out of the caravan, and headed for the boot. It wasn't until he was safely cocooned in its claustrophobic comfort that he remembered the beans.

Another string of expletives ensued. What should he do? Show himself or remain hidden?

That, he decided, all depended on who was coming up the track. Surely it had to be Frank.

'Bloody Frank!' he muttered.

But Frank never came up here at night. Frank only surveyed his collection of clutter in daylight.

The door to the boot had never locked from the inside, but Rhino had rigged up a piece of string that looped over a nail. It was enough to hold the door shut when you didn't want visitors. Not that many people came knocking at the door of the plastic boot.

He waited, his breathing heavy, listening with his ear held flat against the narrow gap. The sound of the engine came closer.

Greasy sweat trickled down his grimy face mixing with the snot from his nose. As whatever it was turned into the field, the beam from the headlights raked across the tumbled bits of junk outside. Rusted cars. Rusted refrigerators. Builders' rubble. Sheets of corrugated iron.

The car was coming closer.

Rhino slunk back as far as he could in the confined space. It was dark inside the boot, but the beam of headlights flashed in through the kiddie size window landing on the dark red holdall behind him.

He lay himself protectively over it, patting it with his meaty hands. What a hoot to be handed it — on a plate so to speak. What a turn up! What friends. What a . . . well, there were disadvantages, i.e. the money wasn't his, but hell, he'd do his damndest to hold onto it. A windfall. That's what it was. A bloody windfall!

Once the difficulties were over and he was safe, he wouldn't be living in a moulded house masquerading as a boot, though he did appreciate it. Once all this was over, he had a good mind to get it renovated so kids could play in it again like they used to.

He would move on. He'd buy himself a caravan, a better one than the old rust bucket across the way that Frank occasionally used. He'd probably opt for one of those motor home types and he'd live in it all the time and learn to drive so that he could go anywhere. At some point he might even buy himself a field like this where he could collect any stuff he fancied.

The moon shone bright again. The two men in the 4x4 climbed out, their shadows falling long and black across the cold ground. One of them dipped the headlights before leaving the vehicle.

Rhino held his breath. The dreams of better times were all in the future; first he had to avoid the two heavies out to take his windfall. One of them nodded in the direction of the open door of the caravan.

Shit!

The gas ring was still lit, the can of beans glowing red. Numpty! He should have turned it off.

The heavies swore at the patches of broken ice beneath their feet. Where there was no ice, there was mud. The men were not amused.

One of them took a tyre iron from beneath the seat, weighing it in his right hand in an effort to get his grip just right for a hefty swing to the head of the man they were looking for.

They'd asked the right questions about Rhino, knew he was big, knew he could take care of himself if need be. They also knew that he had what they wanted. Edna, the dirty old bag woman, had told them he'd come into money. A lot of money.

'Some people out at Northend gave it to him and they're dead so it's his now. So he gave me his wagon,' she'd told them. 'For nothing.'

She'd turned wary when they'd began asking her his whereabouts, his usual haunts, his friends — if he had any.

The wariness had turned to fear when Blind Bob had started shaking her.

Blind Bob wasn't blind in the physical sense; he was blind to people's pain and deaf to their pleas for mercy. Edna had annoyed him because she'd been prattling on like his mother used to prattle, sidestepping the issue, never quite getting to the point.

He'd used the tyre iron to shut her up. He'd never liked his mother anyway. Edna had gone the same way.

Claude had shaken his head at Bob's impatience, but said nothing. That was why they got on so well together; Claude didn't prattle. Claude was a man of few words.

'I smell sausages,' murmured Blind Bob. 'Somebody's cooking supper. Reckon they got enough for uninvited guests?'

Claude grunted. Blind Bob did like his little joke. He himself had never had much of a sense of humour. It went with his silence. Why speak or laugh when you didn't need to? A grunt was as good as a word.

'Looks as though he saw us coming. Ran off or hiding?'

Claude didn't bother to grunt a response. Like two wolves hunting down their prey, instinct and reason combined. They divided, each of the opinion that the man they were looking for couldn't have gone far — not with supper on the gas.

Rhino watched as they squelched their way across the crusted ground. One of them swore when a puddle of thin ice cracked beneath his shoe into the slop beneath.

One went round one side of the caravan, one the other. Claude dropped down to look beneath the scruffy van; Blind Bob drew up an aluminium beer barrel, one of several left to fester in the grass. He stepped up on it and peered along the roof.

Intent on their search, neither noticed the beans exploding from their tin and extinguishing the blue flame. The gas kept coming. Neither of them heard it hissing from among the smoking beans. Beans can be highly flammable; and unburned gas can be explosive.

Used to working as a team, their attention switched from the outside of the caravan to the inside. It was the only place he could be.

They came together at the door in mute agreement. They were going inside to open every cupboard, upend every couch to find him.

Blind Bob went first. 'Coming, ready or not,' he called into the darkened van.

Claude followed him silently. Only when Blind Bob took out his phone and turned on the light did Claude see the mishmash of smoking beans and sausages and the match box suddenly bursting into flame. And the sound. The hissing of unlit propane.

'Get—'

Claude, the man of few words, had spoken his last one. The caravan exploded with such violence that the paintwork of the 4x4 was scarred down one side. A huge yellow flame leapt skywards. Bits of metal flew up into the air then rained down, clanging and clattering on the fridges, rusting cars, and acetylene bottles.

Rhino's temporary home was blown onto its side, its red roof seared black and smoking. The door was blasted off its hinges.

Rhino was knocked unconscious. He didn't hear the ambulance. He didn't hear the fire engine. His arms were still wrapped around the red bag and the money.

CHAPTER NINETEEN

John Rees had arrived unexpectedly.

'You didn't phone, so I figured you were busy and thought I'd pop round. You're not rushing off anywhere, are you?'

Honey shook her head. 'Not at all.'

Here was her opportunity to make amends; Doherty was hovering in the background, but was still rather huffy. She had no doubt he would come round, but in the meantime John was here. What was that old saying? A bird in the hand . . .? A man in the hand counted the same. Though she assured herself they were only friends. Doherty was still her fiancé.

'How about we . . .?'

She'd been just about to suggest they sneak out and have lunch somewhere intimate, when her phone burbled like a strangulated parrot. It was Doherty . . .

'Excuse me for a moment.'

She felt her face reddening as she turned sideways on to take the call.

'There was an old woman who lived in a shoe . . .'

It was hardly what she was expecting him to say.

'Is this some kind of riddle?'

'Don't you remember your nursery rhymes?'

191

'That wasn't one of my favourites. Is there some significance?'

'We've found Rhino. He was hiding out where you wouldn't expect to find him. In a shoe, or a boot, however you want to describe it, the kind provided for kiddies in pub gardens when their parents want some drinking time.'

'What's he got to say for himself?'

'Nothing much. He's injured.'

'Badly?'

'Not so badly as the other guys. A caravan explosion. Gas according to our experts. Baked beans and sausages according to Rhino. It's proving difficult to separate the body parts from the sausages.'

'Seriously?'

'No. Not really. They were only small sausages. As for Rhino, real name Henry Lester Landemore. He's in hospital. Not serious but he's saying nothing, not to us anyway. I need you to prompt him. He told you about the Crooks, but won't say a word to us. There's no guarantee he'll open up to you, but it's worth a try. I'll pick you up in five minutes.'

'That's cutting it fine. It'll take you longer than that to get here.'

'I'm parked outside. You've got five minutes. By the way, he had company in the shoe — two million in fact.'

The phone disconnected.

Honey felt her neck getting warm; then her face. She turned to John.

'I . . .'

'I take it the call was from the cop and it's a rain check. Something pretty heavy's come up, right?'

'We've got this case we're working on . . .'

'Of course you have.'

'I'm obliged to go with him.'

'Of course you are.'

She managed a guilty smile. 'So glad you understand. And we will have lunch, just as soon as this is over.'

John's return smile was weak, understanding, and . . . he obviously didn't believe a word of it.

'I could be waiting a long time for you and the cop to be finito.'

'I meant . . .'

He grinned a little sadly. 'I know what you meant. See you when I see you.'

She couldn't bear to see him go, and she couldn't bear not to meet up with Doherty.

A quilted jacket and a pale pink pashmina were all she had time to grab before hurtling out of the door and into Doherty's car.

At this time of year the hood was up. The interior smelled of warm leather (Doherty's jacket), warm plastic (the car), and warm air from the heater.

Doherty eased the car away from the kerb. The traffic hung around out by the roundabout where Pulteney Street and the A36 converged.

'Rhino is suffering from concussion, though not as though you'd notice. I've placed a guard on the door, just in case.'

'Do you think he's in danger?'

'There are two million reasons why somebody might want a more personal crack at his head. However, my first priority is that he's likely to do a runner.'

'So the money? Where did it come from?'

'He's not saying.'

'What about Edna? Did you tell him about her?'

'I did. That's when I decided to put the guard on the door.'

'And the money?'

'In custody.'

Rhino was sat up in bed in a side ward, a uniformed bod outside. Blinds had been lowered over the glass upper halves of the partitioning.

The television was on. Rhino was eyeing it in bleary-eyed amazement. He didn't notice them enter.

'Portuguese.'

The quizmaster on the TV programme repeated the question.

'What nationality was Henry the Navigator?'

'Portuguese, Portuguese, Portuguese.' Rhino was transfixed, as though repeating the answer might inspire the quiz competitor to do the same.

'Rhino!'

The man jumped at the sound of his name. His eyes flickered from Doherty to Honey.

Doherty moved to one side of the bed. Honey stayed at the foot.

'Hi,' she said waggling her fingers. 'Remember me?'

He shook his head and went back to the TV screen.

Doherty didn't waste time. 'Rhino. I want to know where you got that money.'

Rhino did not respond, his lips forming an answer to the next question asked on the screen without him making a sound.

Doherty reached for the remote lying on the bedside table and turned it off.

'The money, Rhino. Where did you find it?'

Rhino closed his eyes and sucked in his lips, almost as though he were wishing them away.

Honey had what she thought might be a good idea.

'I like quizzes. How about we turn the TV back on?'

She jerked her chin at Doherty. He frowned then obliged. The TV came back into life and Rhino opened his eyes.

The same quiz show was on.

'Who was the only king of England to be called "the great"?'

Honey played dumb. 'Oh, let's see . . .' Of course she knew. She was Lindsey's mother and Lindsey lived and breathed history.

Rhino's piggy eyes glinted bright and were fixed on the screen.

'Alfred! It's Alfred!'

The contestant dithered.

Doherty shook his head, eyes also on the screen. 'Where the hell do they get these people from?'

'Is Alfred the right answer, Rhino?' Honey asked the big man who was almost exploding where he sat.

''Course it is. Hey, this dude shouldn't be on this show. Wanker!'

Honey noticed Doherty's finger hovering over the off switch and threw him a warning look.

She addressed Rhino. 'Do you think you could do better, Rhino?'

His eyes shone with enthusiasm. 'You bet I could! Being in my line of business means I read a lot. I read everything and anything so I pick up the knowledge. Right?'

'The stuff you collected in your trolley?'

'Good stuff!'

Honey ignored the look of frustration on Doherty's face. If frustration were eggs he'd be an omelette.

'Right,' she said nodding gravely. 'I can see that you would pick up a whole load of knowledge like that. It must be like having your own personal library.'

'You bet,' said Rhino rising to the chance of conversing with somebody on his wavelength.

'I bet you I can name all of Henry VIII's queens and what happened to them.'

Rhino almost bounced out of bed with excitement. 'Go on then!'

'Do I get a prize if I get it right?'

His excitement faltered. 'What d'ya mean?'

'Well, if I get the answer right, then I deserve a prize. They give prizes on that quiz show you've been watching, don't they?'

He nodded, warily at first then he beamed. 'Right. I'll be the quiz master. You answer the question.'

'And the prize?'

'Simple,' Doherty burst in, suddenly as keen on Honey's quiz question as Rhino was. 'If my colleague here gets it right, then you tell us how you acquired that money.'

Rhino squinted at the television. Then he eyed the remote control that Doherty still gripped in his hand.

'Can I have the remote control back after?'

'If I answer my question, you tell me where you got the money. I will then ask you a question . . .'

His eyes were bright with enthusiasm. 'Not just one question. Ten. Ask me ten like they do on the TV.'

'Five,' said Honey, already racking her brains for two decent questions.

Rhino narrowed his eyes and thought about it. 'OK. Five, but if you get your question wrong then I get the remote control back anyway.'

Honey folded her arms and nodded. 'And I will not need to ask you any questions.'

'You have to ask me quiz questions! I want to be asked quiz questions first!'

There was no getting away from it. In a matter of minutes, Rhino had become an armchair quiz addict.

'OK. Whatever happens I'll ask you five questions.'

His nodding sent his tangled hair bouncing.

'OK. OK. Your time starts now. Name the six wives of Henry VIII. Full names, mind.'

She rattled them off. 'Catherine of Aragon, Anne Boleyn, Jane Seymour, Anne of Cleves, Catherine Howard, Catherine Parr.'

Rhino looked impressed. 'Brilliant!'

'There,' said Honey feeling mighty proud of herself.

'Your turn,' said Doherty addressing Rhino. 'Where did you get the money?'

Rhino ignored him. 'OK. Now tell me which ones were beheaded, divorced, or survived,' he said addressing Honey.

Biting her bottom lip helped her focus. She vaguely recalled a little rhyme Lindsey had taught her.

'Catherine of Aragon was set aside and died in her bed, Anne Boleyn lost her head, Jane Seymour died after giving birth to a son, Anne of Cleves was divorced, her marriage done. Catherine Howard lost her head too so they say, and Catherine Parr lived to marry another day. Howzat?'

She and Rhino did high fives. Doherty was all serious scrutiny and purposeful intent.

'So where did you get the money?'

Rhino frowned.

'The man ain't got no idea of my trade. No idea of the responsibility.'

Doherty prowled from the window he'd been looking out of and hovered over Rhino.

'Where did you get the money?'

'Can we guess?' Honey asked suddenly. 'Would you play the game if we did things that way?'

Rhino closed one eye and squinting scrutinised her with the other.

'Only if I still get my five questions.'

Doherty threw back his head and turned back to the window in disgust.

'Right,' said Honey. 'First starter for ten.'

'What?'

'Ten points. Did you steal the money?'

Rhino shook his head.

'Did you find the money?'

Again he shook his head.

Honey frowned. She was thinking of the evidence that someone had been staying in one of those attic rooms at the guest house. She saw Doherty looking at her and knew he was thinking of getting the DNA evidence rechecked.

'Did somebody give you the money?'

'Uh uh,' he said wagging his finger. 'Do you think somebody gave me the money?'

Honey thought about it. 'Yes. Yes I do. You were staying with the Crooks, weren't you?'

'That's not proper guessing.'

She glanced briefly at Doherty who was looking fierce.

Rhino looked too. 'Not very patient, your boyfriend, is he?'

'He has issues.'

Doherty eyed her menacingly over folded arms.

'What did you give them that was valuable, Rhino? You gave them something useful?'

'I told them I had it. Showed pictures it did. Shiny pictures.'

Honey frowned. 'A catalogue?'

'They always throw them out in bags at the side of the rubbish bins. Lovely stuff some of it. Glossy pictures of old furniture.'

'Bonhams?'

It was only a guess, but the moment Honey saw Rhino's expression, she knew she'd hit the nail on the head.

His face froze.

Doherty took the opportunity to play at being bad cop.

'Enough of your bloody games, Rhino. Edna was murdered. You know that don't you? Did you murder her, Rhino? Did you murder her and take the money from her?'

'No! No!' Rhino looked horrified, 'I didn't do it! I didn't do it! I was given the money. I gave him the shiny book and the tool. It was with the book. I found it outside Bonhams. Mr Crook gave me money for other bits of paper I'd found. But the book was special. And the key. The tool was special too. He told me it was of interest. That's what he said. Of interest.'

The big man pulled the bedding up to his chin like a shield against more questions — or something else.

Doherty rounded on him.

'What tool? What was the tool for?'

Rhino shook his head. 'I don't know.'

'So what do you know? Do you know the two men who died when the caravan exploded?'

'I don't know.'

'Did you kill them too?'

Rhino's scraggy hair flew around like ropes in a gale when he shook his head.

'I didn't kill them. The baked beans killed them.'

Honey saw Doherty's face twitch and knew he was on the verge of laughing. She couldn't stop smirking herself. The vision of a tin of baked beans being responsible for the death of two men was pretty funny. OK, perhaps it wouldn't have been so funny if they had been nice people, but they'd been thugs. If you hand out the aggro, at some stage it's bound to come bouncing back at you.

'So who were they?'

'The same dudes who killed Edna.'

Doherty straightened, his expression ripe with thoughts and one question in particular.

'How do you know they killed Edna?'

The piggy eyes stayed fixed on Doherty and were full of fear. 'You can't let them get me.'

'How do you know they killed Edna.'

Rhino swallowed. 'Because I saw them.'

Doherty was one hundred per cent attention. 'You saw them kill her?'

'Not exactly. I saw them following the old fool. She was yakking and yakking like she always did and didn't see them. They didn't see me. I was hiding. There's a row of rubbish skips behind the big hotel . . .'

'Which hotel?' asked Doherty.

'The one near the traffic lights.'

'Rhino, there are hundreds of traffic lights in Bath. Which ones are we talking about?'

'The ones where the traffic goes across and up Lansdown Hill.'

Honey and Doherty looked at each other.

'You mean the bins at the back of the Travelodge?'

He nodded. 'It was only temporary, but I knew the bins had been emptied so I thought it would be warm for the night. I'd handed my trolley over to Edna because I'd come by the money. I heard them ask her where I was and heard her say she would take them to me. Of course she didn't take them to me at all; she took them away from me, gave me chance to get away. So I went to stay in the country for a while.'

He was referring to the boot.

'What about the money?' asked Doherty.

Rhino pointed at Honey. 'Guess.'

Doherty swore. 'This is getting ridiculous. Mr and Mrs Crook were murdered for that money and the same men murdered Edna!'

Honey saw fear flash through the street dweller's eyes. Doherty hadn't necessarily hit the button but he'd said enough to scare the man. She took a wild shot on what that was.

'You were living in the attic for a while at Moss End Guest House. That's when they gave you the money?'

Now Rhino looked really scared. 'I didn't kill them. Honest I didn't.'

Honey came round, pushed Doherty to one side and sat on the side of the bed. She covered Rhino's huge paw, or should that be hoof, with hers.

'Did you see them being killed?'

The big man's skin broke into a shiny sweat. 'They said they were going away and I could stay at the place until they left. We'd done good business. Honest business,' he said, nodding his head as though wishing they would agree. 'They had an interest in recycling. That's what they said. Just like me. They called me the King of Recycling,' he added proudly, 'but said it would be best if I stayed out of sight for a while. I could watch the TV while they were away. They didn't mind.'

Honey wondered whether it was worth explaining to Rhino that recycling as far as Boris and Doris were concerned was about gleaning information from utility bills and till receipts and cheating people out of their money and even their identities. She figured he wouldn't understand. It seemed Doherty thought the same.

What she couldn't understand was why they had invited him to stay in the attic.

'No more quizzes! No more playing games, Rhino. You saw who killed Mr and Mrs Crook. Who were they? How many were there?'

'I heard them coming up the stairs — Boris and Doris. They gave me the bag and some air tickets and told me to take it down the back stairs and meet them at the train station. So I did.'

'But you didn't see the killers?'

Rhino shook his head. 'No. I saw Boris and his missus come shooting down from the roof and into those pots. So I took off. Such a shame. Nice people. Fancy ending up in those pots. They reckoned them pots was the best thing about the place. Fancy ending up dead in them.'

Honey was thinking. The giant urns; it all came back to them. Even Rhino kept mentioning them. And then it came to her.

'What were the photos of, Rhino?'

He blinked at her. 'The pots.'

'And the tool?'

'They were outside Bonhams for the auction. Some time back it was. They were too big to go inside. Nice and comfy. And there was a tool — sort of tool. It looked like this. I found it inside one of the pots.'

He hooked two fingers.

'What the hell is that supposed to mean?'

Doherty wasn't getting it; but Honey was.

'It's a key. Two prongs that fix into a turning plate. They use them to undo the fuel and water tanks on boats. It keeps the tanks firmly sealed and watertight.'

'I kept it to hang excess merchandise from my cart. Kept it for ages I did. And the ticket. There was a ticket as well.' He shook his head. 'Lovely ticket it was. Just like on a car . . .'

Rhino was getting a faraway look. Doherty cleared his throat loudly to bring him back to reality, instructing him instructions that he was to stay where he was until they could take a statement.

'We can assume that the whereabouts of the money was beaten out of the victims before they were killed and shoved out of the window,' said Doherty as they drove back into Bath.

'Why bother to slide them out of the windows and straight into those pots? They could have left them where they were. They might not have been discovered for days.'

'That's very profound thinking, Mrs Driver.'

She threw him a haughty scowl. 'Quit calling me Mrs Driver.'

'OK. I suppose it's time.'

'Time for what?'

She saw his wide grin picked out by passing headlights. The day was closing in; winter gloom settling around and not lifting except in streets of brightly lit shops.

'Making up.'

'Dinner? Champagne? Romantic music?'

'My inclination is a night in with a Chinese takeaway. I can provide the music and no problem with the wine. I've got an Asti Spumante in the fridge.'

'And for dessert?'

His smile said it all. 'Honey. We'll forego the chocolate fudge or lemon meringue pie. We can take a bite out of each other.'

The empty wine bottle and the remains of the Chinese meal were sitting on the coffee table. Once the burning passion had been well and truly satisfied, their conversation returned to the two million pounds, the three murders, and the significance of the ridiculously large Greek-style urns sitting outside the door of the guest house in Northend.

'It could be the money Boris Crook embezzled from the company — what was the other partner's name?'

'Belper,' said Doherty. 'But according to him it was a lesser figure than that and Boris had promised to repay it very shortly. Suddenly he was in funds.'

'Then he found the money. Boris, I mean. And it still goes back to those urns. If what Rhino describes is a key then there has to be a corresponding keyhole — or rather two for the prongs to go in. It wouldn't be that noticeable, flush to the decoration on one of those ghastly ornaments.'

'The DNA on the bed linen at Moss End checks out as Rhino's.'

'He was in hiding, or rather being hidden. He knew something Boris and Doris wanted kept secret until they'd made a clean getaway.'

'I don't think it would be a bad idea to pay a visit to Mr Belper to double check the facts. It wouldn't be the first time a company director has under-declared a company's capital — and therefore its tax dues.'

Just as Honey was about to invite herself along for the ride, both their phones gurgled into life.

To Honey's surprise, she found herself talking to her mother.

'I need to speak to you. It's about Bert Watchpole.'

Honey pulled a scary face to convey who it was to Doherty, but he was too involved in his own call, face intense and looking bloody angry.

'Are you listening to me, Hannah?'

Her mother's voice was shrill and she'd referred to her as Hannah, not darling or daughter. Rarely did she call her Honey.

'Yes. I'm here.'

'Where are you?'

'With a friend.'

'Is it that *policeman* friend of yours?'

The tone was mercurial, as though Doherty was a sex maniac and Honey an unwilling sex slave, which wasn't exactly incorrect . . . at least the sex bit wasn't.

'What's this about Bert Watchpole?'

'Ah, yes. Antonio has been making enquiries on my behalf . . .'

'So that's where you've been. In the arms of your Italian stallion!'

'Hannah! That is so vulgar! Antonio is a charming and kind man.'

'He's swept you off your feet, which is why I haven't heard much from you in the last few days.'

'You're old enough to look after yourself. Anyway, as I was saying, Antonio has been making some enquiries on my behalf and it seems that the woman who was carted away by ambulance the same night as Bert disappeared, has gone back to her apartment in Lansdown Crescent. I've promised Rhoda that I will pay this Maggie Stripes a visit and ask her whether she saw what direction Bert went in. There's even a chance she might know where he's gone. Apparently they were both keen on china figures — you know, Dresden, that kind of thing.'

'My mother has become an amateur sleuth,' Honey mouthed to Doherty, her hand over the phone.

Normally he might have rolled his eyes in disbelief. Not on this occasion.

Her mother was giving her an order. 'I want you to come with me. Antonio is driving us. I'll be round for you at eleven sharp.'

The phone went dead. No argument.

Honey eyed Doherty. 'Is the world about to end?'

He grunted. 'The guard I placed outside our street dweller's hospital ward decided he needed a leak. Rhino's gone.'

CHAPTER TWENTY

'Hey. Remember the vibes I received; small men in pointy hats,' shouted Mary Jane as Honey, her mother and the suave Antonio set off in his car for Lansdown Crescent. 'This I gotta see. Gotta see if I was right.'

Antonio's driving was far superior to that of Mary Jane. Honey sat relaxed in the back seat. Although she'd not been that keen to do this trip, once they started all the cares of the hotel fell away. Thinking came easily when the driving was smooth and hosts of car horns weren't honking and terrified pedestrians running for their lives.

Weak winter sunlight attempted to break through the grey day. Trees stripped of the last of their leaves waved skeletal branches in the biting east wind.

'It feels cold enough to snow,' remarked Antonio.

'I don't think so,' said Honey. 'Too early.'

Antonio shrugged his shoulders. 'It smells like snow.'

Feeling relaxed and self-assured, Honey went on to tell him that snow rarely fell before Christmas. Seeing as he hailed from sunnier climes perhaps he didn't know that.'

'I have lived here for forty years,' he told her. 'I think it will snow.'

Gloria Cross turned the collar of her fur coat — the real thing — up around her face and leaned towards Antonio.

'If it does snow, we'll just have to cuddle up with something warm.'

He grinned lasciviously. 'Or something hot.'

Honey grimaced.

Compared to the naked trees they'd passed, the bay trees still sporting their neat leaves, looked like plastic, unmoving in their pots.

'This one,' said her mother, pointing at the same door Honey had entered with Doherty only a short while ago. She hadn't let on that she had visited Mrs Nobbs and didn't intend to. The case seemed too trivial and her mother would probably agree with the vandal who'd mutilated an army of plastic gnomes.

Antonio insisted on accompanying them.

'How can I possibly leave two lovely ladies without a male escort? Anything might happen.'

'Looks like it already has,' murmured Honey, noting that Antonio's palm was placed in the vicinity of her mother's bottom.

The woman who answered the door was the same person Honey had seen in Mrs Nobbs' apartment. Her hair was as sleek as on the last visit and her pale pink knitted suit was complimented by a triple strand pearl necklace.

On seeing Honey and recognising her, she said, 'I don't know anything about the gnomes!'

Gloria Cross dismissed the woman with a wave of her hand. 'Good grief, woman. Gnomes are neither here nor there. We're here about a man, not a gnome. You are Maggie Sinclair, I take it, lately of Flat 22, Overton House?'

The woman answered with a feeble nod, then peered at Antonio.

'If it's anything to do with the selling of my flat, you'll have to deal with my solicitor. I just want to get rid of it.'

Antonio was charm itself. 'You are looking as lovely as ever, Mrs Sinclair. We were worried about you when the ambulance came.'

One wrinkled hand resplendent with some very expensive rings, nervously fiddled with the strands of pearls.

'It was a private ambulance.'

'Ah! That might explain it, though we have had private ambulances call before . . .'

'I . . . my son arranged it specially . . .'

Honey stood silently taking everything in. The more she took in the more puzzled she became. Something here was not quite right. Mrs Sinclair was not right . . . Mrs Sinclair . . .

'Maggie. May I call you Maggie?' asked Antonio, his voice as smooth as olive oil.

Maggie? Maggie Sinclair?

Honey recalled what Mary Jane had said. The initials M and S. She'd thought Mary Jane was referring to the Marks and Spencer's cakes. M and S also stood for Maggie Sinclair. And the small men with pointy hats? The gnomes!

Maggie didn't look pleased to be called by her first name. In fact she didn't look at all pleased that they were there.

'I don't know what you want here . . .'

Gloria adopted an efficient but senior sympathetic stance. 'Look, my dear. We're not here to harass you and neither am I interested in purchasing your latter abode. So be a dear and concentrate on what I am saying. We're looking for a man who disappeared from Overton House at the same time as you were taken away by ambulance. All we wish to know is whether you saw him at the time of your sudden departure.'

The woman stared at them. A scurrilous look had entered the velvet brown eyes. The rose-pink lips, glossy as a plastic, fixed into a defiant line.

'Oh come on, sweetie! You and he were interested in antiques. His wife told me so.'

'So who can blame him for leaving her? The only interest that woman had was in *eating*.'

Like most people who are guilty and turning nervous, Maggie was fidgeting, first with her hands, then her necklace, then glancing furtively over her shoulder.

'What woman?' Honey asked.

Maggie Sinclair turned to her wide eyed. 'What?'

'What woman? You described Rhoda Watchpole perfectly as a lady of rotund figure who sits eating all day. We did not mention either her name or her husband's name yet you knew who we meant.'

Gloria adopted an ultra-superior attitude. 'I think we should come inside and discuss this further. Nobody wishes to air their dirty linen on the doorstep.'

'No! Go away. Go away before I call the police.'

Maggie attempted to close the door, but the pointy toe of Gloria's pink leather boot was made of stern stuff.

The two women glared at each other, senior savagery in all its primeval — and pensionable — glory.

'Remove your foot!' shouted Maggie.

Gloria Cross could be a pitbull when she wanted to. 'You know more than you're letting on, Maggie Sinclair! Let us in or I'll hit you with my handbag!'

Honey flattened herself against the wall. Antonio was flapping his arms saying, 'Ladies. My beautiful ladies . . .'

His appeals not only fell on deaf ears but were stopped in midstream by the backswing of Gloria's handbag catching him across the mouth.

The sound of the front door opening and a draught of outside air preceded somebody yelling, 'Hey! Hey! Is this Lansdown Crescent or Soho on a Saturday night?'

'Aubrey! You're back!'

Maggie Sinclair threw her hands to her face.

'Not to stay, Mother.'

His tone was grim and his face was long enough to trip over. 'I've just come to fetch a few things. I take it *he* is still here?'

The bitterness of the man's voice and the look on Maggie Sinclair face said it all.

'Aubrey! There's no call for you to behave like this. I always said that I might not stay at Overton House. I went there purely for the social scene.'

'Which you brought home with you,' her son said bitterly. 'Another man to fill your lonely days.'

'And you attempted to discredit him . . .'

Suddenly, as though becoming aware of what she'd said, Maggie heaved a big sigh.

'Why don't you let them all in, love. Might as well get everything out in the open.'

An upright man of senior years stepped into the hall behind her.

'Excuse me,' muttered Aubrey, and swept in.

They were shown into a room that shone with light thanks to the three huge Georgian windows which graced it. There was a roll-end sofa in front of the windows, a break-front bookcase, elegant lyre-ended side tables, deeply upholstered chairs of Sheraton design, and carpets rich with colour.

There were also lots of china ornaments; Dresden, Royal Doulton, and Worcester.

Bert Watchpole, for it was definitely he, made them tea which he brought in on a beautiful white tray with gilt edging.

Whereas Rhoda was fat, Bert was exactly the opposite. The old nursery rhyme popped into her mind.

Jack Sprat could eat no fat, his wife could eat no lean . . .

His long, lined face dropped at least two inches at mention of his wife.

'Bert, she's missing you.'

'Who said my name was Bert?' he protested.

'Maggie did — in a way.' Gloria Cross was astonishingly forthright. Honey thought it quite admirable.

'You don't have to tell her that you've found me,' he said. His eyes, as pale as sparrow's eggs, looked at her imploringly and then at Maggie. 'We're in love,' he added.

The two lovebirds groped for each other's hands. 'You don't have to be young to be in love,' said Maggie. 'And the young aren't so good at judging when it really is true love. Older people have a lifetime of experience behind us, we know the real thing when we find it and seeing as we've only got a few years left, we might as well have what we really want. Don't you agree?'

Honey folded her arms and studied the pale pink and green Chinese carpet. Five thousand pounds was a lot of money, but hey, could she really be that cruel to this old couple?

'Aubrey is my son by my first marriage to Bert Abingdon. When we divorced I married Bert Sinclair. Pure coincidence of course. It's not really that I have a weakness for the name Bert.'

She and Bert were sitting on the roll-end sofa holding hands. They exchanged a sugary smile.

'I moved into Overton House because I was lonely after my late husband died. I wanted to meet people and lovely as this place is, there's nobody here during the day and when they are home at night, all of them are tired after working. Some people only live here intermittently — a great shame. These houses were made to be lived in. So dull without people.'

'So you met Bert at Overton House,' said Honey.

'Yes.' Another exchange of sugary smiles. 'We fell in love. I'm surprised you didn't notice, Antonio. I would have thought that seeing as you are a member of the most romantic race in the world . . . well in my opinion anyway, you might have noticed.'

'I should have, I should have known,' murmured Antonio with an apologetic shake of his head and a wave of his hands.

Honey was intrigued. This old couple had fallen in love but had contrived to keep it secret. What a sneaky old pair.

'So it was all a smokescreen. Mrs Sinclair was whisked away in a private ambulance. While everyone watched the drama, Mr Watchpole sneaked away. Would you like to elucidate?'

Bert Watchpole leaned forward, seemingly eager to divulge his clever plan.

'I got the ambulance from a firm that hires them out to TV and film production companies. Nobody checked whether an ambulance had been called and I still had my driving licence . . .'

Suddenly Maggie's son came charging in, his face contorted with anger, one arm waving towards the door and something that was creasing him up.

'Mother! There are frogs in the garden! Stone frogs! Does that woman not have any *taste* . . .'

He was livid.

'Aubrey! Please stop shouting and leave. You have caused us enough pain! Leave Mrs Nobbs to put whatever she likes into the garden.'

'First it was bloody gnomes. Now it's bloody frogs!'

'Aubrey. Do you want me to tell the police that you've wasted their time?'

Maggie's face held no motherly love for her son. On the contrary, she looked as though she meant what she said, her eyes almost disappearing beneath her bundled brows.

Aubrey, being the age he was, read the signs, sniffed, and left.

Maggie, poor woman, for Honey now pitied her, apologised for his behaviour.

'I know he's my son, but sometimes he's quite obnoxious. Anyway, I think it will do him good to find his own way in the world. He's been living on my money and in my house for long enough. Hopefully he'll find a nice woman and settle down — if he can find one that will have him, that is.'

Maggie chuckled.

Honey liked the woman. She could see what Bert had seen in her, though wasn't quite sure what Maggie saw in him. He was hardly handsome in the way that Antonio was handsome. But he seemed a kind man; a patient man.

On the plus side, she now knew who had vandalised Mrs Nobbs's garden gnomes. The other parts of the jigsaw fell into place once Maggie told them of how Aubrey had tried to get Bert arrested.

'He pretended we'd had a burglary and blamed it all on Bert. Aubrey collected up a few things and hid them in the shed. Anyone else would have sold them off, but my son merely hid them in the garden shed. Quite pathetic really.'

Honey decided it would do nobody any good to mention Aubrey's part in the desecration of the plastic gnomes. Not to Maggie.

She did mention it on the way back into town. 'So much for men in pointy hats.'

'Mary Jane. A first-class performance,' declared her mother.

Mary Jane beamed.

Gloria Cross sighed. 'But what about poor Rhoda. What will she do with herself?'

Honey had that one worked out. 'Pile on the pounds thanks to Marks and Spencer cream cakes.'

'I think you too are a genius, my darling Gloria,' said Antonio. 'Tell me, would you ever consider moving into Overton House? There are flats available. Some are suitable for two.'

'Well . . .'

Honey cringed. Could she cope with having an Italian stepfather who gushed over every woman he came into contact with including those not far off receiving their centenary birthday card from the Queen?

The question was shoved on hold when her phone rang. It was Doherty.

'No news on Rhino and I've been to see Boris' business partner, John Belper. Care to meet up and discuss ongoing strategy?'

'Professional strategy or pleasure?'

'We can diversify depending on how the mood takes us.'

CHAPTER TWENTY-ONE

The Zodiac Club was the haunt of the hospitality trade and as such only came alive after most tourists were tucked up in bed.

A vodka and tonic appeared under Honey's nose with plenty of ice and lemon. Doherty was drinking Jack Daniel's.

'John Belper and Boris Crook had been in business for some years selling internet advertising, which included mailing lists. They'd gather email addresses, package them, and sell them on to marketing firms. A lucrative business, so he told me.

'With the profits they made they began investing in property and in a rising market did very well. Then the partners had a bit of a falling out and Boris did a midnight flit taking a chunk of the firm's profits with him. He used those profits to purchase the property in Northend.'

'It didn't take long to find him.'

'Apparently not. That's where the water gets muddy. Yes, we know Boris Crook had a deal going with Rhino with regard to collecting discarded paperwork. It seems he had it in mind to set up a new internet venture independently along the same lines as the other. But he couldn't possibly have acquired the money to repay John Belper in such a short period of time. Yet Mr Belper was adamant that's exactly what had been promised. In fact it was Boris Crook who contacted him and told him so. Why would he do that?'

'Unless he found that two million amongst Rhino's stuff, which we know he didn't.'

'So the money came from somewhere else. But where?'

'How about the identity of the victims of the exploding beans?'

'We're doing dental and DNA checks, so hope to have something shortly. Thing is the goons were only the tools; somebody was behind them pulling the strings. They were paid to get rid of the Crooks; paid to find the money. They knew Rhino had it. One of the Crooks had told them. But they didn't know where Rhino was. So they made enquiries of the street people and came across Edna. She knew about the money and some of the places where Rhino was likely to be. They went round a few before going to the field and finding Rhino doing his nursery rhyme bit.'

Honey turned the glass round and round on the bar top as she thought it through. A little alcohol oiled the brain cells; too much would deaden them. At present her intake was just about right.

'The two thugs were working for somebody else. I wonder who?'

'We'll know more when we know who the baked bean baddies were.'

'I wonder where Rhino is now.'

'Gone to ground.'

'Do you think he's safe?'

Doherty regarded his drink with stoical reticence. 'He's streetwise. He knows places the rest of us don't know. Whether anyone is searching for him . . .' He shrugged. 'The media reported the caravan fire and the destroyed 4x4. The registration of the 4x4 was false of course. But we never released details about the money we found.'

'In that case let's hope Rhino's found a safe refuge. But I was wondering . . .'

His eyebrows arched beautifully above deep-set eyes. 'Whether I was still good in bed . . .?'

She grinned. 'No, but it was up there on my list of questions to ask of national and personal importance. I was wondering why they let Rhino stay in the attic at Moss End?'

Doherty shook his head. 'I don't think he was staying there. I think they were keeping him there. They wanted to get away. The idea was to keep him there until they'd made a clean getaway. It was Rhino who had given them the key . . .' He rubbed at his chin, stubble rasping against his fingers.

Honey twirled the glass and set the ice cubes clinking.

'And Rhino wouldn't have minded being kept there. Besides three meals and an en suite bathroom, it had a television set.'

'It was still on when Scene of Crimes went in. I've had somebody give those urns a going over. We managed to get them transported to Manvers Street. We found two holes that weren't holes; set into one of the dancing figures. You wouldn't have noticed them. They looked like eyes. And guess what?'

'A secret compartment. The money was hidden in there. So where did it come from?'

'Dishonest sources. My thinking is that Rhino mentioned the key when he was doing his deals with Crook. Crook listened to Rhino's story of how he came across it. At the same time he was interested in a newspaper Rhino gave him. Do you remember?'

Honey nodded. 'So?'

'Something in that newspaper triggered off something about the key. Plus the auction catalogue. A nice shiny picture of the urns inside it. I reckon Boris Crook had seen those urns before. I reckon he put two and two together. He was a colonial.'

Honey nodded. 'So I understand.'

'From South Africa. He did something with conveyor belts. Travelled all over.'

Honey pouted. Selling conveyor belts all over Africa sounded a pretty boring pastime. But then, Boris Crook hadn't looked the sort to climb Kilimanjaro or paddle his own canoe up the Zambesi — or was it down the Zambesi?

'What are you thinking?' she asked.

Doherty looked down into his drink and shook his head. 'I don't know. That's the bloody trouble. I just don't know.'

'We should have quizzed Rhino more at the hospital. He might have given us a lead without even knowing it.'

Doherty eyed her accusingly. 'Well if you hadn't been hogging him with all that quiz stuff . . . The man was obsessed with general knowledge.'

'Which means he can read and write and what's more, retain information. His trolley was full of old newspapers and magazines that day I met him outside Manvers Street. He told me himself that he was a mine of information and read a lot of what he toted around. Even I referred to it as a wandering library and he agreed with me. What if he'd read something and mentioned reading it to the Crooks?'

'So what was it?'

Honey sucked in her lips as she thought about it. 'Do you still have the supermarket trolley Rhino handed over to Edna?'

'It was hardly priority on our victims' effects list, but I'll see what I can do.'

'He might be lying about them telling him to take the bag and meet them at the station.'

'Probably not. I know I'm a cop and we tend to believe the worst of people, but Rhino strikes me as relatively honest.'

'That's big of you.'

He eyed her. 'Thank you.'

'I think we're agreed that their night time visitors would go after Rhino once they'd told them he had the money. Two million pounds is nothing compared to two lives, even if it means running a guest house for the rest of your days.'

'But they were wrong. They were both killed and . . .'

'Thrown off the roof and bull's eye — straight into those hideous Greek-style urns.'

'Back to the urns again.'

'It's always back to the urns. Can we change the subject?'

'OK.' Honey told him about Rhoda and the missing husband.

'Are you going to claim the five thousand pounds?'

Honey shook her head. 'And neither is my mother. She's suddenly finding it all very romantic. The Italian warden at Overton House has got a lot to do with that. He's got white hair, brown eyes, and a Mediterranean complexion. Heads turn when he passes and he knows how to charm a woman.'

'And has he charmed you?'

'I'm not into smooth men. I like them a bit rough around the edges.'

'Is that what I am? Rough around the edges?'

'Would you prefer to be Prince Charming and have women falling at your feet?'

'No,' he quipped. 'I'd prefer you falling into my bed.'

That night she made an excuse not to go home and slept at Doherty's. In the middle of the night she sat bolt upright after a dream, staring into the darkness of the room as though there was something to see.

'What's up? You OK?' Doherty sounded groggy but concerned.

'I had a dream.'

'A nightmare?'

'No. Just a dream. It was about the urns.'

'Shit!'

Doherty crashed back upon his pillow, one arm across his face.

'I suppose you want to tell me about it,' he said, forcing himself to push his grogginess aside.

'I saw Boris and Doris upside down in those urns but they weren't dead. They were alive and looking for something.'

'What? Worms? Daffodil bulbs?' He stopped making fun and sat up. 'Money?'

When she looked at him there was just enough light coming in from the street outside to see the expression on his face.

'If we're to find out where the money came from, we need to find out more about those urns.'

'Bonhams are checking. How about I start with Alistair and then on to Miss Porter? Mrs Hicks will have a forwarding address.'

She lay back down, Doherty's arm behind her neck.

'Did you see the naughty figures parading around those urns?'

Honey smiled in the darkness. 'Yes. But I didn't know you did.'

'I wouldn't have thought some of those positions were possible.'

'Well, you know what they say. You don't know until you try.'

CHAPTER TWENTY-TWO

Miss Ginny Porter was an energetic soul with iron-grey hair and a soul-searching face in that she had a very direct way of looking at you. She looked the sort who had never blushed in her life and never balked from asking an awkward question.

She was wearing jeans and a navy-blue jersey sporting an RNLI motif on the left breast. A green and blue neckerchief was clasped at the throat with a scarf clasp that sparkled as though it were set with diamonds and emeralds, though in reality it had to be made of paste.

'It's a lovely bungalow,' said Honey admiring the patch of well-kept garden outside the window. 'And you're on a bus route.'

'Beats being in town,' said Miss Porter as they followed her into the kitchen. 'I wouldn't have a garden in town. I'd have to live in one of those bloody awful retirement flats along with a lot of old crocks. Not for me. Shared enough billets when I was in the Navy.'

'You were a WREN?' asked Honey, referring to the women's branch of the Royal Navy.

'Oh yes. Then when the old-style Navy gave way to the new, I resigned. Luckily my father had left me quite a packet. The title went to my brother. He's an earl. I'm plain old Miss

Porter, but you can call me Ginny. No point in standing on ceremony on this ship.'

The kitchen she led them into was modern and bright with a southerly aspect over fields and the weir on the River Avon at Saltford. It smelled of home cooking in a gentle way; fresh produce and carefully prepared meals for one. The cupboard doors were white, the worktops black marble. A utensils rack hung over the central island.

A collection of herbs growing in pots were ranged along the kitchen window ledge. One of the pots held a pair of hyacinths, their leaves piercing the earth by about three inches.

Doherty pulled out one of the high stools ranged beneath the black marble work surface for Honey to sit on before pulling one out for himself.

Doherty outlined the investigation and told her about the part her plastic Greek urns had played.

'I suppose you think I have no taste buying such monstrosities!' She laughed and it was obvious she wouldn't have been offended if they'd agreed with her.

Miss Porter continued to talk, her hands stilled in the process of slicing the carrots each time she wished to make a specific point about her leaving Moss End Guest House and moving into a bungalow in what was essentially a suburb rather than city or country.

Honey asked her about the urns. 'I wouldn't have thought they were quite your thing.'

'You're quite right. They were not my thing at all. My own fault really. I should have checked that I'd bid for the right ones, and then to enter "last bid" — well — I really did get egg on my face.' She laughed and shook her head at her own stupidity.

'Was there much interest in the urns from other bidders?' Honey asked.

Miss Porter offered her a piece of fluted carrot which she accepted and munched on contentedly. It was sweet and fresh; probably grown in Miss Porter's own garden.

'Not really. Apparently they were a late addition to the auction. Somebody did come along some months later and ask if I would be interested in selling them, but I told them I couldn't possibly do that. You see, I'd already signed and exchanged contracts for the sale of Moss End and the urns were listed on the inventory. I couldn't possibly break a legal contract, even for the money they offered me.'

'Who was it that offered you the money?'

Carrots finished, Miss Porter began shredding cabbage. 'I never saw them,' she said as she sliced the cabbage head with a heavy, sharp blade. 'Somebody phoned me and said they were willing to buy them. They offered me a few thousand. I told them I very much appreciated their offer, but couldn't possibly oblige. Moss End was sold and the urns were sold with it. If they wished to approach the new buyers, they were welcome to do so.'

* * *

Honey voiced the number one question as they hurtled back along the main A4 into Bath.

'Who was it offered to buy them?'

'And why?' added Doherty.

'Perhaps you need a psychic on the case,' Honey suggested.

'And of course you've got just the person in mind. The answer is no. This is straightforward police work. Besides, the more your American friend is kept off the road, the less likely she is to be arrested for dangerous driving. It's safer for all concerned, including the residents of Bath.'

'But . . .'

'I'm sure Casper would agree with me.'

There was hidden meaning in Doherty's last remark. Honey sat silently letting the grey-looking fields flash past.

Honey gave it one last try. 'She did get it right about the plastic gnomes and Bert Watchpole.'

'*No*. My final word. No Mary Jane. No otherworldly mumbo-jumbo.'

She could read all the signs; the clenched jaw, the hard look in the eyes. Doherty was adamant. The police would not be requesting the skills of a mumbo-jumbo practitioner. But, hey, that didn't mean she couldn't give it a go.

* * *

It was five o'clock, the night had settled in dark, damp, and drizzling with rain.

The whole thing ended up a bit like a family outing; Lindsey wanted to come, Honey's mother wanted to come, and Mary Jane was as restless as a cat about to have kittens. Yes, of course she would do it, and wasn't it mighty fine that her vibes regarding Bert Watchpole had been correct.

Lindsey was bubbling with laughter. 'I can't believe that none of you claimed the reward for finding Mr Watchpole. Five thousand pounds! That would have bought a cruise in the sun, Grandma . . . sorry . . . Gloria.'

'True romance is worth more than five thousand pounds,' snapped Gloria, who was sitting in the front passenger seat beside Mary Jane. Not out of choice, but purely because Honey and Lindsey had leapt into the rear seat like a couple of kangaroos being chased by a pack of dingoes.

On arrival Mary Jane stood outside the metal gate with her eyes closed and her arms held wide. This was her method of picking up whatever vibes there were around the place. It was basically akin to going into a trance, but deep trances were something she tried to avoid. She was getting older and not so good at bouncing back out of them.

'Gloomy old place,' said Gloria, who was not a great one for old places though she made exceptions for Buckingham Palace, Windsor Castle, and Balmoral. If they were good enough for Her Majesty the Queen, they were good enough for her.

Lindsey gave a so-so shake of her head. 'I'm not one for early Georgian myself, but it's not that bad.'

'I feel a door,' said Mary Jane.

Jerked out of their conversation, everyone else looked around them searching for the door.

Honey's mother pulled her pure wool coat around her slim shoulders. 'Well there's a gate in front of us. Might as well go in.'

The gate squealed when she pushed it open.

Mary Jane was still standing with her eyes closed.

Honey caught hold of her arm. 'We're going in, Mary Jane.'

'I'm OK with that.'

The eyes opened and the long arms came down. She halted halfway to the front door and tilted her head back.

'They came down there. Like kids on a slide.' Her head jerked back to normal. 'And ended up in there.' She nodded at each of the urns in turn.

'My,' exclaimed Honey's mother. 'Isn't she brilliant. She knows exactly what happened here.'

Lindsey grinned. 'Don't we all? It was in all the newspapers and on TV.'

Gloria readjusted her handbag and scraped some mud from off the heel of her shoe. 'I don't read newspapers and I avoid watching the news on TV. I don't want to know what's going on in the world.'

Mary Jane remained transfixed. She was eyeing the urns.

'Pretty ugly,' said Lindsey. 'I mean, who in their right mind would have these?'

Honey pointed out that Miss Porter had bought them by mistake.

'In my humble opinion, the owner who put them up for sale should have burned them. They're hardly decorative.'

'They came from a nightclub. Naked dancers used to jump out of them — or something. I don't know the exact details.'

There were moments in Honey's life when sudden inspirations of genius flashed on in her mind like a chain of fairy lights. This was one of them.

'That's it. We don't have the exact details.'

Keen to see Mary Jane do her stuff, the others weren't really listening to what Honey was saying. What was a brilliant take on a murder case compared to a dotty dame from La Jolla?

Gloria peered at the figures on the urns and decided she wasn't seeing enough detail so undid her handbag. A rare thing was about to happen . . . Gloria Cross was about to be seen in public wearing spectacles.

'These figures are doing lewd things,' she said, more with wonder than condemnation.

Lindsey peered closer too. 'They're certainly not authentic, but then they wouldn't be.' She tapped the side of the urn with her knuckle and nodded. 'Plastic. Part of a stage set.'

'In a nightclub,' Honey added. 'We know that much, but not which nightclub, but there are ways . . .'

She sidled off over the rough flagstones of a patio shaped like a half moon. Doherty was on voicemail which meant he was either interviewing somebody, in conference with a senior officer, or having forty winks.

She left a message. 'These urns; where did they come from? Alistair at Bonhams would know this, and do you recall his cousin, the freelance bouncer, mentioning he'd seen them before at a nightclub? Which nightclub? Who owned it? And does it tie in with any piece of news hanging around in Rhino's old trolley, the one he passed to Edna?'

When she came off the phone, Lindsey was peering up into Mary Jane's face.

'I think she's in a trance.'

'That's what she does,' whispered her grandmother. 'Now don't go waking her up. It's dangerous to wake her up before she's ready.'

'How do we know when she's ready?'

'She puts what she's feeling into words. Sometimes it doesn't make sense; well, quite a lot of the time in fact, but it's great fun,' finished Gloria, her gloved hands clasped tightly together in front of her face.

The spectacles, Honey noticed, had gone back into the bag. Her mother hated imperfections.

'Mother,' she stated, 'that pair of spectacles take nothing away from the fact that you're drop dead gorgeous. I'm sure Antonio would be intrigued by them, not put off.'

Gloria sniffed. 'I intend looking drop dead gorgeous whether Antonio approves or not!'

Pushed back firmly into her place, Honey looked at Mary Jane.

'Not much seems to be happening,' whispered Lindsey.

'It takes time to tune in,' Honey replied.

Gloria shushed them. 'She has to concentrate very deeply,' she mouthed silently.

Mary Jane seemed to have gone into a deeper trance than before, her head thrown back, arms fluttering like a butterfly trapped behind a glass screen.

'Can she see through closed eyes?' asked Lindsey.

'No, of course not. She's seeing with her *inner* eye.'

'Her mind,' Honey added, not so sure now that it was a good idea.

Suddenly, Mary Jane began to wail. 'Ohhhh! Ohhhh! Blood. Blood and broomsticks!'

Grandmother, mother and daughter exchanged surprised looks.

Honey shrugged her shoulders. 'I presume she's tuned in to the night of the party. A few witches were there — it was a Hallowe'en party as well as Alison's birthday party. The blood is self-explanatory.'

'Keep your voices down,' whispered Gloria who seemed to be acting as a kind of master — or mistress — of ceremonies.

'Oh, this is terrible,' Mary Habe cried. 'Those poor people. Three men all intent on doing away with them.'

Honey was looking at her watch, distracted, wondering how much rain was going to frizz her hair and trickle down her spine. But the mention of there being three men jolted her back to the present.

Three? But surely there were only two? She told herself that she had only seen two . . . but that didn't mean there wasn't a third. He could have gone round the back in order to block off their escape. She reminded herself that Rhino had exited by the back route. If a third man had been there, Rhino would not have got away.

'Sparklers. Lovely, lovely sparklers. That's what Doris is telling me. It's all about lovely, lovely sparklers. And friends.'

'What . . .?' Honey began but her mother thrust a palm towards her in a stop gesture and went on to ask the question Honey had been about to ask.

'What friends, Mary Jane? What friends?'

'The sparklers. She's telling me that the sparklers are best friends. Oh dear, oh dear, oh dear. It's all over.'

Mary Jane blinked herself back into reality.

'Did I come up with anything useful?'

'Could be,' said Honey, 'though I don't know of anyone named Sparkler being attached to the case.'

'Hannah! You really are dim at times! Sparklers are diamonds. Diamonds are a girl's best friend.'

Honey slapped her hand on her forehead. 'Of course, of course, of course!'

She was about to phone Doherty again stopped herself. He'd been downright cynical about using Mary Jane's talents. But what was the next best thing to do? She decided it was to ask the other partygoers if they'd seen anything suspicious — a late arrival who just might have been in the company of two walking bed sheets.

There was the sudden sound of squealing metal behind them and all eyes turned to the gate.

'Oh. I wondered who it was,' the arrival said, addressing Honey. 'Are you all policemen?'

'No, Miss Hicks,' said Honey, addressing the older woman. 'We're not. We've been conducting a little experiment. Mary Jane here is a professor of the paranormal, a psychic in fact. She's helping with enquiries.'

'How very interesting.'

Mrs Hicks leaned more heavily on her stick, her cat circling her legs until it espied Mary Jane. Its orange eyes stared at her intently and it made a sound, something between a meow and a purr.

Miss Hicks looked down at the cat, then without moving her head looked up at Mary Jane. For one instant Honey was sure that the old lady's eyes were as orange as those of the cat. At the same time something seemed to illuminate Mary Jane's face, as though suddenly she'd been picked out by a spotlight.

A slow smile spread across Mrs Hicks' lips. 'A real one. Well, that makes a nice change to these charlatans that ask leading questions and appear on my television set nowadays. Would you like to come in for a cup of tea?'

The invitation was unanimously accepted.

Honey was obliged to make her apologies. 'I just have a couple of phone calls to make and I'll be right with you.'

The metal gate swung slowly shut on its spring leaving Honey with only her phone for company. Streetlights shone on the other side of the wall surrounding the house. All was total darkness on the inside of the wall and darker still in the house behind her.

The drizzle was unrelenting so she took shelter in the porch, cloistered like a sentry between the giant urns.

She flicked to Doherty's number. Again it went straight to voicemail. Where was the man?

She knew the next step should be to ask those at the party whether they'd seen a third man. With that in mind she phoned Alison's landline number. Four or five rings and the phone was picked up but it wasn't Alison. It was coochie coo lover boy!

'Hi, Maurice. It's Honey Driver. Is Alison there?'

'Honey! Nice to hear from you. I'm afraid Alison is in the shower. We're going out to dinner. Can I get her to phone you back?'

'Well, seeing as you were also at her party, perhaps you can help. You see it's been brought to my attention that there could have been a third man involved in the murder of Mr and Mrs Crook and that it has something to do with diamonds being exchanged for a lot of money. Two million in fact. I was wondering if you or Alison had seen any suspicious characters who shouldn't have been there.'

'Good grief. Do the police know about this?'

'Not yet. I won't go into detail, but they wouldn't necessarily respect my source.'

She could have told him that Rhino had said there were only two men, but she didn't. He'd think she was mad if she told him that it was a psychic who had insisted there were three and that diamonds were involved. *Let sleeping dogs lie*, she said to herself. Explain the complexities of the investigation when it's all done and dusted — and when Doherty had calmed down once he'd found out about Mary Jane's involvement.

Maurice was chewing things over. 'I see,' he said slowly. 'Now let me think . . . did I see anyone who looked as though they shouldn't be there? It is possible I might not have noticed seeing as everyone was in costume . . .'

Honey held her breath. A hit on the first phone call. How great would that be?

'Anything at all.'

'My memory. It is not what it was,' said Maurice, his South African accent more noticeable as his speed of delivery increased. 'I'm trying to visualise that place.'

'I can understand that. I'm looking up at the outside of it now and trying to recall who exactly was at the party whose face I didn't see.'

'Like Spiderman and the Mummy?'

'Exactly like that, though those individuals have checked out.'

'And you're there now?'

'I am. And it's dark, cold, and raining.'

'Look, I am more than willing to help you, but perhaps my memory needs a nudge. How about I meet you there? It might help. I'll drag Alison along too. We can have supper afterwards.'

'She won't mind coming out here?'

Maurice laughed. 'Of course not. You know Alison. She'll want to be in on the action.'

The light drizzle was turning into a thick mist. The orange gleam of the streetlights was muted as though a muslin veil had been thrown over them.

Honey shivered and tossed up whether to stay put or sneak back across the road for a hot cuppa. And a chocolate biscuit. Miss Hicks looked the sort to offer chocolate biscuits to visitors.

A mental toss of a coin, and Honey trotted across the road.

A fire was glowing behind the old-fashioned glass of the Parkray.

Her mother seemed very disappointed at her arrival. 'We were holding hands and trying to conjure up the murder victims so they could tell us who killed them, but you came banging at the door and spoilt it.'

'There's nothing like being made to feel welcome,' murmured Honey.

Mrs Hicks handed her a cup of tea. 'Never you mind. Have a chocolate digestive. There's milk and dark.'

Am I psychic or what, thought Honey, taking two biscuits.

The orange-eyed cat purred from Mary Jane's lap. Lindsey eyed her mother over her teacup.

'Is all well on the crime liaison front?'

'I think we're getting there,' Honey exclaimed with satisfaction. 'But I do have to go back over there once I've drunk this tea. I really needed something to warm me up. Thank you,' she added on being handed her third chocolate biscuit.

'I'm presuming you're meeting your policeman friend,' said her mother. She scraped a crumb from the corner of her mouth while awaiting a reply.

'No. I'm meeting Alison and Maurice. I asked Maurice whether he'd seen anyone at the party who shouldn't be there. If Mary Jane's information is correct, then there was a third man implicated in the murder. He's still out there.

Still dangerous. I figured that seeing as I saw two of the killers, perhaps one of the other guests may have seen the third. Hence my phone call to Alison, the birthday girl. Maurice, her latest man friend, I can hardly call him boy, arranged the party for her. We thought it would be a good idea for them to come out in the hope it jogs their memory.'

The tea and biscuits were consumed over an analysis of Mary Jane's trance and why it worked sometimes and not others.

Mrs Hicks informed them that she rarely went into a trance state herself; she just got feelings, like instincts, and followed them up.

'And you're a white witch?' Gloria asked her.

Mrs Hicks poured herself another cup of tea. 'Of course. Deal in bad spells and they come back to deal with you. Anyone else for tea?'

The sentry-box shelter outside the front door of Moss End Guest House did nothing to protect Honey from the chilly mist that had fallen on the village. The mist was turning into a fog which made the streetlamps dotted through the village look mysterious and magical. Honey felt the cat brush against her ankles on its way past. The night was cold. Only a cat would want to go out in this weather. A secretive night. A secretive animal.

The sound of the odd passing car was almost muted, the cars driving slowly, the driver peering over the wheel, stomach taut with nerves as he or she searched for the taillights of the car in front.

If she'd been the nervous sort, she might have run back over the road to warmth, friendliness, and more chocolate biscuits.

But you're not nervous, so you're staying put come hell or high water.

* * *

Doherty was down in the darker recesses of the police station, the place where they stored larger pieces of evidence.

They'd found the secure cap that the two-pronged key fitted. They'd also found out that the urns had come from a London nightclub — called Seraphina — just as Alistair's cousin had said. Following investigations, a report had been emailed through. The club's owners had been found dead under suspicious circumstances. Ownership had passed to a 'sleeping partner' who had proceeded to sell everything off. The sleeping partner had flown in and out of the country on business. The nature of business was none too clear, though Scotland Yard had their suspicions.

'We think he was smuggling diamonds, but we've got no proof. We did a search of the premises but didn't find anything.'

Doherty took a flashlight from the workbench.

'Saucy stuff,' laughed one of his team. 'Take a look at the size of some of the assets on these geezers.'

Doherty focused the beam on the naked figures, the light making them look as though they were dancing. One of the figures looked as though it was dancing more vigorously than the others.

Why that particular figure?

He trailed the beam back over the figure of a centaur. A well-endowed centaur. There was something about the centaur that wasn't quite right and his manhood had nothing to do with it.

It was his tail: thick, bushy, and round like a table tennis bat. The centaur was also the biggest figure in this line of the frieze. All the other rows were smaller. He also seemed be painted more heavily, in a blacker paint than the rest of the figures.

He traced the outline of the centaur — even the over-large manhood. Sensing it gave in to pressure, he pressed the oddly shaped tail more firmly. Something clicked.

Les Cutler, his fellow team member, came and looked over his shoulder.

'A compartment! Well, will you look at that!'

Doherty turned off the flash. 'So there it is; one urn contained a locked compartment big enough to hold a bag of money. This urn had a smaller aperture; big enough to smuggle diamonds. Get fingerprints here. Now. These urns came in from abroad and the diamonds came in with them. When the diamonds were sold, the other urn was used to hide the money in. Unfortunately a mistake was made when it came to selling them. Whoever hid the money didn't move quick enough. They were sold before he could retrieve it.'

* * *

Honey stirred from the corner of the porch. She listened intently, willing a car to pull up outside the house, then she could get this over and get into the warm.

She snuggled back into her corner and when she looked up she saw she had company.

'Maurice! Where did you come from? I didn't hear the gate squeak. It usually makes such a . . .'

'I wanted to surprise you. I came up through the car park.'

He spoke quietly, not nearly as brusque as he usually was.

She thought about the car she'd heard earlier. It had to have been Maurice's car. A feeling of unease crept up her spine, reminding her of the time a boy named Darren Hughes had slid an ice cube down her back years ago. Even he wouldn't have managed to make her shiver so much as she shivered now.

'Where's Alison? I thought she was coming with you.'

She tried to sound light-hearted as though nothing was amiss when all her faculties were warning her that something most definitely was.

'Alison won't be coming. She's indisposed. She'll be all right though. Just a little something in the fizzy drink she's so fond of.' He shook his head. 'Women and champagne. Can't understand it myself.'

'I prefer red wine,' Honey blurted, as though keeping things light would keep him at bay. Deep down she knew it would not. Maurice was here on a mission. Things began to add up. Diamonds. South Africa. Smuggling. The two urns and the nightclub in London.

She'd trod on his toes, upset his apple cart, put her nose into things she had no business knowing about. And now, grim-faced, he was standing between her and the gate. Doing a runner was out of the question.

Although doing a great imitation of a half set blanc-mange, she put a brave face on it.

'Are you going to explain to me what you were involved in?'

'No. You're not on my need-to-know list.'

Nor on your need to live list, Honey thought. Suddenly an awesome shiver threatened to bring on convulsions. Not that she'd ever had convulsions, but if one did come on, it might get her out of here — or make his job of killing her easier.

'Right! I'm going to scream.'

He clamped a hand firmly around her mouth. 'No you're not. You're going to die.'

CHAPTER TWENTY-THREE

The tea party across the way was just about at an end when a phone began to ring.

All three women looked for it, diving into bags and, in Mrs Hicks's case, looking behind the clock, in drawers and beneath a knitted cat.

It was Lindsey who traced the source. 'My mother's left her bag behind.'

She took out the phone and clicked receive call. 'Hey. Doherty. What gives?'

Mary Jane stared at the phone Lindsey was using. 'I've got a funny feeling.'

'So have I,' echoed Mrs Hicks, who had insisted they call her Olivia. 'It's not my real name, it's just a name I like,' she had said.

'OK. Get here quick as you can.' Lindsey ended the call.

All three women were looking at Lindsey. Her face had gone pale, her bottom lip hanging slightly as though she didn't know quite what to say.

'Tell it as it is,' said Mary Jane.

Her grandmother was all eyes.

'That was Detective Chief Inspector Doherty. There's been a development. Bonhams confirmed where those urns came from. Some special surveillance department at Scotland Yard confirmed that they were sold with the rest of the contents of a London club that was under surveillance. They also said that the urns had come in from South Africa.'

'I knew it!' Gloria Cross sprang to her feet. 'A lot of diamonds come from South Africa.'

Lindsey surveyed all of them with wide frightened eyes. 'So does Maurice Hoffman, the man my mother has arranged to meet.'

Gloria Cross sprang immediately into action. 'Where's my coat? Does anyone have a gun?'

Lindsey looked horrified. 'Grandma! You don't know how to use a gun.'

'When my daughter's in danger, I can do anything. I'll just point it and fire.'

'I've got this.' Mrs Hicks — Olivia — grabbed her walking stick.

'Are we all in on this?' Lindsey asked.

'One for all and all for one,' shouted Mary Jane. 'Just you wait till you see what I've got in my car.'

The three septuagenarians and the youthful Lindsey Driver, medieval historian and unofficial guardian to a disorganised mother, trooped out of the door.

* * *

Honey was cold. She didn't know where Maurice had got the key to the back door, but it explained a lot of things. Her thoughts went back to Alison's party. A group of guests had trooped up the pub to purchase some much-needed drink. Maurice had ostensibly gone with them, or at least he said he had. But one of the others who went reckoned he'd got lost on route.

'It's a straight walk but old Maurice got waylaid. Had a leak did you, old chap?'

Maurice had laughed the joke off and said that the cold weather affected his waterworks. He preferred the sunshine of South Africa.

'Up you go,' he said now, pushing her up the stairs, pointing the muzzle of a gun into the small of her back.

'I suppose that's unregistered.'

'No, but that doesn't prevent it from shooting live bullets.'

'Someone will hear it.'

'I doubt that very much.'

He marched her up the first flight of stairs then the second up to the attic bedrooms. They went up in darkness. Honey wondered at her chances of flicking on a light switch. A sudden light in a darkened house would shine out like the beam from a sea bound lighthouse. Lindsey and the others were only across the road and if they looked up from their tea and tittle tattle long enough, they might see it. *Might*. What were the chances of changing might to must?

Making a brave stand and living a bit longer fought an ongoing battle for a while. Living a bit longer finally won out — at least for the time being.

Three stairs down from the top landing she was almost sure she heard the meow of a cat. Hopefully it was a lucky black cat and of immense proportions; big enough to eat murderous Maurice before he murdered her.

The attic rooms were eerie and cold. A draught limbo danced through the ill-fitting windows. Honey shivered.

Light from the street lamp outside formed a chequerboard effect of alternate orange and black. It was only barely enough to see by, but enough to see that not much had changed since she'd last been here. The police tape was still stretched across the door to each room. Rhino's bedding was gone, courtesy of the forensic boys, and something scurried and scratched behind the skirting boards.

She mused as to whether Rhino actually saw the vermin that was doing the scratching; probably appreciated the company.

She tripped when Maurice pushed her roughly into the room that had not been occupied by Rhino.

'Steady. Wouldn't want you to break your neck accidentally. If a job's worth doing, it's worth doing well.'

She'd read somewhere how fear can hone your senses and make you superhuman. Whoever had penned that particular gem of wisdom hadn't been close to being thrown out of a window.

Honey stared at the four small panes that made up the whole; like the kind of a window in a house a child might draw. She knew it wasn't a sash but pivoted on fixings embedded into the wooden frame. Boris and Doris had been shoved out through the lower aperture.

'I have to point out I could do with losing a few more pounds. That's a pretty small opening.'

Maurice laughed. 'Honey, I really love your sense of humour. Alison said you'd always been funny. She reckoned it made up for your taste in clothes and complete absence of beauty regime. And fat people are always funny. That's what she said.'

'So nice to have friends like her.'

Honey made an instant promise to herself that if she ever got out of this, she was going to tell Alison exactly what she thought of her dated clothes and plastic tits.

'Don't worry,' said Maurice. 'I'm not so stupid as to shove you out there. I don't have a point to make, just tracks to cover.'

'Well that's a relief. I can't stand heights.'

He laughed again, one hand clasping his stomach, the other holding the gun. 'You're absolutely killing me.'

'So glad I can keep you laughing till the very end.'

'Oh, but you're a dry one. Alison was right about that, too.'

'Are you really serious about Alison?'

He took out a man size cotton handkerchief and mopped at his streaming eyes.

'What a bloody stupid question at a time like this. Most people go with "can I make a last request".'

Honey shrugged, feigning nonchalance. 'Just asking.'

'Well seeing as you've asked I may as well answer. It depends whether I still have a use for her. She's a good alibi one way and another.'

'Marriage?'

He gave her a look. 'That's not funny. That's silly.'

There were plenty of times in her life when Honey had needed to think on her feet. Like the time she'd been trying to coax a cat out of a tree then saw the reason why the cat had taken shelter up there in the first place.

A Rottweiler lurking beneath the tree had switched his attention to her, teeth bared, jowls slobbering with the need to bite something.

The cat had looked pretty surprised to see her shin up that tree and sit on the same branch. The fire brigade had been surprised too — and amused.

However, this particular scenario with Maurice ranked high above the encounter with the Rottweiler; in fact it outranked every other scrape she'd ever got into.

She played the card that might at least get her behind a lockable door.

'I need the bathroom.'

'No point.'

'I may wet my pants.'

'OK. You pee, I'll stand and watch.'

Honey wrinkled her nose. 'That's gross.'

'It works for me. The bathroom has a bolt on the back. I would not want you sliding it across. Beating it down would waste valuable time.'

Using the bathroom had been her number one card. What next? The perpetrators of crime liked to boast, Doherty had told her. She'd been snuggled up to his naked torso at the time. The possibility that she might never snuggle up to him again sent a jolt through her body.

Honey, if you want another of those flesh touching moments, get in there and appeal to his lousy, rotten, murderous ego.

'Well, I can see you're on the ball,' she said brightly.

Maurice took time out from trying to lift the wooden cover of the water tank.

'I need a hand with this. Get on the other end of it. And don't try anything.' The gun waggled at her.

'I can see you're serious.'

She got on the other end of the wooden cover. She couldn't see the water within, but she could smell it; slightly metallic because it hadn't been used of late. Hanging baskets only required water during dry months.

Use every opportunity to get under his skin. Ask questions. Get to know him.

'Can I ask you something?' The first thought that entered her mind was to ask him why they were removing the lid of the tank. No point. She already knew the answer — or thought she did. Boris and Doris had had their heads bashed against the wall of the water tank before being thrown out of the window. Unlike the old lath and plaster walls of the attic, the lead lining of the tank was unyielding. Easy to smash a skull against it. Try it against the bedroom wall and the old plaster would cave in before her skull did.

Musing on these profound and less than happy thoughts, Honey helped him lift the lid. Whatever wood had been used it was damned heavy. There were nails all around its edges proving that at one time it had been fixed down.

She used both hands, he used one. She thought about dropping it. The thought of it landing on his toes and the gun going off made her change her mind.

'Why did the men wearing bed sheets tip the victims into the urns?'

They heaved the lid on its end so it rested against the wall.

'They were stupid. They were making a point.'

'By dropping them into the urns? What's the significance in that?'

He sighed, frustrated. 'I already told you. They were stupid. They wanted to make a point. Now I am making a point. Strip.'

'What?'

'Strip off your clothes.'

'I'll catch my death of cold!'

'That's exactly the point. You will die quicker without any clothes on.'

'You're going to throw me out of the window with nothing on?'

'No. That will be far too messy and noticeable. I am going to immerse you in one of these old water tanks. Nobody will find you for months, at least not until the house is sold or a possible purchaser notices the smell of your decaying body.'

'Nice scenario,' she managed to quip, despite her racing heart.

He pointed the gun. 'Strip.'

Honey unzipped her padded jacket and laid it to one side. Her hands shook as she peeled off her sweater, then her skirt. Goose pimples erupted where she'd never thought them likely to exist. Even her teeth started chattering.

Keep your head warm and your body stays warmer longer. She kept her hat on. It was hardly the most flattering of hats, being woollen, of blue and grey Sinclair and vaguely resembling a tea cosy. Maurice must have been clued up on survival tactics too. He reached out and snatched her woollen hat.

'Hey, that has sentimental value. My mother knitted it for me and you can't believe that it'll keep me from freezing to death all by itself!'

Gloria Cross had never knitted a thing in her life. But these were desperate times.

'You've got it all wrong.' Maurice shook his head. 'You look stupid wearing a hat and your underwear. Your boots too. Take them off. And your tights.'

'My tights? Excuse me, but here again I don't think they're likely to make much difference,' she said, disliking the prospect of standing in just her underwear.

'I know that. It's just that I dislike tights. Alison only wears stockings. They are sexier. I might as well enjoy the view,' he leered.

Much as she disliked pandering to him, taking things slowly might keep her alive a bit longer — long enough for Lindsey and the others to come looking for her.

Slowly, very slowly she pulled her tights down over one leg at a time. OK, they weren't stockings, but she did her level best.

The house had been left unheated and it was November. Even the most seasoned exotic dancer would have had trouble holding a smile let alone a sexy pose.

Finally the tights were on the floor along with everything else.

Aware that Maurice's eyes were raking her from head to toes — loitering on the in between bits, she hugged herself.

Please, she thought inwardly. *Not the underclothes!*

Her bra was not the prettiest one she owned, but it was the most comfortable. Ditto the pants.

He did a twirling motion with the gun. 'Turn round.'

A sinking feeling, as though she'd swallowed a pound of pig iron, settled in Honey's stomach. This was it. He was going to knock her on the back of the head and then shove her in the water tank.

'Those pants are hideous. Alison wears thongs. Mostly lace thongs. They divide the buttocks most attractively.'

She couldn't help snorting. 'They're like dental floss. Yuk. Very uncomfortable.'

'Alison was right. You don't do yourself any favours. What have you got against lace and half cups?'

Honey ignored his question. A soft shape glided across the floor behind Maurice. He didn't see it, but Honey had.

Peregrine, Mrs Hicks' cat, and where the cat was Mrs Hicks wasn't far behind.

The mouse that had been scratching behind the wall suddenly made a run for it — straight between Maurice's legs.

The cat shot through them too. Totally unprepared, Maurice staggered, reached out with the hand that held the gun to steady himself. The back of his hand was grazed by a nail sticking out from the upended wooden lid.

'Fuck!'

He staggered backwards. The gun fell with a soft plop into the water tank.

Honey darted for the stairs, but Maurice was too quick. A pair of strong arms wrapped around her.

'No you don't! Your bath awaits you!'

Although she struggled, he picked her up and dropped her into the tank, holding her in with one hand. With his free hand he heaved the lid on top of her, stooping only to grab the cat and throw that in too.

The cold was intense. Mind-numbing. Peregrine, as frightened as she was, lay on her chest. Honey's chin was under water. She could feel the cat's claws digging into her bra. Whatever she did she had to calm the poor creature or she'd be scratched to death.

Through chattering teeth she spoke to him, telling him how clever he was and she knew Mrs Hicks would find them.

She said all this in a hushed voice, lying there in the darkness, feeling her body slowly lapsing into hypothermia. The water reverberated to the sound of Maurice hammering each nail home with nothing more than the heel of his hand.

She was in a water-filled coffin. Freezing water and the possibility of being clawed to death; Honey's teeth chattered. Despite the darkness she forced herself to keep her eyes open. The cat's furry coat helped. As long as she kept her back arched he wasn't knee-high in water. Bless him, he even settled down and began to purr. Did he know something she didn't?

CHAPTER TWENTY-FOUR

Olivia Hicks was careful not to let the gate slam. She held a finger to her pursed lips.

'We need a pincer movement,' Mary Jane whispered, the hefty weight of a tyre iron lying over one shoulder.

Gloria Cross, who had been testing the weight of her handbag by swinging it around her head, agreed with her.

'You go round the back that way,' she barked. Gloria pointed at the gap between the main building and the coach house. 'Lindsey, you go around that way.'

She directed her granddaughter in the other direction, to a set of steps, the top treads shrouded in mist.

Surprised at her grandmother's leadership skills, Lindsey sprang to it, disappearing into the darkness at the top of the steps, Mary Jane similarly hidden between the alleyway between the two buildings.

Mrs Hicks was standing silently, her eyes closed and both hands resting on her walking stick.

Gloria touched her shoulder. 'What do you know, dear?'

Olivia's eyes flicked open. 'He'll come through there.'

She pointed to the patch of absolute blackness Mary Jane had disappeared into.

Honey's mother winced. 'Is Mary Jane in danger from this Maurice person?'

'I don't think so. Mary Jane has a strong aura.'

'And a hefty tyre iron,' murmured Honey's mother.

The two elderly women positioned themselves at the end of the alley. The only light came via the streetlamp out in the street behind them.

Olivia explained quietly that the alley led to the back of the house and garden. 'Beyond that are fields.'

'So whoever comes out of the house has to come this way.'

'That's right.'

Gloria took a deep breath. 'And we'll be ready for whoever it is.'

* * *

Once the brief light from the street was behind her, Lindsey felt her way along the end wall of the house in total darkness. The earth was soft beneath her feet.

Passing around the rear corner of the house, the ground became more solid.

The house loomed dark and brooding between her and the road. Something screeched in the field to the rear of the garden.

Her attention was drawn to a sudden thud somewhere along the back wall of the house. A door! Her guess was confirmed when she heard the sound of feet walking over gravel.

Her mother?

Just as she was about to shout out, she felt a hand on her shoulder. A soft voice whispered, 'No.'

She nodded to whoever it was then thought better of it. If she couldn't see them, they couldn't see her. She reached to pat the hand resting on her shoulder and felt . . . nothing.

* * *

At the other end of the garden, Mary Jane was looking up at the stars. The mist had lifted, though she guessed only temporarily. Beyond the garden she could see the branches of denuded trees seeming to scratch the sky.

She was feeling uneasy about her friend; she wasn't yet in the spirit world, but if they didn't find her shortly she would be.

The mist whirled in again, obscuring the fields and the trees.

Going into trances could sometimes be downright inconvenient. Her concern for Honey was bringing on a trance; not that they weren't useful.

She closed her eyes. The wall of the old coach house was cold but was just about the only thing holding her upright. If she could just concentrate . . .

In that instant, Maurice Hoffman stole past her. Neither saw the other in the darkness. Both were absorbed in the things they did best; Mary Jane with the paranormal, Maurice Hoffman with murder.

The streetlamp beyond the wall lightened the darkness at the front of the house. Mary Jane eased herself away from the wall. Maurice Hoffman was silhouetted against the light from the street.

Unaware that he'd been seen, Maurice smiled with satisfaction. He'd parked his car some distance away, back towards the main A4 road.

He couldn't help his grin. What a night! Honey Driver had fallen for his invitation to meet without a second thought. How stupid was that? And what fun he'd had, watching her undress, admiring her body while pretending that he didn't think much of it. The truth was that she was more to his taste than airhead Alison. Still, Alison was alive and Honey Driver would soon be a deep frozen ice lolly.

Hands shoved in his pockets, head down, it came as something of a surprise when he looked up to see two women ahead of him. One was leaning on a stick, the other had fluffy hair and was wrapped up in fur. She was swinging what looked like a handbag around her head.

'Isn't it a little dark and cold for you ladies to be out and about?' he said, his charm dripping off his tongue like honey from the comb. He thought of the cat he'd thrown in on top of Honey. 'Have you lost something?'

'You could say that.' It was the one with the fluffy hair who spoke. She sounded pissed off.

'If it's a cat you're looking for, I nearly tripped over one back there.'

He jerked a thumb at a spot over his shoulder.

The other woman lifted her head. Her voice carried like ice.

'Cats are aloof from humankind. They act on their instincts but communicate on a different spectral plain.'

He sniggered. 'I don't have a bloody clue what you're talking about. Now out of my way. I've got a plane to catch.'

The woman leaned on her cane as though it were a third leg, her head jutting forward.

'You're not going anywhere, Maurice Hoffman. We know what you've done. And we are going to detain you until the police arrive.'

He burst out laughing. 'You and Grandma Fluff here? I don't think so. You'll need an army of grannies to stop me, lady. Now, out of my way.' He paused for effect; his voice flooded with menace. 'Before I get nasty.'

'What have you done with my daughter?'

Gloria was quivering from her beautifully styled hair to neatly varnished toes, but she was on the attack.

'I don't know what you're talking about.'

'Oh yes you do. And you're not going anywhere. The police will be here shortly. They know about the diamonds. They know about the money you got paid for smuggling them and the money that was stolen from your business partners. We know everything.'

Maurice stiffened.

'You're shivering, Granny. Why don't you get out of my way and go home and warm your toes in front of the fire? Before I do something I might regret.'

'I'm not shivering,' Gloria snapped. 'I'm quivering. With anger. If you've harmed my daughter . . .'

'Let me pass.'

Gloria swung her handbag around her head like an old-time knight with a spiked ball on a chain. She'd read her fill of medieval romance so figured she knew what to do.

'No.' Her shout echoed in the thickening fog. Her body swung on her slender legs as she twirled the bag. Her legs weren't quite what they used to be, they wouldn't stand the stress of running a marathon.

'You shall not pass,' proclaimed Mrs Hicks who was standing right behind her, walking stick raised.

Muttering an expletive that ended in 'off', Maurice Hoffman swivelled round and marched down the path that led to the small car park at the end of the building. He'd chosen this route on arrival, only too aware of the squeaky gate.

Then the sound of police sirens interrupted the quiet night, distant but getting closer.

A younger figure stepped into the car park entrance, a far wider entrance than the one Gloria and Olivia were guarding.

'You're not coming through here either until you tell me where my mother is.'

Lindsey was holding a garden spade above her head.

'I could kill you all,' Maurice growled, turning to face them, though not yet cornered.

He began backing up the way he'd come. The only hope of escape he had was to get through the hedge at the back of the property and take off over the fields.

With this in mind, he began to run backwards into the darkness, his eyes still on them just in case one of the women was fit enough to follow.

'I'll kill all of you,' he shouted. Then he was gone, enveloped in darkness.

Suddenly there was a thud. Then there was a groan.

Heart beating with excitement, Lindsey got out her phone. Her fingers felt like thumbs, but eventually she found the button that switched on the LED torch.

Maurice Hoffman was flat out, unconscious on the ground. A tall figure brandishing a tyre iron stood over him.

'Have I killed him?' Mary Jane sounded a little surprised, though not at all regretful.

Lindsey looked down at him. Her grandmother and Mrs Hicks joined her.

'He deserves to be dead,' said Mrs Hicks.

'I don't think he is,' said Gloria, looking disappointed.

Mrs Hicks turned her head slowly then peered along the dark gap between the two buildings. 'Your granddaughter's vanished.'

Honey's mother shook her head. 'Shame I didn't get to hit him with my handbag. Mrs Thatcher used to do that you know; hit the members of her cabinet with her handbag if she thought they weren't paying attention. I should think it felt most rewarding. Shame I couldn't try it.'

The sound of police sirens preceded the flashing of blue lights and a breathless and worried-looking Doherty came racing through into the car park and up the steps.

He eyed the flat-out figure of Maurice Hoffman then each of the three women.

'I take it Honey is involved in this somewhere. Where is she?'

'In there. Lindsey's gone in to find her.'

He nodded in the sage, serious way he had when he was having trouble digesting a given situation.

'That's OK. But this isn't.' He nodded down at the unconscious Maurice. 'What happened to him and who did it?'

'Granny power,' said Mrs Hicks. 'He told us to go warm our tootsies in front of the fire and to mind our own business. That's the trouble with the young nowadays; no respect. We took umbrage.'

Doherty looked stunned. He shook his head in despair. 'Umbrage is understandable. Unconscious takes more explaining. How did he get to be unconscious?'

Mary Jane raised her arm to reveal her weapon of choice. 'It was dark. He ran into my tyre iron.'

Doherty opened his mouth to say something, but Mrs Hicks had a knack for picking up angry vibes. She could also lay on the defenceless little old lady bit when she needed to.

'Can somebody help me look for my cat? Peregrine doesn't stray from my side. I fear the worst. Oh dear. Oh dear, what shall I do.'

* * *

Lindsey had never been inside Moss End Guest House. It smelled musty and damp. Coming in the back way, the first stop had been the utility room. Bedding was piled high, but there was no lingering smell of soap suds that a busy hotel usually had.

She considered turning on the lights just in case Maurice Hoffman hadn't been working alone. Heart beating nineteen to the dozen, she decided to chance it.

Click! On came the lights. Her surroundings were gloomy. The kitchen was brighter, but no sign of anyone else.

Upstairs!

The word had popped into her head like someone had spoken it. This place was cold and creepy but it didn't explain how come she was hearing things — or not hearing things. It wasn't really a sound more a sudden inclination. She jerked round. Was that a hand on her shoulder again?

Nobody there.

'Gird your loins,' she said to herself. 'You're made of strong stuff, Lindsey Driver!'

Talking to herself seemed to work. She soldiered on into the hallway which served as a reception area.

Nobody leapt out from beneath the Victorian desk, a thing of dark wood with small spindles running around its edge surrounding a green leather surface. It was set in front of the window. The room wasn't big enough to hold much else and there were no creepy corners. There were three doors opening off the hallway. The one to her right seemed the most convenient so she opened it and pressed the light switch. It didn't come on and the room was big with a high ceiling.

'Mother? Honey Driver? Are you there? One tap for yes, two for no.' Her humour was short lived. She sounded nervous even to herself.

Upstairs.

That voice again. Where had it come from? She looked all around her but she was all alone.

The stairs were steep and enclosed between wood panelled walls. A brass handrail ran up one side. The landing at the top of the stairs was like the inside of a cave. Not a vestige of detail showed. Total darkness.

'Right,' she said out loud. 'I'm only going up these stairs if the light works.'

The light worked. Whoever was urging her on — whether it was in her own head or an outside influence — they seemed to be on her side.

At the top of the stairs a narrow corridor went off to her right. To her left was a quarter landing and a bathroom and nothing much else. She worked out she was at the very end of the house. The higgledy-piggledy corridor to her right was the way to go.

Halfway along the corridor a set of stairs went up to the attic bedroom.

'I know this,' she said to herself, almost in wonder only this time it was nothing to do with an unseen presence whispering in her ear. Her mother had told her that the bodies of the victims were thrown out of the attic bedrooms at the top of the stairs. The only way was up.

'But I'll only go up if the light works. Light switch,' she muttered, found it and switched it on. 'Thanks — whoever you are.' She headed up the stairs.

* * *

Wet and freezing, Honey was slowly slipping into unconsciousness. It was as though she no longer had a body, just a brain that felt as though it were surviving all by itself. Bits of her were closing down. Her toes went first. Then her fingers.

'Isn't it wonderful that I've got an ample bosom,' she murmured.

Peregrine purred in response. OK, he was only a cat, but even he must have appreciated the fact that her bosoms were the only part of her beside her head that was above the waterline. Which meant he was above the waterline too, and as a cat, he preferred things to be that way.

Still, a body couldn't survive as head and bosoms alone, and she couldn't keep her back arched indefinitely.

The cold was taking over. No matter how hard she tried, she couldn't prevent her eyes from closing.

'You mustn't,' she muttered to herself though her voice wasn't even a whisper. The words had only surfaced in her mind and never got to her lips. She reasoned that other people had survived similar situations.

'Hold on. Like the people on the *Titanic*.'

She knew most of them who'd gone into the water had been dead in minutes. Cold was a swift killer. The body just shut down. Fast.

* * *

Lindsey looked to either side of her. The attic rooms were unlit and gloomy. The wallpaper hadn't been changed in years; gold stars on dark blue.

The smaller of the two rooms held only a narrow bed and a bedside table. Closets were set into the only wall not curbed by the slope of the ceiling.

The larger of the rooms contained much the same furnishings, but also two large boxy affairs painted a hideous green.

For some reason her eyes kept going back to those boxes. They were the size of a decent coffer, the sort of thing a housekeeper would keep her linens in. Yet they couldn't be that, she thought. Not up here.

She attempted to open the smaller of the boxes. The moment she saw the water she knew that this was an old-style water tank, probably Victorian and no longer used to supply the house with water.

There seemed little point in opening the lid of the other one, except . . .

Try it!

The larger box had a wide lip running all the way round — easy to grip. It should have opened as easily, more easily anyway, than the smaller of the water tanks, but it didn't.

'Some plonker's nailed it down,' she grunted as she tried to heave it open. A sudden sound caused her to pause. It was faint. She stayed perfectly still, her ear against the wooden lid. That sound again. A faint meow.

A cat had fallen into the water tank!

Her thinking progressed on a more logical train. No. Not fallen in. The lid was nailed shut.

She began hammering on it.

'Mum! Are you in there?'

There was a faint sloshing of water. A small voice calling for help. And more meows.

Hammering on the lid and screaming for her mother to hold on, Lindsey was oblivious to the quick rat-a-tat of masculine feet racing up the stairs.

'She's in here! She's in here! But I can't open it. It's nailed shut.'

Doherty didn't hesitate. Using the tyre iron he'd confiscated from Mary Jane, he prised open the lid.

A pair of orange eyes looked up at them. The cat meowed, purred, then jumped off Honey's chest, onto the floor, and off down the stairs.

Honey opened her eyes.

'I feel so tired,' she murmured. 'Take me to bed please.'

Doherty caught hold of her shoulders, raised her up, and held her tight.

'You bet.'

CHAPTER TWENTY-FIVE

It wasn't often Honey held a dinner party for family and friends, but she figured on this occasion that they all needed it.

Just for once her mother was all for the idea of dining with Doherty.

'I've been a widow a few times,' she declared. 'Losing husbands is one thing; losing a child — even a middle-aged child — is far more devastating.'

'I'm so glad you're accepting Steve,' Honey said to her.

'The man saved you,' said Gloria, her diamond earrings rattling as though in applause.

The man. It was noticeable that she didn't call him by name, but there, her mother didn't surrender anything that easily.

She did add that she couldn't stop long because Antonio had invited her to his place.

'For an authentic Italian dish?' Honey asked.

Her mother's eyes sparkled. 'He *is* an authentic Italian dish.'

Honey laughed.

By ten o'clock Lindsey was preparing to go clubbing with friends.

'I need to party. Finding my mother half-frozen wearing one of her old bras and a pair of outsize knickers was a fact-finding tour I haven't quite got over yet. I need to chill out, though not in cold water.'

Honey thought how lucky she was and said so.

'If you hadn't persisted in searching that gloomy old house . . .'

'And if Mary Jane hadn't come armed with a tyre iron . . .' Lindsey caught the look on Doherty's face. 'Sorry. I hear you turned in a statement saying it was black as night round there and he must have fallen and hit his head.'

Mary Jane eyed Doherty blankly as though she hadn't heard what either he or Lindsey had said.

'Things could have turned out differently. All of you could be dead. Maurice Hoffman's fingerprints were inside the small safe in that urn. They'd been made in South Africa and ordered by the Seraphina Club in London, purely to be used for smuggling. Rhino had an old placard from the club in his trolley. Boris saw it, saw the key, and called up the details on the internet. He'd been out in South Africa for a while and had seen the reported theft of diamonds. He'd also seen bits of paper connected to Maurice Hoffman and the club. Trading people's details was his business. He put two and two together, found the money in one of the urns, but didn't count on being found by Hoffman and his cronies. He had hoped to be able to retrieve the money from Rhino after the two thugs came calling. Unfortunately . . .'

There was silence as everyone digested the details.

Finally, Lindsey stood with both hands on the chair back. Her expression was thoughtful, one eyebrow raised higher than the other. She was biting her bottom lip, her eyes fixed on the fatty rind she'd left on the side of her plate.

'It was an odd night,' she said, her voice soft though her vowels were clipped. There was something she wanted to say but didn't know how to say it.

Honey reached across and covered her daughter's hand with her own.

'Don't look so worried, love. I know it must be a trial to have a nutcase of a mother like me. You go out and enjoy yourself.'

'It isn't that . . . I really don't know how to say this, but something . . . someone . . .'

'Moss End is haunted,' Mary Jane piped up, casually. 'The presence isn't exactly the same as Sir Cedric. I mean, *he's* perfectly ordinary.'

All heads turned in her direction. Only Mary Jane could possibly talk about ghosts being ordinary.

'I can explain,' said Mary Jane. 'Olivia and I had a little chat about it and we both agreed it was a special place. There's a door there into the great beyond. It's like an express elevator for spirits; they come and go through it like we do in a department store.'

'Ghosts!' Lindsey exclaimed.

'Not ghosts,' said Mary Jane, her face upturned, eyes fixed on the fancy plasterwork around the light rose.

'What exactly do you mean?' Lindsey asked, her face full of interest.

'It means that it's a kind of spiritual super-highway; a bit like the internet but without the microchips.'

'So you felt it too?' Lindsey sounded awestruck.

Mary Jane blinked like an owl that just woke up.

Honey didn't want Lindsey to feel odd about what she experienced at Moss End Guest House. She exchanged a nervous look with Doherty. Doherty, sipping wine, looked totally unconcerned.

'All right. I'll admit it myself,' said Honey. 'I felt there was something going on there, but they weren't interested in me. And spirits kind of like to help out now and again.'

Lindsey pulled her chair back out and sank back into it. 'Like angels?' she asked.

Mary Jane did a so-so toss of her head. 'You could say that. Helpful beings that may or may not have ever lived; they exist. Sometimes they like to help out those who are living. Well,' she said suddenly, knees making a cracking sound as she got to her feet. 'I'm turning in. Thanks for the dinner. It's good everything worked out and that I'm not being sued for bashing that guy over the head.'

Honey tuned herself out of the conversation. She was worried for Lindsey. She truly felt for her. Despite the joking, she knew Lindsey had been as much affected by her ordeal as she was herself.

'Lindsey?'

Her daughter shook her head. 'I'm OK. Honestly I am.' She sighed deeply. 'Thank goodness for Mary Jane. Mary Jane, you are absolutely amazing.'

Mary Jane, a bright delight in her favourite shocking pink and pistachio green velour lounging suit, looked surprised. 'I am?'

'You knew there was something spiritual about that house.'

Mary Jane shrugged. 'I picked up on the atmosphere, but Olivia filled me in on the detail. That's why she's there you know. She keeps an eye on the place. Her and that cat of hers. What a cat, huh? Did you see those orange eyes?'

* * *

It was good to finally be alone. Lindsey had opted to stay with friends overnight. They had the coach house to themselves. The sheets on the bed were freshly laundered, the room was warm. Only the fact that Doherty was lying in bed beside her with only his chest hair providing any modesty prevented her from falling asleep.

She stroked his chest and kissed his shoulder.

'It's good to be alive. And great that you rescued me.'

'Me and my trusty tyre iron.'

'It was lucky Mary Jane brought it with her.'

'Hmm. Lucky for her that she didn't kill him.'

He sounded grumpy, or at least disengaged from the conversation, as though something was bugging him. She watched his face as her fingers made circles over his chest. In an effort to snap him out of it she played the sympathy card.

'I don't think I've ever been so cold in my life.' She backed it up with an involuntary shiver.

Doherty still remained silent. Wooden. His attention remained fixed on the wall where the flat screen television was flickering with a soap that he always declared was absolute dross.

Honey thought about the interlude with John Rees. John had visited her in hospital. She'd been kept in purely for observation. John had sat awkwardly beside the bed because it wasn't just the doctors doing the observing. Doherty was there too, grim-faced, arms folded across his chest, eyeing John as though daring him to gush with affection. She'd pointed out to him afterwards that John could not be arrested for visiting her in hospital.

The fact was, Doherty had not been amused about either John or the car accident. On the other hand she hadn't been too happy either. Being relegated to second place in his affections behind a damaged car hadn't exactly pumped up her ego.

There was no alternative but to tear his attention away from the television. Plan A. Confront the problem. Plan B . . . well, she'd work through plan B if plan A fell flat.

'Right! Can I have your undivided attention, please!'

She threw back the bedclothes, getting between him and the TV, her knees to either side of his, thighs apart.

Bearing in mind the fact that she was wearing nothing but her favourite perfume, it came as something of a surprise that his gaze fixed on her face. Only her face. Not that he never looked at her face; it was just that at certain moments he was partial to scrutinising other bits of her body.

'OK. I'm sorry about your car. I'm also sorry about flirting with John Rees. But you have to understand that you telling Ahmed that you loved your car more than anything else was a definite contributor to my flirting. I mean, Ahmed wouldn't lie about a thing like that, now, would he? He's about to become a married man.'

Doherty stared at her, lips slightly apart. Funny, he was still looking into her eyes. He'd often told her that he loved her eyes, but they hadn't necessarily been top of his list of admirable parts of her body.

'You're wrong.'

Now it was her turn to look surprised.

'I am? Which part of that statement am I wrong about?'

'Ahmed about to become a married man. His family have brought over half a dozen possible brides for him to meet. He hasn't married any of them.'

'Really?'

'He wants to be an actor.'

Honey wasn't really interested in Ahmed's career prospects. First and foremost she wanted to know where she stood with the love of her life.

She sighed, her breasts rising and falling with purposeful intent. Doherty still looked wooden. Being downbeat wasn't normally part of her make-up, but his manner was pushing her that way.

In the end she felt beaten. 'Oh well. We all have our hopes and dreams. Where would we be without them, huh?'

Doherty chewed his lips as though he were thinking something through. Lashes fluttered over half-closed eyes.

Her hormones did acrobatics. Those little telltale signs convinced her that he was about to regain his former interest in the rest of her body.

She waited.

Nothing happened.

What was she reading him wrong?

'You're deep in thought. Do you want to call it a day?'

He shook his head.

'Are you ill?'

He shook his head again. 'Just nervous.'

She'd never known Doherty to be nervous. He was her big brave policeman; well not too big. Just right in fact.

'Anything I can help you with?'

She felt like melting when he raised his eyelids. Those eyes. They took her back to the first time they'd met. Casper St John Gervais, chairman of the Hotels Association, had lumbered her with the job of Crime Liaison Officer. Bribed with the promise of business being put her way, she'd accepted the post. Nothing much would occur, she'd thought, but it had. An American tourist had gone missing from a down-market guest house. They'd clashed at first, though not for long. But this. Was this the end?

'Your boobs are good,' he said suddenly. 'Perhaps if I concentrate on them rather than your face I can say what I want to say.'

Honey straightened. 'Like hypnosis?'

'Could be,' he said, dropping his gaze from her face to her breasts.

'Do you want me to swing them? Like they do with a pendulum or a pocket watch?'

He shook his head, his eyes flickering, obviously deep in thought. 'OK. Here goes. Honey. My car is all fixed which means we are all fixed. We're back to where we were. The two of us against the world. OK?'

She nodded. 'Seems OK to me.'

THE END

9 781804 056493